Loyal - A Fairy Tale Retelling of Red Riding Hood

The Crown and the Sceptre

Kristina J Jordan

Published by Kristina J Jordan, 2021.

This is a work of fiction. Similarities to real people, places, or events are entirely coincidental.

LOYAL - A FAIRY TALE RETELLING OF RED RIDING HOOD

First edition. September 14, 2021.

Copyright © 2021 Kristina J Jordan.

ISBN: 979-8201535377

Written by Kristina J Jordan.

Also by Kristina J Jordan

The Crown and the Sceptre
Free A Fairy Tale Retelling of Rapunzel
Strong - A Fairy Tale Retelling of the Princess and the Pea
True A Fairy Tale Retelling of Puss in Boots
Pretty - A fairy Tale Retelling of the Frog Prince
Loyal - A Fairy Tale Retelling of Red Riding Hood

CHAPTER ONE

It was just another Tuesday.

Until the letter arrived. Obscure. Tiny. An innocent cream envelope half buried in the innocuous stack of correspondence laying in the silver tray. Pretending it wasn't about to change Katherine's life with its momentous news.

Katherine almost didn't open the letter.

She was late... extremely late for an appointment at the weaving guild. She was distracted by perfecting a brand-new weaving pattern; one Katherine knew would be the talk of all the Lovanian court ladies.

Letters were just another annoying duty, designed to keep Katherine from what she loved. Possibly an invitation to an event she would prefer to avoid. Or a notice about the silk guild. Maybe, if Katherine was lucky, a letter from an acquaintance, but that was a rare occasion. Village girls in Annecy weren't big letter writers.

Katherine sighed, giving in to duty. Swiping the letters on her way through the house, she held them in one hand, pulling off her leather slippers with the other. Fresh tea waited on the polished table in the centre of the room; Katherine poured a cup, adding a dollop of honey before sinking onto the settee to open the correspondence.

And there it was.

That cream envelope, unfamiliar handwriting streaking across the front. A niggle of curiosity darted through Katherine's chest as she eased the silver handled letter opener under the thick paper, drawing out the letter.

The handwriting was elegant writing, curving and swirling across the margins. Katherine scanned it, eyes growing wider and wider as they skimmed the page. With a tiny cry, her fingers froze. The letter floated soundlessly to the thick carpet like a snowflake landing on ice.

"Lukard," Katherine's voice choked, tinged with desperation.

A middle-aged man silently appeared from behind the carved wooden door.

"Mistress Katherine?"

"Send for the carriage. I must speak to Princess Lucie. Immediately."

"FROM WHO?" LUCIE WHISPERED, anxious not to waken the sleeping child in her arms.

"Mother." Katherine waved the crumpled pages, not dramatically— Katherine hated drama— but with more force than usual.

"Wait a minute, I'll put this cublet down and we'll go to the sitting room and talk properly." Lucie lifted the sleeping child and carried her to the cot. She laid her down, stroking the downy head as the child murmured and shuffled in sleep.

"There." Lucie turned to her older sister. "She'll sleep for at least an hour. I'll have tea and cake brought to us."

Lucie led Katherine to her elegant sitting room, opening the French doors leading to Queen Isabella's formal garden. Lavender scented air wafted in on the cool breeze, ruffling the curtains and skimming Katherine's hot skin. Lucie settled next to her sister on the brocade settee.

"Now, can I see this letter?"

Katherine handed the letter to Lucie and waited silently, while her sister scanned the words. Concern grew in her eyes as she turned the page in her hand.

My daring family,

The way I disappeared from your lives was unforgivable. I knew that then and I know that now. I have regretted every day—no every minute—that my husband was forced to raise my sweet, brave girls alone. If there had been any other way, I would have stayed. I left to protect you. Protect you against my Iasian family. A family both powerful and wicked. I can't explain much in this letter, but what I can say is that the danger is increasing. Your existence has been discovered and you are in danger. I cannot explain in writing, even with my precautions this letter may go astray.

Althea will tell you how to find me.

Come quickly and come carefully.

Your loving Mother, Avella.

"I don't understand." Lucie turned to her sister, eyebrows pinched. "Father told us mother got the fever. It must be a hoax, someone getting at the throne, perhaps?"

Katherine shook her head. "That's what I thought. But certain things never added up with mother's death. You were a tiny baby, so you wouldn't remember... but everything happened suddenly. Too suddenly. One day, mother was there, and the next she was just gone. I never actually remember mother being ill. I assumed I was too young to remember. But maybe... maybe mother was never sick."

Lucie pressed her lips together in a fine line, "Would Marion remember? She's old enough to have noticed." She handed the crumpled letter to Katherine.

Katherine folded the thick paper, gently sliding the pages into the envelope. "I'm afraid to tell Marion; she felt mother's absence the most. It would be awful to raise her hopes, then dash them. I can't tell Father. He's traveling south on guild business and won't return for weeks."

Lucie nodded, "I understand. We need to tell Marion soon, though. It would be worse if she found out we kept it a secret."

Katherine's shoulders slumped. She rubbed her finger up and down the edge of the envelope. "You're right. I'll tell Marion tonight. I'll send a message for her to come to the house for dinner. It will be easier without the children."

Lucie squeezed her sister's arm. "You won't be alone. I'll join you. Frederich's always complaining I don't go out anymore; he won't mind being on his own for an evening."

Katherine shot her sister a grateful look. "Thanks, Marion hates when I bring mother up, and you know her health is fragile. I'd hate this to be the reason she falls ill again."

"What happens after you tell Marion? Have you thought about it?" Lucie hesitated, pleating the fabric of her dress.

"Go find mother, of course." Katherine turned to her sister, surprise flashing in her eyes. "Don't you want to meet her?"

Lucie faltered. "I don't know... I mean, if this is true, mother left us. Alone. For years. Now that I have my own babies, I can't imagine *ever* doing that."

"Mother had a reason," Katherine argued. "You read the letter; she was terrified of putting us in danger. Wouldn't you do anything to keep your children from harm?"

"I suppose...." Lucie frowned. "But surely there was another way. Surely mother could have let us know she was alive and safe."

A soft rap at the door interrupted the sisters; Lucie put her finger to her lips in a warning gesture. "The castle grapevine is unbelievable. We'll finish our discussion later." Lucie opened the door, smiling at the maid pushing the cart of tea and pastries.

After arriving home, Katherine meticulously washed her hands before opening the door to the greenhouse— or what *was* the greenhouse. The first thing Katherine did when her father moved them into the manor house was to convert the expansive greenhouse into a silkworm nursery.

Katherine closed the door to keep the nursery temperature stable. The delicate silkworms were susceptible to every tiny change in their environment. She lifted a mulberry leaf, examining the fat creamy nub attached to the bottom of the leaf. All was well with the cocoons. Katherine sighed happily.

She checked the other cocoons, looking forward to her favourite time: unravelling the cocoon, twisting the slender filaments into strands of silk thread. Katherine spent a few more moments in the quiet nursery, hovering over the silkworms, delighted they were developing properly.

In the years since Katherine started growing her silkworms, her business had expanded. Now Katherine's silk guild employed women in nearly every village, all involved in some part of silk production. Some grew mulberry trees for the silkworms to eat, some raised the tiny brown moths to create the cocoons, and some specialized in Katherine's favourite part of the silk process—spinning and weaving to create the fabric that was quickly becoming a prominent segment of the Lovanian economy.

"Sleep well, little friends," Katherine whispered to the silkworms, glancing around to make sure no one was listening. Jasper rubbed Katherine's ankles with his furry head as she emerged from the cocoon house, begging for chin scratches.

"Did you think I was talking to you, Jasper?" Katherine lifted the small cat, rewarding him with a cuddle. She locked the nursery carefully, smile fading as her thoughts returned to the present situation. Katherine didn't look forward to dinner. Marion had grieved the loss of her mother hard. The burden of raising two younger sisters had fallen mainly to her shoulders; Katherine didn't enjoy dredging up the past.

She strode across the courtyard, taking a shortcut through the kitchen where delicious savory smells greeted her. Mabel usually cooked only for Katherine and sometimes her father, Pierre; she was always delighted to welcome actual guests. Katherine was far too easy to please, often preferring a simple meal of bread and toasted cheese or a bowl of soup to the elaborate productions Mabel took pride in.

"That looks lovely." The rich scent of roast beef and creamy sauce wafted through the steamy air.

"It's my favourite recipe," Mabel puffed under Katherine's compliment. "Not everyone has a princess for a dinner guest. And a duchess."

Katherine flinched at the still unfamiliar titles. Raised in the tiny village of Annecy, her highest aspiration had been head weaver at the Annecy guild. Katherine missed those days, the satisfaction of creating a new pattern, the glow of accomplishment at creating beautiful things. She gave herself a shake. *You're lucky to be where you are. Who you are,* Katherine reminded herself sternly. She crossed into the dining room, running a critical eye over the table settings. It was her sisters; they wouldn't complain if something was out of place. All the same, Katherine liked things done correctly.

Lukard appeared at the door, silent as a ghost.

"You're guests have arrived," he announced, no hint of expression on his face.

"Thank you." Katherine smoothed her already sleek golden hair and glided to the door.

"Marion," Katherine greeted her eldest sister, a warm smile lighting her face. Her sister looked well, glowing. The illness that plagued her was now merely a distant memory. "How are you? And George and the children?"

"Wonderful." Marion returned the smile, handing her velvet wrap to Lukard. "Obviously, the children begged to accompany me; there's nothing they love more than seeing Aunt Katherine. But it's lovely having a quiet evening on our own. Has Lucie arrived?"

"I have." Lucie appeared around the corner.

The three girls waited politely as three gold rimmed bowls of soup were set before them.

"Mabel always makes such delicious food," Marion sighed, inhaling a spoonful of fragrant creamy soup. "If you're not careful, I might just steal her away."

Katherine forced out a weak laugh. Marion threw her sister a quizzical look, a wrinkle appearing between her eyebrows. "Are you all right? You seem... quiet."

Katherine hesitated, her hands growing cold. "I admit, I invited you tonight because I have to tell you something. It's about.... mother."

Marion tensed, "What about her?"

"We think.... we think mother's still alive." Katherine lowered her eyes.

"What? How is that possible?" Marion dropped her spoon, ignoring the soup that splashed onto her fine silk dress.

"She sent a letter." Katherine drew out the envelope. Now creased, the envelope hadn't left Katherine's person all day.

"It's a lie." Marion insisted, a turmoil of emotion boiling in her hazel eyes. "Mother is dead."

"But what if she's not dead?" Katherine searched her sister's troubled face.

"I know she is. I saw it myself," Marion's voice cracked, eyes luminous with unshed tears.

Katherine froze, a strange mix of emotions sweeping over her.

Disappointment.

Sadness.

Shock.

Her sister had never mentioned this before. "What did you see?"

"It wasn't the fever." A single tear trembled on the end of Marion's lashes. "Father spread that story because he didn't want people knowing the truth. Mother killed herself."

"You saw that and never told us?" Lucie's eyes filled with sympathy. She reached out, putting her hand on Marion's.

"It was the end of winter. The snow was melting, and the river was full. Mother left late one evening; she told me she needed to take care of something at the shop," Marion's voice trembled.

Katherine nodded, mother had often helped her father in the trading business. Even she remembered that.

"In the morning, Mother hadn't returned, so I went searching for her. She wasn't at the shop. They told me she never came. That was unlike mother. She was always at the shop or home with us. I went home and into the garden. I thought maybe she fell in the greenhouse or orchard. Then I saw it." Marion choked back a sob. "A pile of her clothes, shoes and a note. By the river." Marion's cheeks were wet. "Mother didn't want to live anymore."

"But you didn't see her jump. You just saw the pile of clothes and the note." Katherine hated speaking the words aloud when Marion was distressed, but she couldn't hide the excitement edging into her voice.

"Well.... No.... I didn't," Marion dragged the words out.

"Mother might still be alive. We can't ignore this. What if she needs us?" Katherine leaned forward. "She's our *mother*."

"I don't know if I want to see her." Marion set her jaw, wrenching the words out.

"You don't?" Surprise flitted through Lucie's eyes.

"No. Why should I? Mother abandoned me. Abandoned us. Now she wants to prance out of the woodwork? After years of neglect? I don't think so. You have children." Marion narrowed her eyes, turning to Lucie. "Would you leave your children? Ever?"

Lucie lowered her lashes, pale fingers pleating the edge of the napkin. "I wouldn't want to. But I would. To keep them safe, I would do anything."

"There must be something else mother could have done. At least sent word that she was alive. All those years.... Wasted." Marion's eyes sparkled with tears. Angry tears.

"I'm going to find her." The words spilled from Katherine's mouth before she could reel them in.

Lucie and Marion jerked their heads up.

"But what about the guild? Your work?" A troubled look crossed Lucie's face.

Katherine waved a hand. "Do you think the guild matters compared to our mother? Besides, the guild practically runs itself now. Mary has experience; she'll step in as guild-master."

"But how will you find her? The letter didn't say where mother lives," Lucie protested.

"Althea will know."

"Althea's so far away now that she's moved into the forest. You can't travel there alone." Marion said, hand tightening on her spoon.

Katherine pinned her sister with a stubborn look."I travel alone on guild business all the time. How is this any different." She set her jaw, as Marion lowered her gaze.

Three days later, Katherine was in her warehouse. Located in the middle of the Corvan city, it was where the guild stored fabrics and materials ready for sale. She raised a lantern, scanning a row of fabrics.

"You can't traipse around the country alone. Not with Avella's family searching for us. Tell her, Frederich." Lucie nudged her husband.

"I'm afraid Lucie's right. It's too dangerous," Frederich agreed, the reluctance at being drawn into the sisterly argument clear on his face.

"I'm only travelling to Althea's cottage," Katherine insisted, folding a length of fabric she'd pulled from the bolts of colourful silks that lined the walls from the floor to the ceiling; patterns created by Katherine and her guild members. "I need to go that direction, anyway; weaver̶   Althea's village asked to join the guild. I want to collect

ulled out a bolt of red fabric, this one a sturdy wool, aterial through her fingers.

"Yes—you're safe for now. But what happens after you speak with Althea? I know you're planning to run off to wherever you think Mother lives. At least take Frederich's guards."

Katherine rolled her eyes. "I don't need babysitters. I've travelled alone for years now, without incidents." She folded the red fabric, adding it to the neat pile at her feet.

"What's that material for?" Lucie eyed Katherine's stack of fabrics.

"I'm having these sewn into clothes to test the dyes. Red usually fades quickly, but I think I've finally got something that works." Katherine packed the fabrics into a canvas satchel.

"It's beautiful." Lucie examined the deep, rich colour. "What's the dye from? I haven't seen this shade."

"Resin from the Lac trees. Father brought it to me from eastern trade ships, but I'll need to order a lot more if I want enough for guild production."

Lucie crinkled her nose, losing interest in the subject. Katherine could talk about weaving and fabrics all day long. "Well, back to the main point. Are you planning to find Mother after you talk to Althea?"

Katherine looked her sister straight in the eye. "Yes."

Lucie sighed. "There's no stopping you? Could you at least take Lord Gunther with you? His estate is near Althea's cottage, and there's no one better when it comes to protection. Frederich and King Erich trust him implicitly. And you know Lord Gunther has a soft spot for you."

Katherine recoiled. "Lord Gunther? He's a buffoon. We can't stand each other."

"No, it's you who can't stand Gunther. What happened between you two anyway? You used to get along so well."

Katherine tensed. She had been friendly with Lord Gunther. Very friendly. And hoping for more than friendship. Until the day she discovered.... Katherine shuddered, cheeks flaming as she quick' forced her thoughts away.

"We just don't." Katherine clamped her lips together, face flushing bright pink.

"Fine. But you have to admit, Gunther's one of King Erich's best council men—even if he is young. You couldn't be in better hands." Exasperated, Lucie plopped on the only chair Katherine had in the warehouse, a rickety wooden affair that had seen better days.

"Lucie's right." Frederich placed his hands protectively on his wife's shoulders. "Lord Gunther is a good man, and he'd do anything for your family. We'd rest easier if you asked him to accompany you." Lucie shot her husband a grateful look, eyes warm with affection.

Katherine steeled her spine, shaking her head mutinously. No way was she going anywhere with that horrible, obnoxious man, and she wouldn't be caught dead near his estate either. Katherine made a mental note to steer clear of Gunther's lands while travelling to Althea's cottage.

Lucie sighed. "I don't understand why you insist on being so stubborn, but have it your way. At least promise you'll turn around immediately if you see any—and I mean any — danger." She exchanged glances with Frederich, full of hidden meaning Katherine couldn't quite decipher.

"Fine," Katherine relented. Her littlest sister did have her best interest in mind. Besides, how would Lucie know the reason she and Gunther didn't see eye to eye? It wasn't a story Katherine planned on sharing. Ever.

"Good, it's settled." Lucie squeezed Katherine in a tight hug. "I'll miss you, and so will the little ones."

Katherine softened. She would miss her sister. They were close, and Katherine loved nothing more than being aunt to Lucie's three children. "I'll miss you too." She embraced Lucie, breathing in the scent of perfume and floral soap.

After Frederich and Lucie left, Katherine finished packing. She planned to leave first thing in the morning, and she determined not to stop until she saw mother's face again. The last thing Katherine tucked in her saddlebag was a tiny book, so ancient and worn, its pages crumbled at the slightest touch. The book was the only remaining thing belonging to her mother; Katherine had carried the slim volume carefully ever since it came into her possession.

Katherine fastened the bag with guilt laced fingers. She should have told Lucie and Marion about the book long ago, but something always stopped her.

"Maybe, just maybe, mother will explain what you're about," Katherine directed her comment to the volume that nestled, hidden, silent, and full of secrets inside her bag.

CHAPTER TWO

Katherine rubbed her hand against her aching spine. She seldom rode now that she conducted most guild business from the city. This would hurt come morning, but Katherine couldn't stop now. Delays at the guild held the journey to Althea's by three days. Not only that, Katherine's awareness of her proximity to Lord Gunther's estate prickled the back of neck. Lord Gunther was the last person Katherine wanted to run into. She gazed at her surroundings, scanning the rich landscape of fields and orchards. The clip clop of hooves in the distance caught her attention. Katherine turned in the saddle, eyes instantly alert.

Silly, likely a farmer heading for Corvan, Katherine chided. The twist in the road meant Katherine couldn't see who was behind her. Her heart sank when she spotted an elegant black horse. His master, a powerful man with thick black hair, lounged easily in the saddle. A dart of admiration ran through Katherine's unwilling mind; she quickly squelched the wayward thought, pressing her lips tightly together.

"Lord Gunther." Katherine nodded, hiding her discomfort under a polite expression.

"Katherine." The booming voice caused Katherine's horse to skitter sideways. "I heard you were travelling my way."

"You did?" Katherine reined in her mount; this was a conversation she wouldn't easily escape.

"Your sister told me." Gunther bared his teeth in a grin.

"I see." Katherine noted to herself to never tell Lucie her business again. Lucie was well aware of her dislike for Gunther. What was she thinking?

"Yes, I was riding this way myself. I thought I might bump into you." Lord Gunther drew up beside her, his towering figure looming over her.

Katherine glanced at Gunther's face, wishing he didn't have to be quite so handsome. "I guess you did. I'm on my way to Althea's cottage." She hoped Gunther would take the hint and leave.

"Oh, wonderful, I'm headed that way myself." Gunther rode easily beside her. "I haven't seen you lately; has guild business been keeping you busy?"

"I'm afraid guild business is taxing at the moment. The guild's expanding, and even then, we can't keep up with demand for our silks." Pride laced Katherine's voice. It had taken a monumental effort to convince enough women to join the guild to make it a success.

"I see." A strange expression flitted through Gunther's eyes. Katherine thought she might have detected a flicker of hurt. Impossible. Gunther has the emotion of a rock, unless it involved strategy and fighting, he has no interest. Katherine flicked her eyes away.

"I really am very busy," Katherine insisted. They neared the turnoff to Althea's cottage, a shady lane with tall hedges looming on either side.

Gunther nodded goodbye, his tall figure disappearing around the corner.

"Hello dear." Althea met Katherine at the door. Althea had been elderly as long as Katherine remembered, but she was shocked at the change in her. Althea's grey hair had faded to soft white; the lines in her face had deepened. Still, Althea's eyes were bright and keen as she ushered Katherine into the cottage, taking Katherine's satchel in her knobbly hands.

"Tea?" Althea hobbled to the kettle and moved it over the range.

"Please." Katherine stretched her aching legs in front of the fireplace.

Althea produced a steaming mug of tea and a plate of honeyed bread. "Now," her kind eyes looked into Katherine's, "you're not here for a mere chat; what brings you?"

Katherine twisted her hands in her lap. "I received a letter." She reached into her pocket, sliding out the envelope. Katherine felt an arrow of loss as the smooth edges left her hands; the letter hadn't left her person since the day it had arrived.

Althea unfolded the pages, scrutinizing them in silence. The frown on her face deepened as she read.

Katherine waited silently, holding her breath as Althea folded the pages and returned the letter.

Althea sighed, a faraway look in her eyes. "I should start from the beginning. I knew your mother when she was a child. Avella was Iasian, from nobility, important in the royal court."

Katherine nodded. She had heard Avella's story before, but she realized what Althea was about to explain much more of the story.

"Your mother was a lovely child, very sweet, easy to love. But her mother and sister were a different matter entirely. Her mother thought only of marrying her daughters to the prince. He was not a nice man, but Natalia didn't care about their happiness. When your mother showed signs of power—a gift Avella couldn't control— she sent Avella to her grandmother, your great-grandmother. All so she could present her eldest daughter, Madelaine, in court.

"Your grandmother, Sorchia, was a cruel woman, much worse than her daughter. She saw your mother's powerful gift and wanted to use it for her own ends. Sorchia had a grudge against the royal family and planned to destroy them at any cost. When your Avella refused to help Sorchia, Sorchia locked her up in an abandoned tower. That's when your father came along. Pierre found Avella and helped her escape from your grandmother."

Katherine listened intently. Katherine knew little of Avella's family. Pierre avoided the subject whenever she or her sisters brought it up.

"Your grandmother was furious; she chased Avella and Pierre, nearly killing your father. When your mother returned to her family estate, Sorchia burned the entire manor house down. Avella realised the only way to gain peace from Sorchia would be to disappear. So, with the help of your father, that's what she did."

"That's when they opened the business in Annecy—but what about you? How did you come to live in Annecy?" Katherine widened her eyes, thirsty to know more about Avella's story.

"When Sorchia couldn't find Avella, she came after her sister, Madelaine. Her sister was a beautiful girl; Sorchia disfigured her, destroying any chance Madelaine had for a good marriage. Madelaine was a proud girl— the toast of the court in her coming out year. She could have had her pick of any suitor. Even the prince was eyeing her. In her fury, Madelaine vowed revenge on your mother and her family until they were ruined, just as she was."

"Is that why Avella couldn't return after Sorchia's death? Because of Madelaine?"

Althea nodded. "It broke Avella's heart, but she desperately hoped you'd survive if Madelaine didn't know you existed. Madelaine was stubborn and cruel; she wouldn't give up."

"So now..." Katherine's voice trailed off into a question.

"Now, Sorchia is long gone... but Madelaine...."

Katherine held her breath.

"Madelaine knows about you, Pierre and your sisters; she must be closer to discovering you," Althea admitted.

"After all these years?"

Althea nodded, an apology in her eyes.

"That's why Avella couldn't give you her location in the letter."

"In case Madelaine intercepted it?" Katherine finished the sentence.

Althea nodded.

"I know you and you sisters might be angry with Avella for leaving, but remember, Avella gave up a lot to keep you safe. Her road wasn't easy."

Katherine's eyes softened. "I know. And Lucie knows too.... but Marion..."

"Marion cared for you and Lucie when Avella left. With your father travelling on business, it wasn't easy. I helped when I could, but I couldn't draw suspicion. I had to be very, very careful."

"You and Avella stayed in touch all these years. How?" Katherine sipped her tea, wincing; it was cold.

"Avella grows herbs in her garden. She sends them to me and includes messages using a code we agreed on beforehand. I haven't seen Avella since she left, and I rarely hear from her, but I know she's healthy."

Katherine twisted her hands in her lap. "And what of her sister? Madelaine?"

"Lucie will be safe from Madelaine. She's in the castle with King Erich's guards to protect her; Frederich will see to that. And Marion will be safe as well, her husband's estate has nearly as many guards as the king. Madelaine wouldn't dare attack the kingdom's crown princess in the king's fortress. But travelling alone, you need to proceed with caution. Madelaine's had years to plan this revenge, and she's like her grandmother Sorchia. She feeds her grudges."

"Does Madelaine have a gift? Like Lucie?"

Althea drew her brows together. "Your mother worked with fire, just like Lucie. But Avella's magic is sealed. I performed the sealing myself; it was the only way Avella could stay hidden. Your grandmother had a gift, the gift of growing. As for Madelaine, Avella didn't mention her gift. But from what I've heard, strange things happened in that manor house. You must realize it's possible Madelaine does have a gift."

Katherine shivered at the dark tone piercing Althea's voice.

"I want to find Avella. It's worth the risk." Katherine set her jaw.

"I thought that's what you'd say." Althea smiled. "Avella lives on the border of Louixe, a little harbour town. It isn't close."

"That's all right. I need to do this."

Althea nodded. "I wish I could accompany you; these rattly bones don't travel well. But I'll do what I can to help. Do you have your cloak with you?"

"Will this work?" Katherine brought out a pile of red fabric and draped it across her knee; she'd fashioned a cloak from the fabric, lining it with thick, warm wool and crafted a hood for it.

"Perfect." Althea fingered the rich cloth. "I'll ward it; if Madelaine sends someone to look for you, you won't be recognized while wearing the cloak. You might not have power dear, but you're a Rapunzel, power will still respond to your blood." Althea got slowly to her feet, hobbling to the wooden table in the kitchen. Reaching up, Althea lifted a glass jar of dried leaves, throwing a generous pinch into the mortar.

Curiosity aroused, Katherine watched as Althea continued mixing ingredients, pounding them into a smooth brown paste. She daubed the concoction on the hem of Katherine's red cloak, muttering quietly. A shimmer of energy, almost imperceptible to Katherine's unpracticed senses, shivered through the room, making everything brighter, sharper. Katherine's eyes widened, goosebumps trickling across her skin. Then it was gone.

"That should hold until you return. Don't worry if you can't see it; the ward will still be there." Althea returned the red cloak to Katherine, who clutched it to her chest. The cloak pulsed under her fingers, tinged with unfamiliar energy.

"One more thing." Katherine took a deep breath, gathering her courage. "I have this. It was Avella's." She drew out the little book, being careful not to jostle the pages.

Althea stepped back, surprise flashing through her eyes. "Where did you get this book?"

"I took Avella's book the night of the cabin fire; I meant to return it to Father; he enjoyed having that reminder of mother.... But something in the book called to me... I kept it. My sisters don't know I have it," Katherine admitted.

"That book belonged to your grandmother, Sorchia." Althea sat back down in her chair. "Your mother took it to escape. But she couldn't read it."

Katherine stared at the tiny book. "Can I learn how?"

Althea shook her head. "I'm not sure you would want to read it. Your grandmother was a dangerous woman; that book is ancient and possibly evil. I don't think your mother realized what she had."

Katherine slid the book into her inner pocket, relieved when it disappeared from sight. Perhaps she should tell Lucie and Marion about the book. It didn't feel right to tell them when she'd found it; Marion was so ill and Lucie was distracted by Prince Frederich. After that, it was too late.

"No matter." Althea patted Katherine's smooth hand with her gnarled fingers. "What's done is done. Bring it with you and let your mother decide what to do with it."

Althea insisted Katherine spend the night in the cottage, showing her to a cosy bedroom tucked under the eaves. Katherine lay awake, the feather coverlet pulled to her chin. Moonlight streaked silver paths across the floorboards. Katherine fell asleep watching it march its steady path.

The next morning, Katherine breakfasted early. She planned to arrive in the next town by nightfall; the idea of spending the night in the woods didn't appeal to Katherine, especially knowing that Madelaine was hunting for her.

It was hard to feel afraid in sunny daylight, though. Dappled light scattered across the lane, shining like golden coins. Katherine wore the red cloak, pulling it close against the morning chill. She turned back as

Althea stood on the front step, framed by honeysuckle vines, waving as she rode down the path.

Katherine hummed a tune as she meandered down the path. It was nice to escape the constant grind of guild business. Katherine loved the silk guild— loved anything to do with fabrics— but she missed being a weaver, only responsible for creating. Sometimes, the guild felt like endless streams of accounts and paperwork. Katherine glanced at the deep green leaves against the cloudless blue sky, wondering if she could produce the dye to make that exact colour combination.

"Hello again," a deep voice jolted Katherine from her thoughts.

"Gunther? What are you doing here?" Katherine gave Gunther a stiff smile.

"Didn't you know? This forest is on my estate." Gunther grinned, his tall horse prancing underneath him.

"Oh." Katherine's voice was small. She hadn't realized Gunther's lands were this extensive.

"That's all right. I will allow you passage." A playful expression crossed Gunther's face.

"Thank you." Katherine turned primly to face forward.

"Well...."

Katherine raised her eyes, waiting for Gunther to finish speaking.

"Aren't you going to tell me where you're going?" Gunther kept his playful expression, but there was steel behind his words.

Katherine sighed. Gunther was too stubborn and wily to be avoided. "If you must know, I'm going to the Luixe border." Katherine kept her answer short, although she knew it was futile to keep things from Gunther.

"Oh, is that so? I fancy a trip to the Luixe border myself. I haven't been in ages." Gunther's horse kept pace beside Bardot.

"Gunther." Katherine's fingers clenched the reins. "I know you have no intention of going to Luixe. Why are you doing this to me?"

Gunther frowned. "I only want to make sure you're safe. It's dangerous to travel alone."

Katherine huffed. "There's nothing dangerous in this forest; I've lived around here my whole life."

"Actually, that's not true."

A frisson of apprehension crept down Katherine's spine. "What do you mean?"

"I mean, wolves have been spotted nearby. In these woods."

"Wolves?" Katherine scoffed. Everyone knew wolves didn't live in this part of the forest. Only Lucie had ever seen wolves, but in a different forest, near Iaisa. Powered by the magical chateau, the wolves must be long gone now.

"I don't believe it." Katherine was determined to shed Gunther at any cost, someone who only pretended to like her. Katherine's face burned hot with an unwelcome memory.

Gunther reached out and grabbed Bardot's reins. "Katherine. Listen."

Katherine raised reluctant eyes to Gunther's.

"If you don't want me along, fine. You've made it clear how you feel about me. But I'm going to give you some advice and I want you to listen."

Katherine bit her lip and nodded. In spite of how she felt about Gunther, he was smart. She respected his opinions.

"First, don't travel after dark. Stay in the towns at night. If you do get stuck in the woods, light a fire and keep it burning as bright as possible. Wolves are afraid of fire and they won't go near one. Second, don't go off the path. I know you're brave and capable, but these woods are tricky."

Katherine locked eyes with Gunther. "I won't."

"Good." Gunther dropped the reins. "And if you run into danger, anything at all—if anyone so much as looks at you wrong—you ask me for help."

Katherine brushed a strand of hair from her eyes. "I will."

With a creak of leather and metal, Gunther whirled and was gone, cantering up the forest track.

Unsettled, but determined, Katherine continued her journey. But her fear of the wolves ruined her enjoyment of the otherwise pleasant solitude. Every tiny crackle made her jump. Every whispering leaf turned into predators creeping through underbrush. The sweep of the wind no longer comforted her with its caress but frightened her with its mysterious noises.

Finally, lulled by the sunshine and the fact that town was a mere hour's ride away, Katherine relaxed. Then it happened. A rabbit skittering through the bushes, scampered in front of Bardot, startling the usually dependable horse. Bardot reared, whinnying in distress, and Katherine tumbled. Fortunately, she landed on the grassy verge, and besides a few bruises, was unharmed. But the horse panicked, catching his foot in a hole. Katherine scrambled to her feet, grabbing the reins.

"Shh.... You're all right." She calmed the terrified animal with soft murmurs, stroking his satiny neck. Bardot rolled his eyes, bobbing his head up and down.

Katherine ran shaking hands down Bardot's legs, checking for injury. When he flinched, Katherine peered closer. A long scrape on his front leg leaked blood. Wiping her grimy fingers on a cloth, Katherine opened her satchel, taking out a long strip of fabric.

She poured a bit of water on the wound, soothing the still frightened beast, then wrapped it tightly in some cloth.

"I guess we'll take it easy," Katherine said, resting on a mossy log. She would walk to town and hope the farrier would tend to Bardot when she arrived. But how to get there; Katherine mulled over the question in her mind. Katherine had no way to assess the seriousness of Bardot's injury; she didn't want to put undue strain on the horse's leg.

Regret lanced her chest, as Katherine wished she hadn't been so quick to dismiss Gunther's offer of help. He might be brusque and annoying, but being army trained, he was certainly invaluable in emergency situations.

"Can you walk beside me for little ways?" Katherine asked Bardot, who, unfazed by her indecision, tore mouthfuls of juicy grass from the roadside. Katherine took Bardot's reins and began walking, progressing slowly; she stopped often to rest and check for signs of heat in Bardot's injury. The horse went willingly. Comforted by the fact that Bardot didn't seem to be in visible pain, Katherine kept up a steady pace.

Orange sun slanted between the trees, and the chances of reaching the next village before dark were slim. Foreboding trickled down Katherine's spine as she realised, despite her advancement she would be forced to spend the night in the forest.

Don't worry, there's no danger in this forest unless you're afraid of deer and hedgehogs, she thought to herself. Dismayed, Katherine scanned the thick underbrush, looking for a clearing to sleep. The sun dipped behind the trees and as the sky purpled, Katherine led Bardot off the path, letting him drink from the brook before setting up camp.

Gunther's advice to build a fire burned into Katherine's memory. She quickly gathered sticks and branches, piling them under a beech tree. By the time she completed this task, twilight had settled. She felt through her saddlebag; with a wave of relief, she felt the cold metal box holding her flint and tinder. Grateful her father had taught her how to light a fire and keep it burning, Katherine soon had a merry blaze crackling.

The flickering flames bolstered Katherine's spirit as she foraged through her pack, producing dried meat and bread. This was not the comfortable inn with a hot meal Katherine expected, but it would suffice until morning.

After her makeshift meal, Katherine curled into her bedroll, staring at the fire until she fell into an uneasy sleep.

Bardot woke Katherine, panicked, whinnying. Fear knifed through Katherine's chest as she jerked upright. The fire had nearly fizzled out;

Katherine rushed to fumble for more wood, coaxing the glowing coals into a healthy blaze.

"What is it, boy?" Katherine found Bardot's shadowy figure. There was no sign of danger, but tendrils of fear raised every hair on Katherine's neck. She stroked his neck, comforting herself as much as him.

Katherine listened carefully, but only heard the faint rustle of an evening breeze whisking through the trees. When Bardot calmed, Katherine returned to her bedroll, but she couldn't sleep. Gunther's warning about wolves reverberated through her mind. So, she spent the rest of the night huddled, feeding the fire, keeping it blazing. When the morning sun turned grey shadows to gold, Katherine was still awake, eyes dry and gritty from lack of sleep.

Not in the mood to cook, Katherine ate the rest of her loaf, forcing the dry bread down with sips of water. When she went to check on Bardot, she found, to her dismay, the injury had worsened, swollen and hot to touch. Bardot flinched and whinnied in pain when Katherine pressed the skin around the injury.

Katherine cleaned and wrapped Bardot's leg as best she could, but knew the horse needed proper care. Katherine wished desperately Althea were there with her poultices; she would know exactly what to do. Katherine went in search of aloe near the brook. Marion always grew aloe in the garden for scrapes and burns, and Katherine hoped it would help. She wandered along the stream's embankment, scanning the undergrowth for the pale green spiky leaves.

"Are you lost?" a deep voice drifted from behind a stand of trees. Katherine jumped, nearly sliding into the rushing water.

"Who is it?" she pressed a trembling hand to her heart.

"Sorry, I didn't mean to frighten you." A rugged man stepped from behind a beech tree. A grey cloak wafted from his shoulders.. not wool or fur... a fabric without a discernible weave or pattern—one not even Katherine's critical eye recognized.

"That's all right." Katherine's thumping heart slowed, no longer slamming against her ribcage. "I wasn't expecting to meet anyone this deep in the forest."

The mysterious stranger stepped toward Katherine, the grey cloak flowing like a living thing. "Are you lost?"

"Not exactly." Katherine attempted to evade his question. There were no rumours of bandits haunting this stretch of road, but you couldn't be too careful about strangers. Katherine clutched the red cloak tight around her shoulder, grateful for the extra layer of protection Althea's ward afforded.

The man slithered closer; Katherine shrank back against the vine covered stream bank.

"We can help." His smooth voice trickled through the morning air.

"We?" Katherine glanced around the forest.

"Come on out." The stranger waved. Three others—all wearing that same grey cloak— appeared, ghosts against the shadows of thick trees. One man and two women.

"Hello." A woman stepped forward, her wide smile showing white pointed teeth. Dark hair, waving and tousled, hung free to the small of her back. "Did you say you were lost?" The strange woman placed a warm hand on Katherine's arm. Katherine glanced down, seeing long nails, a faint rim of dirt underlining the bed.

"Not lost. My horse injured his leg. I was hoping to find aloe to relieve his injury."

"No aloe grows at this streambed; it's far too dark. But if you return to the cabin with us, we could give you some. Eleonor here grows aloe in our garden. In fact, we have an ointment that would probably be better."

Eleonor's smile widened as the man spoke, white teeth gleaming against her polished skin.

"Thank you, that's very kind. But is the cabin far? I could get the ointment and return to Bardot." Katherine hesitated to trust the motley group. There was something... off about them.

The man's eyes narrowed. "It's just, I'm not sure how long he can walk... the horse, I mean." Katherine rushed to answer, not wanting to offend her strange benefactors.

"I see. Why don't you let Eleonor look at your horse?"

Katherine reluctantly led the group to her makeshift campsite where Bardot waited, his liquid brown eyes patient. He rolled his eyes when the strangers appeared in front of them, unimpressed by their desire to help. Katherine soothed the horse as Eleonor approached. He flinched when she touched him, stroking her hands down the length of his injured leg.

"Just a flesh wound. With proper rest and care, Bardot will heal in no time." Eleonor straightened. "The ointment will prevent infection."

Katherine breathed a sigh of relief. Her journey had hardly begun, and she couldn't afford delays. "Do you think the horse could walk to the village?" She turned to Eleonor.

Eleonor frowned. "It's probably not a good idea to strain the injury. Why don't you stay overnight with us; you could see if he's improved by morning?"

Eleonor ignored her leader's glare as she made the offer.

"That's kind of you. But I couldn't impose." Katherine lowered her head against the unwelcome gaze boring into her.

"It's no bother," Eleonor insisted, untying Bardot's halter. "Zelia and Jules can help you gather your things."

Katherine watched, helpless, as Zelia and Jules, the two strangers who had been in the forest with Eleonor, quickly helped Katherine as she gathered her belongings, rolling up her bedroll and tamping the fire with damp earth. Moments later, Katherine followed the four strangers through leafy underbrush as they forged through the thick, green foliage. They burst through, entering a clearing where a small, roughly made cabin was situated.

"This is your cabin?" Katherine gazed at the dwelling with curious eyes. It was tidy but old, weathered boards displaying signs of age. But the neat garden and freshly swept front step told Katherine that someone took pride in the small forest home.

"Yes." Zelia opened the front door, wiping her feet on a cheerful woven mat. "It isn't much, but it's home."

Katherine followed Zelia inside, surveying the interior with wide eyes. She was greeted by a kitchen area with a comfortable chair near the fire. A wooden ladder led to a loft upstairs, two side doors led to what Katherine presumed were bedrooms. Yellow cloth covered a bowl warming on the hearth; bread rising, Katherine sniffed the warm yeasty smell.

"What do you do in the forest?" Katherine was curious about the lack of animals and farmland. Most country people owned chickens and at least a goat or two. In spite of the healthy garden, there were no signs of livestock.

Eleonor winced. "We do all right with the garden," she answered, directing Katherine to sit at the fire. Eleonor rummaged on a kitchen shelf, pulling down jars and bottles, while muttering to herself.

"Ah, here it is." Eleonor opened a jar, filling the room with a strong herbal scent. "This should have your horse better soon." She held it to her nose, sniffing as she closed her eyes in concentration.

Katherine followed Eleonor outside to a modest shed. Bardot was munching the oats Katherine had given him, and hardly noticed when Eleonor smeared a thick layer of salve over his injured leg. She wound a loose bandage around it and gave him a pat.

"He'll be all right in the shed tonight." Eleonor latched onto the shed carefully.

"Why, are there wild animals here?" Katherine furrowed her brow. She should have taken Gunther's advice a little more to heart.

Eleonor brushed off her question. "Rarely, but it's better to be safe." Her eyes darted to the front of the cabin where Alerion, the one Katherine had spoken to first, was sitting wrapped in his grey cloak. Alerion seemed to be the leader of the strange group; Katherine watched closely as the others deferred to him, almost seeming to fear him at times.

Katherine pondered the mystery of the small group. They didn't seem to have an occupation, but were secure enough to afford plentiful supplies. Katherine noted the overflowing kitchen shelves. Zelia whiled away her time in the kitchen, baking bread, while Eleonor pottered in the garden with her herbs. Not enough herbs to sell, Katherine noted with an experienced eye, just enough for personal use.

Alerion and Jules sat outside in front of the cabin. Jules whittled a piece of cherry wood with a sharp knife and Alerion stared into space, a grim expression on his face.

When Katherine tried to ask Eleonor questions about her life in the forest, she was either redirected or totally ignored. At dinner, Zelia placed a generous platter of roasted meat in the centre of the table. Venison. They must hunt. Katherine guessed it was Alerion. He looked like a hunter—how he slunk noiselessly place to place, and his eyes. His eyes were watchful and predatory.

"Have some more." Zelia pushed the plate toward Katherine.

"No, I couldn't." Katherine leaned back from the table, rubbing her full stomach. She took the mug of tea Zelia offered. There was no milk; a dollop of honey spiced and sweetened the tea. The peculiar family sat around the table in silence, watchful eyes locked on Katherine, as if they were waiting for something.

Wooziness came in waves over Katherine. Not enough sleep, Katherine yawned. Katherine's thoughts became vague and muddle; the faces blurring together. The last thing she remembered was Alerion's golden eyes hovering over her. She tried to protest as she felt her body being lifted and carried, but her mouth refused to move.

KATHERINE PRIED HER gritty eyes open. The tarry black surrounding her was thick and silent. She blinked, adjusting to the darkness. A bedroom, she felt the cotton pillowcase under her cheek. A single beam of moonlight shone through a crack in the curtains. Katherine huddled under the covers, her head still muddled from the... the tea she realized with a start. Zelia put something in the tea to make her sleep. But why?

Katherine swung her feet to the floor, trying to be as quiet as possible. She tiptoed to the door, pressing her ear against the wooden frame. Murmuring voices drifted through the thin walls.

"Why did you bring that girl here? What were you thinking?" Katherine recognized Alerion's voice. His voice was tight, angry.

"I wanted to help. She's no rules against that, does she?"

A creak and a muffled thud. Someone had thrown another log on the fire.

"Fine, help anyone and everyone, if you must. Remember, we have a job to do, and there are consequences for failure."

"I know," the voice was resigned. Eleonor, Katherine recognized the timbre. "But we've been searching for so long, and there's no sign of them. Not even a whiff. I mean, what if they don't actually exist? What if someone else got them first? Maybe they're a figment of her imagination."

"With that scar? An overactive imagination wouldn't cause that," Alerion answered back. "Someone did that to her. Besides, you know what will happen if we fail. To us... to them. All we need is the Rapunzel blood. Just one drop will lead us to the others. Then we'll be free. We almost had it once; we won't let it get away again," he growled at the end of the sentence.

Katherine shivered. Rapunzel.... that was her mother's family name. She clutched the edge of the red cloak. The cabin was chilly, so she'd never taken it off. They must have put her in bed without removing it.

Katherine shivered, realizing the only thing protecting her from being discovered was a thin layer of red fabric.

"So what now?" It was Jules. "Do we wait until the girl leaves before we carry on searching?"

"No. We hunt tonight." Alerion's tone left no room for argument. "Did she take enough potion to sleep until morning?"

"She did," Zelia answered.

"Then we go." Crackling energy whipped through the air, leaving Katherine gasping for breath, the bitter taste of magic burning through her mouth and nose. She pressed her eye to the crack in the door, hoping to glimpse them. What was happening?

A flash of grey, not the cloaks. Fur. A gleam of pointed teeth.

Wolves.

Katherine bit her lip, holding back a whimper. In a flurry of motion, the wolves leapt out the cabin door. Katherine ran to the window, peering through the gap in the curtains. Four wolves... enormous wolves. Running like wind, they disappeared, melting into the forest like wraiths.

The second the wolves vanished from sight, Katherine dashed for the bedroom door. She desperately fumbled with the latch, wrenching the handle with all her might. Locked. Bolted from the outside. Not giving up, she ran to the window. Also locked. There must be something she could do.

Katherine looked around wildly, searching for something to break the glass. The bedroom was bare, not even a hairbrush on the wooden dresser. Katherine's eyes settled on the brass lamp on the nightstand. That would do. Katherine hefted it in her hand, feeling the weight of the metal. She flung it at the glass, ducking to avoid any shattering glass. The lamp banged uselessly against the glass, then rolled to the floor.

Katherine picked up the lamp, pounding on the window again and again. But her efforts were useless. They'd warded the cabin with protection. Katherine curled under the quilt and let the hot tears flow.

CHAPTER THREE

Glaring sun streaked through fluttering curtains. Katherine rubbed bleary eyes, momentarily confused. She gasped as last night's shocking events rushed through her mind. Katherine flew to the door, grasping the metal handle. It clicked, opening easily under her hand.

"There you are," Eleonor said, smiling. "We didn't want to wake you. Did you sleep well?" Katherine shuddered as Eleonor's pointed teeth gleamed in the bright daylight.

"Yes." Katherine pushed back her tumbling blonde hair.

"Good." Eleonor slid steaming hotcakes onto a red plate. "We were about to eat breakfast." She poured four circles of creamy batter into the griddle, watching the batter bubble and turn crispy on the edges.

Katherine's stomach growled. She was hungry, and the hotcakes smelled delicious. Eleonor set out a pitcher of honey and plonked a tall stack of hotcakes in front of Katherine. "Go ahead; I've fed your horse. The others will be in shortly; trust me, they wouldn't think to leave any hotcakes behind."

"How is Bardot?" Katherine hoped the wolves hadn't frightened Bardot.

"Bardot's injury is mending well." Eleonor's voice was animated as she flipped the hotcakes. "But he'll need to rest; you can stay another day until he's healed."

"Oh, I couldn't take your bed another night." The idea of being locked in the cabin another night sent chills racing up Katherine's spine. The sooner she escaped this cabin—these strange wolf people—the better.

"It's no trouble," Eleonor insisted. "In fact, to be perfectly honest with you, it's lovely to see another face. I love my family, but the clearing gets lonely."

Katherine nodded, mouth too full of honeyed hotcakes to answer. After breakfast, Eleonor led Katherine to the shed to visit Bardot. The horse whickered happily, greeting her with a friendly nudge of his nose.

"How are you, boy?" Katherine ran her hand down Bardot's injured leg. Eleonor was right. The horse's leg had drastically improved, the heated skin cooled, the swelling barely perceptible. Bardot flinched as Katherine's touch traveled over it. Was the injury still sensitive to her touch? Hoping she was wrong, Katherine fastened Bardot's harness. Leading him into the clearing, she observed signs of a limp. Bardot followed, willing to please his mistress, but Katherine saw the horse still favored the sore leg. Katherine gulped. She was stuck at the cabin another night.

The day dragged slowly; Katherine warily avoided Alerion. The group seemed strangely normal—human—in spite of last night's revelation. Eleonor was especially friendly, asking Katherine multitudes of questions about the outside world Eleonor craved contact with; Katherine wondered why she stayed with the others if she didn't like the isolation.

That night, when Zelia brought Katherine tea, she only pretended to drink, a futile attempt to avoid being ambushed again. Although Katherine watched for an opportunity to dispose of the tea, with a sinking heart, she realized the intense gaze of four pairs of eyes made this an impossible task.

Katherine feigned a yawn, letting her eyes droop. Maybe she could pretend the tea was working. She sipped excruciatingly slowly, working her empty throat, letting her head droop to the side. She peeked through slitted eyes, glimpsing the triumphant expression on Alerion's face. Her plan was working, just a few more minutes. Katherine rested her head on the table, allowing her eyes to drift shut.

Katherine's heart pounded, mouth dry with fear as powerful arms lifted her. She felt herself deposited once more in the hard, narrow bed.

Click. The bedroom lock fell into place. Katherine's eyes snapped open.

She waited, forcing her breaths to stay even until murmuring voices rose again. Katherine slithered upright on the bed before tiptoeing to the door.

"... has no idea." The words drifted through thin wooden walls.

"She barely touched the tea tonight; are you positive?" There was an impatient edge to Alerion's voice.

"No, she's definitely asleep," Jules assured Alerion. "She didn't stir when I set her in bed."

"All the same. I'll be glad when the girl's gone. Keeping her another day was ridiculous. If Madelaine knew you'd brought strangers to the clearing, she'd have your skin. Mine too," Alerion grumbled.

"But it's lonely here. I wanted to see another human, even for a little while. Besides, the girl needs help," Katherine answered.

"She's not a pet," Alerion grunted. "See that she's gone tomorrow. I'm travelling back to Iasia to see Madelaine the day after tomorrow; if the girl's still here, it won't be safe for anyone." He growled, the fierce sound raising hairs on Katherine's neck. "Besides, I caught a whiff of scent." Alerion said.

"You did?" Katherine heard excitement colour Jules' voice.

"Near the healer's house. Madelaine told us the healer would be the key to discovering the Rapunzel girls. I've been checking regularly."

"Where did the scent trail lead?" Zelia asked.

Alerion growled again. "The scent was strong. Definitely Rapunzel blood. I smelled that magic. One of them visited the healer. Recently. What's more, your friend here has been there too. I didn't scent her, but I recognized the horse's scent."

"The injured horse?" Zelia sounded doubtful.

"I know it was the horse." Alerion answered. "The Rapunzel scent ended at the healer's cottage. I tried to backtrack, but the scent went cold. We should have watched the healer's cottage better; I blame myself."

"You don't think the healer killed the Rapunzel daughter, do you?" Jules asked.

"Her? No, the healer woman is too soft to kill. Besides, I would have smelled blood. The cottage was clean."

"Where did the Rapunzel girl go if she's not at the healer's cottage?" Zelia sounded puzzled.

"I don't know." A burst of noise. Light flared under the crack around the rickety wooden door—another log thrown on the fire.

"You girls find out what the girl knows. It's unusual for a woman to travel alone through the forest. If she spoke to the healer, she could be the key to the missing Rapunzel girls. We need to know what it is. I'll return to the healer's cottage tonight to follow the scent again. The Rapunzel girl might return."

Shuffling footsteps crossed the floorboards; Katherine assumed the wolf people were leaving. Katherine crept back to her narrow bed, heart pounding against her ribcage. She pulled at the neck of the red cape. Earlier, Zelia had encouraged Katherine to remove the cape and thrown her a suspicious glance when Katherine insisted she was cold. She fell into an uneasy sleep. Tomorrow, she could leave.

In the morning, Bardot's leg was almost recovered. He didn't even notice when Katherine ran her hand up over the injury.

"You should give the leg one more day, just to be sure." Zelia worried her lip as Katherine examined the injury. Katherine's mind whirled; she had to leave without making the wolf people suspicious.

"You're right," Katherine agreed, stroking Bardot's soft nose. "If it's not too much trouble, I could stay another day."

The relief on Zelia's face was palpable. Katherine followed Zelia to the cabin, determined to slip away at the first opportunity. That opportunity didn't arrive until lunchtime. Katherine waited until Zelia and Eleonor were busy in the kitchen before slipping to the shed, skirting the front of the cabin where Jules and Alerion sat.

"Be quiet," Katherine whispered to Bardot as she hefted the saddle onto his back. She threw her satchel over her shoulder and mounted. Maybe she could find her way to town before the wolves caught up. A wave of relief rolled over her as Katherine left the small clearing, travelling into the sun dappled forest.

When she was out of earshot, Katherine urged Bardot into a trot; Bardot was willing, and Katherine was soon slipping through the trees. If she was on the road, perhaps there would be other travellers. Surely she'd be safer there; the wolves wouldn't dare attack in full view.

To Katherine's horror and dismay, the wolves appeared silent as ghosts from the thick trees. Two in front and two behind.

Four pairs of unblinking yellow eyes stared.

There was no way Katherine could outrun wolves in the thick forest, especially with Bardot's injury. Her blood iced in her veins as Katherine realized she was trapped.

She fumbled at her side as Bardot shifted uneasily underneath her body. Katherine's only weapon was the small knife she used to cut twigs for the fire. She clutched the cold metal tight in her hand.

The largest wolf lunged, a growl deep in his throat. Bardot reared, desperate hooves flailing. He caught the wolf in the shoulder, sending it spinning to the ground. The wolf leapt up, limping, but not running away. Katherine swung the knife wildly, shuddering as the sharp metal met flesh and bone.

Searing pain roared through Katherine's arm; a wolf had leapt, slicing razor-sharp teeth against her arm. She flailed the knife again, but this blow only glanced off thick hide. Another wolf circled, teeth bared as it stalked the horse. Suddenly, with a whimper, the wolf fell.

An arrow pinned the wolf to the ground. Another arrow whistled through the air. This one missed.

Hoofbeats thundered behind her. She saw Gunther, a grim look on his face as he fit another arrow into his bow. But he was too late. Another wolf leapt, catching Katherine's shoulder.

Katherine tumbled from the horse, crashing to the ground with a bone-jarring thud. Katherine fought the black spots swimming before her eyes as she reached out, fumbling for anything that might help her fight. An oblong object met her fingers. The book. It must have fallen from her pocket when she fell. A bolt of power shot through her, and through the haze, she heard howling.

Everything went still.

CHAPTER FOUR

"Are you hurt?" Gunther slid off his horse, racing to Katherine's side.

"I'm fine." Katherine struggled upright, cradling her injured arm.

"You're bleeding." Gunther took Katherine's arm, gently rolling up the sleeve. Blood covered his hands as he prodded the injury. Katherine bit back a cry. The pain seared like a hot knife. Gunther used his waterskin to pour water over Katherine's arm, cleaning the wound. His calloused hands were gentle, soothing in spite of the blazing pain.

"Do you have something to wrap it?" he asked.

Katherine gritted her teeth, pointing to her saddlebag. Gunther wrapped the wound securely in a makeshift sling, tying the cloth with a firm knot.

"Can you ride? We should hurry before the wolves return."

Katherine nodded, with Gunther giving her a boost, she heaved herself onto Bardot's back, face pale with the effort. Gunther swung easily into the saddle beside her.

"What were you thinking, lingering in this part of the woods for so long; you should have left here days ago." Gunther scolded, his mouth thinned into a tight line as he glanced at Katherine's unsteady form.

"I got delayed." Katherine said, hesitating.

Gunther shot Katherine a glare. "I can see that... but *how?*"

Katherine bit her lip, she didn't relish explaining the details of the encounter with the wolves to Gunther, but he did save her. Besides, Gunther was smart and resourceful, if anyone could give her insight into the situation it would be him. She took a shaky breath and started to talk.

THE ROSE INN WAS DINGY and run down, but to Katherine, it was the finest palace she'd ever seen. After leaving their horses with the groom, Katherine followed Gunther inside. The smell of fried onions and gravy hung rich and heavy in the air, and Katherine's stomach growled. She hadn't eaten since breakfast.

Gunther and Katherine found an empty table and sat down.

"Let's recap, you think the woman behind the wolves is Madelaine Rapunzel?" Gunther asked Katherine as she scooped a forkful of gravy-soaked mashed potatoes.

Katherine nodded, mouth too full to answer.

Gunther scratched his chin. "The name sounds familiar. I spent some time with the Iasians on Celine's first delegation. Madelaine Rapunzel wasn't in court, but I heard people speak of her." He snapped his fingers. "I've got it."

"What?" Katherine glanced up from her roast pork.

"Madelaine Rapunzel is Iasian nobility. Rumor had it she was injured in a terrible accident and that's why she never appeared in Iasian court. Madelaine was supposedly a remarkable beauty; I guess she didn't want people to see how much she had altered."

Katherine caught her breath; it was the same story Althea told her. It had to be true. She glanced at Lord Gunther, debating whether to disclose Althea's information.

"Do you know where Madelaine's estate was?" Katherine asked.

Gunther shook his head, "No, Madelaine was only mentioned in passing. I suppose we could find out... ask someone. Celine would know."

Katherine tapped her fork on the edge of her plate. She didn't like Gunther, but no one got things done like he could.

"Can you find out where Madelaine lives? I want to pay her a visit." Katherine set her jaw.

"Well, you're not going alone. Not after being attacked by Madelaine's pack of wolves."

Katherine rolled her eyes. "It would take forever to organize guards for a cross border visit."

Gunther's eyes gleamed. "Oh, I wasn't planning on inviting guards." He grinned at the Katherine's perplexed expression. "It's been a while since I've paid a visit to Iaisa. I plan to come myself."

A FEW DAYS LATER, KATHERINE was still arguing with Gunther.

Bardot ambled along the woodland path beside Lord Gunther's tall black horse. Katherine's arm and her shoulder still pained her, but the wound was healing nicely. Katherine obtained salve at the village apothecary that would last until the injury healed.

True to his word, Gunther sent a messenger to learn where Madelaine Rapunzel's estate was located. Much to Katherine's dismay, Gunther was determined to join the expedition and wouldn't be swayed.

Although Gunther pressed, Katherine remained tight-lipped about the reason for her interest in Madelaine Rapunzel. Katherine would find Madelaine, then find how to keep her mother and sisters safe.

She couldn't stop Gunther from riding beside her, but that was where his interference ended; Katherine told herself firmly. As to what Katherine would say when they arrived at Madelaine's estate, that was a question even Katherine couldn't answer.

"Not long now." Gunther glanced at Madelaine. They trotted down the main street of Pacolet, the last town before Madelaine's estate. Katherine glanced around the village with curious eyes. These were the shops and businesses her mother frequented as a child. It was market day. Market Square was busy with people buying, selling, or just there for gossip. Katherine's eyes settled longingly on a colorful fabric stall. This area of Iasia was known for fine wool; Katherine always wanted a chance to explore their wares further.

"Go ahead, we have time." Gunther urged Katherine toward the stall.

"Are you sure?" Katherine hesitated.

"Yes. We'll probably have to spend the night in the inn here, anyway; you may as well. I know you're dying to see the fabrics." Gunther threw Katherine an encouraging smile.

Katherine lost no time handing over the reins and wandering through the stalls, inspecting the merchandise. Katherine fingered the patterns and colours, letting the vibrant blues, greens, and purples slide across her skin.

"Looking for anything particular?" the vender asked, eyeing Katherine's rich red cloak and hoping for a sale.

"I'm not sure I have space; I'm travelling."

"Oh, we can have it sent to you. Where do you live?" the vender's eyes were sharp.

"Lovan," Katherine said, surveying a pattern of interlocking stripes.

"Oh... we don't get many from those parts here." The vender slid his eyes toward Gunther, still waiting patiently with the horses.

"We're just passing through." Katherine drew the red cloak around herself, not caring for the sly look gleaming from the vender's eyes.

"I see. Well, if you choose your fabrics, we can arrange transport for you. Lady Madelaine sends couriers there regularly."

"She does?" Katherine jerked her head up, temporarily forgetting she wasn't supposed to know who Madelaine was.

"Oh, yes; in fact, she's here in Market Square. Madelaine is a regular customer of mine. I'll introduce you." The vendor gestured across the square toward a tall veiled woman. The woman glided toward the fabric stall.

Katherine held her breath, trying not to stare. Madelaine's veil was so thick she could only discern a faint glitter of the Madelaine's eyes behind the dark fabric.

"Lady Madelaine, lovely to see you," the merchant greeted her effusively. "I was speaking to this young woman..."

"Katherine. Just Katherine," Katherine supplied.

"Katherine was saying she would like some fabric sent to Lovan for her." The vender smiled obsequiously.

"Pleased to meet you." Madelaine stretched out a cold, elegant hand. Katherine took it, almost numb with disbelief. This was the woman responsible for the loss of Katherine's mother. A shiver of disgust went through her as she touched the woman's pale skin.

"Of course, I would be happy to arrange that." Lady Madelaine's voice was low, husky.

"That's too kind of you. I couldn't possibly accept such generosity from a stranger." Katherine surreptitiously rubbed the hand that had touched Lady Madelaine on the edge of her red cloak.

"Of course, you can, my dear." There was a nearly imperceptible edge in Madelaine's voice. "I insist."

Katherine's mind raced. She couldn't possibly allow Lady Madelaine to know where she and her sisters lived.

Gunther stepped forward, hand resting on his sword. "If you could send the fabric to my estate, that would be wonderful. Of course, we will compensate you accordingly. Lord Gunther at your service." He bowed stiffly.

"Certainly," Madelaine murmured.

After choosing the fabrics she wanted, Katherine returned to Lord Gunther and Lady Madelaine.

"I insist that you and your husband must stay at the manor instead of that poky little inn. It would be my pleasure."

"Oh, he's not—" Katherine's was cut off by a warning glance from Gunther.

Lady Madelaine clutched Katherine's hand in her cool grasp. "I rarely have visitors anymore, and I've no family nearby; it would be delightful." Katherine threw Gunther a helpless glance as she was pulled along by the woman.

"But I—"

"Nonsense." They arrived at an elegant carriage. Lady Madelaine shooed Katherine into the cool dim interior and climbed in behind her. "My groom will bring your horses."

Gunther climbed into the carriage behind Madelaine, sitting on the narrow bench. Katherine shrugged off the warning bells that were ringing in her head. After all, hadn't they wanted to get close to Lady Madelaine and learn exactly what she was planning and stop her. This was a golden opportunity.

The carriage rolled along a rutted path, the manor rising out of the thick trees. Most of the manor was newly built, the brick still bright red. But Katherine glimpsed some of the original building. Blackened by fire, it stood in bleak contrast to the newly built facade. It must be from the fire her mother had caused.

Katherine wondered at the fact that it was Lucie, her mother's youngest daughter, who had inherited her mother's fire magic. She understood better now why her mother had wanted to seal the magic and why Lucie was reluctant to use her fire unless absolutely necessary.

"Come." Lady Madelaine swept up the stairs toward the entry hall. The manor gleamed, not a speck of dust or dirt marring its shining surfaces. A little brown dog ran to Madelaine, leaping into her outstretched arms and licking her frantically.

"This is Manoy." Lady Madelaine kissed the dog, her voice softening. She removed her cloak, but left the veil firmly in place. One of the servants came forward, offering to take Katherine's cloak.

"No thank you, I'm a bit chilly." Katherine clutched the edge of the cloak, unwilling to give up her protection. Who knew what Madelaine was capable of—especially in her own home.

"I injured my arm," she explained as Madelaine's veiled head turned. "It's more comfortable covered."

Madelaine accepted her explanation, but Katherine wondered how long she could keep her interest at bay. Katherine would need to make her visit short if she wanted to avoid discovery.

"Please, make yourself comfortable. I must give the cook instructions; she's used to only having me alone." With a musical laugh Madelaine glided away, leaving only a trace of perfume behind her.

Katherine turned her curious eyes to Madelaine's drawing room. A receiving room. An adjoining door was ajar—a library—well used by the looks of it. Katherine itched to explore, but clinking china announced the arrival of tea.

"I hope I wasn't too forward bringing you to the manor." Madelaine sat ramrod straight on the edge of the settee. Madelaine still hadn't removed her veil and her cup of tea sat untouched, cooling on the silver tray.

"Not at all, it's a delightful interlude. Your estate is beautiful; I would love to see the gardens; I've heard so much about them." Katherine politely nibbled a raspberry tart. In truth, Katherine had never heard about the Rapunzel gardens, but it seemed an excellent way to finagle a tour of the Rapunzel estate.

"Of course." Lady Madelaine accepted the bait.

Madelaine's gardens were lovely, but not as fascinating as her extensive stables. Even Gunther was impressed by the horses—breeds Katherine and Gunther had never seen before. All beautifully cared for. Lady Madelaine came alive in the stable, cooing and murmuring to the horses, who responded with their own language of nickers and whinnies. *It must be lonely on this vast estate,* Katherine thought, watching Madelaine stroke a velvety nose.

After the stables came the Aviary, the largest Katherine had ever seen. Again, Madelaine's aviary was filled with strange and unusual creatures and birds from far away. Madelaine told her she had even once owned a firebird. It didn't thrive well in captivity, so she freed it.

"What's in that building?" Katherine pointed to a long, low-slung building. Newer than the manor, its mottled stone walls stood out against the lush green gardens like a stain.

"Just a barn." Madelaine turned and hastily led them in the other direction. "I keep animals for milk and meat. You wouldn't be interested." Katherine and Gunther exchanged a significant glance; they had to get in that barn.

CHAPTER FIVE

Even at the dinner table, lady Madelaine kept her veil firmly in place, eating by slipping forkfuls of food under the edge of the thick veil. Katherine noticed that although Madelaine served meat, she didn't partake, only nibbling vegetables and a slice of buttered bread. *Madelaine must never eat meat,* Katherine thought, chewing her tender roast beef. Manoy joined them for dinner, curled on Madelaine's lap and eating titbits sneaked under the table.

"Emory will show you your chamber," Madelaine's husky voice broke the thick silence hovering over the dinner table.

Chamber, not chambers? Katherine's horrified eyes flicked to Madelaine. She must be mistaken; Madelaine couldn't possibly intend for Katherine and Gunther to share a chamber. Katherine slid her eyes to Gunther. To her dismay, Gunther merely winking, looking amused by the predicament. They followed the steward up the wide polished staircase to a richly decorated stateroom.

"I'll sleep in the dressing room tonight," Katherine said, voice stiff.

Gunther sighed, removing a clean tunic from his saddlebag. "I don't relish this situation any more than you, but Madelaine can't get suspicious. I'll sleep in the dressing room, goodness knows I've slept in much worse situations."

Katherine softened, nodding before sitting awkwardly on the bed, fidgeting with the ties of her red cloak. Grubby streaks ran up the crimson hem; she examined them, wondering if she could wash them by hand and dry it overnight. Madelaine would surely notice and be suspicious if Katherine wore the same dirty cloak tomorrow.

As Katherine was scrubbing a muddy stain from the cloak, Gunther disappeared into the dressing room and snoring shortly ensued. Katherine tossed and turned on the four-poster bed, but sleep eluded her. She tossed and turned restlessly, the feather quilt twisting around her limbs. Maybe reading would help her nod off, Katherine thought, lighting a candle and slipping into the darkened corridor. Only a ticking clock broke the silence; everyone was asleep. She tiptoed down the corridor toward the sweeping staircase, thinking surely Madelaine wouldn't mind if she borrowed a book from the library. Katherine crept down the stairs, testing every board for creaks before putting her full weight on the carpeted step.

She held up the light, casting an orange glow over tidy rows of books. Animal Spirits. The Soul of the Horse. Capturing the Stag. Magic and Animals. Natural Magic. Communication and Canines. Katherine shivered, her heart drumming like thunder as she scanned the titles. Every single title on the shelf was related to animals and magic—not just any magic—dark magic. *Was this Madelaine's hold over the wolves,* Katherine wondered. Madelaine must access the dark magic to control the wolves from across the Lovanian border.

Katherine ran her finger down the spine of the book, questions flooding her mind. Disturbed, Katherine returned to her room, falling into an unsettled sleep.

"Katherine. Katherine. Wake up." Katherine bolted upright. Gunther shook her shoulder.

"Breakfast time."

Katherine rubbed bleary eyes. Gunther was dressed and ready, hair combed neatly, eyes bright and energetic.

"Are you all right?" Gunther's brow wrinkled.

"I saw something strange last night." Katherine splashed her face with cold water. "You know those books in Madelaine's library?"

Gunther nodded, his brow furrowed.

"They're all about animals…. and magic. Every single volume."

"That's how Madelaine controls the wolves? With magic? I thought Althea said Madelaine wasn't gifted?"

"Althea said she didn't know. Maybe Madelaine hid her gift. Maybe her gift didn't appear until later…. My mother couldn't keep her gift hidden, perhaps Madelaine found a way to hide the gift."

Gunther's eyes grew thoughtful. "The key to Madelaine's secret is in the barn."

Katherine chewed her lip. "But how will we get in? Madelaine has the barn guarded and locked; she's determined to keep us away."

"If you distract Madelaine for an hour, I could sneak past the guards and look at the barn," Gunther said, eyes glowing.

"I suppose… but how will I distract Madelaine?" Katherine's voice was reluctant. She hated that Gunther was putting himself in danger for her.

"Tell Madelaine we want to go riding on the estate to see the grounds. She's obsessed with horses. At the last minute, I'll tell her I'm sick. Madelaine is far too polite to disappoint you."

Getting Madelaine to agree to ride was easy. She was only too delighted to show off her prized steeds to her visitors. However, getting Madelaine to leave Gunther unattended in the manor house was quite another matter. Madelaine very nearly turned back; it was only when Katherine professed her undying disappointment at not seeing the famous Rapunzel grounds that Madelaine relented. Katherine could almost see the fierce expression hidden behind the thick veil as Madelaine mounted, whispering to the horse who remained still as a stone while she sat poised in the saddle.

Madelaine took a narrow path leading through the woods.

"What's that?" Katherine pointed at a crumbling tower half hidden behind the thick trees.

"That land belonged to my grandmother." Madelaine urged her horse to hurry past the ancient ruin. "My grandmother's land was next to my fathers; when she passed away, the two estates merged into one." Madelaine's voice took on a bitterly hard edge.

"Is your grandmother's house nearby?" Katherine asked, pasting an innocent expression on her face.

"I haven't been to grandmother's house in some time. It must be in ruins now," Madelaine answered shortly, urging her horse into a canter.

Katherine's suspicion's were immediately aroused. Madelaine's tone made it clear she didn't want Katherine investigating Sorchia's house, which only made her more determined to do that very thing.

Katherine searched the thick trees for signs of her grandmother's manor house. A glimpse of crumbling stone flashed through the trees. That must be it. She marked the spot in her memory, determined to investigate further, uninterrupted.

Madelaine was quiet when they returned to the manor house, hardly speaking a word after Katherine brought up the subject of her grandmother. She abandoned the horse with the groom and quickly excused herself, informing Katherine she had a headache and wouldn't be down for lunch.

Perplexed, Katherine returned to her room, where Gunther was waiting.

"Did you find anything?" Katherine sat on the bed to unlace her boots.

Gunther's face was grim, his eyes hard around the edges. "I did. And I understand why your friends the wolves were so eager to do whatever Madelaine wanted."

Katherine's hands froze on her laces. "You do?"

Gunther nodded. "That building is full of cages."

"Cages? I have to see for myself." Katherine said, pulling on her boots.

"Wait, what about Madelaine?" Gunther glanced at the corridor.

"She had a headache." Katherine strode toward the door.

Gunther and Katherine slipped out the servant's entrance and moments later were at the barn.

"Some of those animals are wolves." Katherine whispered. Two rows of cages lined the dimly lit space.

"The same wolf family." Katherine's voice was weak. Her heart lurched in her throat.

Gunther nodded. "Madelaine's keeping other members of the pack prisoner to hold it over the wolves' heads. Wolves are loyal. They'll do anything for the pack."

"Can we free them?" Katherine glanced at the thin scraggly hair of a juvenile fox.

Gunther shook his head. "I tried to open the cages; Madelaine has the locks warded. And they aren't like the cosseted horses in the stables. These animals have been ill treated. Some of them don't look like they'll live much longer." Pity flashed through Gunther's eyes.

Katherine pressed her lips together. "We have to do something. What about..." Katherine stopped herself. She wasn't ready to explain about the book and the strange hold it had on her. She didn't even know how to use the book and she certainly didn't trust it. Katherine averted her eyes.

"What about...?" Gunther pressed, searching Katherine's face.

"What about my grandmother, Sorchia's manor house? Maybe we could look there. I discovered its location it while riding, and Madelaine did her best to avoid it. Maybe there is something of Sorchia's Madelaine doesn't want us to find."

Interest sparked in Gunther's eyes. "Where is Sorchia's manor house?"

Katherine moved to the window, pointing over a wooded hill just beyond the barns. "That way."

Gunther fingered his dagger.

"You mean go to Sorchia's now?"

"Of course. Madelaine's not here at the minute. There's no better time." He grinned.

"Wait, I'm coming too." Katherine retied her cloak more securely.

Together, Katherine and Gunther moved silently away from the barn toward the stables.

"Lady Katherine?"

Katherine jumped, heart in her throat. "I didn't see you." She turned to the steward, who stared with a dour expression.

"Do you require assistance?" the steward glanced at Katherine's muddy boots.

"Just walking in the gardens. For some fresh air." Katherine attempted to keep her voice light and casual.

"I wouldn't advise that."

Katherine froze.

"There are dangerous animals in the nearby forest. Lady Madelaine would never forgive herself if something harmed her guests."

"I'll take my chances." Gunther smirked. He placed his hand on Katherine's back, shepherding her down the path.

"Shouldn't we take horses?" Katherine panted, attempting to keep up with Gunther's long strides.

"No, we'll be all right. That hill's not that far, less suspicious this way." Gunther grabbed Katherine's hand, tugging her beside him.

Katherine was winded when they arrived at the manor. Gaping holes in the roof and thick layers of ivy told Katherine Sorchia's manor had been abandoned for years. Gunther rattled the front door.

"Locked, Madelaine must be trying to keep *someone* out." Gunther muttered, scanning the rough stone walls. He waded through the overgrown shrubbery toward the back courtyard.

"What are you doing?" Katherine squeaked, hopping over clumps of dead grass.

"Getting inside." Gunther was at the kitchen, sliding his dagger between the door and the frame. "It's an old lock; it should pop off easily enough." He twisted the dagger. The rotten wood around the lock splintered, coming apart under the dagger. "See, rotted right through. I do have other skills besides fighting, you know."

"I'm beginning to see that," muttered Katherine as she stepped over the doorframe.

Thick dust and grime covered everything in the abandoned kitchen. Blackened pots hung from green mold-streaked walls. Broken china crunched underfoot.

"Anything important will be in Sorchia's wing." Gunther strode through the wreckage of Sorchia's kitchen. The remainder of the manor house suffered the same condition as the kitchen. Once grand rooms, reduced to moldering shells of their former glory.

"This must have been Sorchia's chamber." Katherine stood in a large stateroom on the second floor. This chamber felt different—personal. Katherine peeked in the dressing room, where a line of dresses hung in neat rows. All grey and black. She fingered one, raising a puff of grey dust. Sorchia's vanity was intact, a tray of dried-up perfumes arranged in front of the tarnished mirror.

"What are these?" Gunther picked up a slim volume from a stack of books teetering on the nightstand. He flipped through pages of spidery handwriting. "Must be Sorchia's diaries."

Crash. Something banged downstairs. Something big. Katherine froze, her heart pounding a staccato rhythm.

"What was that?" Katherine tiptoed to the door, palms sweating.

Bang. Another crash, closer.

"Did someone follow us?" Katherine pressed her ear up against the chamber door.

Clumsy footsteps thudded on the staircase; Katherine drew back, frantic eyes meeting Gunther's. "Someone's coming!"

"So what if they do?" Gunther shrugged. "We'll explain the door was open, and we wandered inside to look around. The place is clearly abandoned, and we're Madelaine's guests. It's not like we're doing anything wrong." Gunther tucked the diaries into his satchel and held out his hand to Katherine.

Slowly, Gunther opened the door and peered out. The banging had stopped; Katherine wondered if the intruder had left.

To Katherine's left, a floorboard creaked and she heard an eerie rumble that sent shivers up her spine. A shadow fell across them.

The blood in Katherine's veins turned to ice. The noises were caused by a creature.

Something not human.

CHAPTER SIX

Katherine gaped; the creature was massive, crusted with pale, matted fur, flaunting terrifying claws, and knife sharp teeth bared in a cruel snarl.

The bear reared, towering over Katherine and Gunther, the crown of its head almost brushing the cobwebbed ceiling. Katherine froze, her vision white around the edges as she focused on the awful sight.

A low grunt emerged from the slavering mouth. The bear dropped to all fours, claws slashing the floor, shredding the dusty carpet to ribbons. Katherine gasped, leaping backwards into Sorchia's chamber and slamming the rickety door.

"We're trapped," she whispered frantically to Gunther. "It's huge and all we have is your dagger." Her frantic eyes searched the room for potential weapons, but there was nothing.

Long claws raked the old door, ancient wood creaking dangerously under the bear's weighty paws. Katherine raced to the chamber window, flinging open grimy shutters. She stared down in dismay, realizing they were far too high to jump; without a trellis, the steep stone walls were impossible to scale.

The bear's relentless assault on the door continued; in seconds, the rotted wood would shatter under the bear's massive bulk. Heart racing, Katherine backed away from the window—where was Gunther? Distracted by the window, she hadn't noticed him leave. Gunther sprinted from Sorchia's dressing room, a wooden pole in his hand.

"Take this." Face grim, Gunther handed Katherine his dagger. "Sorry, it's not much; I'll fight the creature with the pole and distract him. When you get the chance, run."

Katherine opened her mouth in panic, but before she spoke a single word, the door burst open, flying off its hinges and slamming against the chamber wall.

Gunther shouted, thrusting the jagged end of the wooden pole at the creature's gaping red mouth. But the bear dodged the shaft easily, batting it like a feather. The dry wood splintered into useless shards, leaving Gunther empty-handed.

Katherine shrieked. Her hand automatically reached into her pocket, clutching the dry papery surface of her mother's tiny book. She grabbed it tight, squeezing her eyes shut, preparing for the onslaught of sharp teeth and fierce claws. To Katherine's surprise, ringing silence met her. Her eyes cracked.

The bear thudded to floor, grunting, the feral look fading from his beady black eyes. He turned and shuffled down the stairs. Katherine's eyes met Gunther's in shock and disbelief.

"What happened?" Katherine darted to the window, leaning out just in time to see a pale furry shape loping through Sorchia's overgrown garden. She slumped against the windowsill, drained. "It's leaving."

"Why did the bear run?" Gunther threw down the stub of wood he still held. He spun to face Katherine, eyes flooding with questions.

"I—I don't know..." Katherine's eyes followed the bear as the creature lumbered through a gap in the stone wall, disappearing from sight. "Do you think my aunt sent the bear?"

Gunther nodded. "Undoubtedly. But why did the bear leave so suddenly when the creature had us cornered? The same thing happened with the wolves; you must have an inkling." Gunther pinned Katherine with suspicious brown eyes, waiting for a reasonable answer.

Katherine lowered her head, realizing now wasn't time to nurse bygone grudges. Gunther deserved an honest answer. She took a deep, shaky breath, collecting her tumbling thoughts.

"You can't say a word to anyone.... Not even my sisters. Promise."

Gunther's solemn gaze met Katherine's. "You have my word."

"I think—I think it was this book." Katherine hesitated, then drew out the slim volume with a shaking hand, holding it out to Gunther.

Gunther took the book, gently thumbing through worn pages with calloused fingers. "Ancient magic. Where did you get this?"

"The book was mother's; father kept it after she... disappeared. I grabbed it the night of the Annecy cabin fire, and my father and sisters never knew. I guess I didn't show them the book then because so much was happening so fast. When I finally had an opportunity, it was too late. But I think... I think it was originally Sorchia's." Katherine shrugged, her cheeks flushing.

"I've little experience with magic, but this feels powerful." Gunther placed the book back in Katherine's waiting hand. A tingle swarmed up her arm as the familiar magic coursed through her blood.

Katherine nodded. "The moment I touched the book, the bear left. Do you think the bear felt Sorchia's magic?"

"Yes." Gunther's rumbled. "That bear was under Madelaine's enchantment, an animal like that wouldn't dare come inside the house to attack unless forced. Madelaine must have sent it to find us, maybe even kill us."

Katherine shivered. "We can't stay at Madelaine's estate, but if we leave, I'm worried she'll follow with her enchanted creatures; I can't let her track us to Avella." Her mind raced with possibilities.

Gunther's jaw twitched. "We'll return to Madelaine's estate and learn everything we can, then go find Avella. I've got Sorchia's diaries; if the book is important, Sorchia will have written about it. We'll learn as we travel." He patted his bulging satchel.

Katherine followed Gunther through the broken-down manor house, pausing when her red cloak caught on a broken bannister. She tugged, ripping a corner of the fabric as it tore against splintered wood. *I can repair the cloak later,* Katherine thought before she hurtled down the staircase, eager to escape the heavy darkness of Sorchia's grim presence.

Katherine burst into the glaring light, sucking in deep breaths of fresh, earth scented air. She'd never been so relieved to see sunshine. After brushing off the worst of the dust and dirt, Gunther and Katherine trudged through the forest toward Madelaine's manor.

"DID YOU HAVE A PLEASANT walk?" A smooth, husky voice startled Katherine. Madelaine, seated in the shadows, another heavy veil shadowing her face, greeted them.

"Yes, your estate grounds are lovely." Katherine forced a pleasant smile.

"Wonderful." Madelaine rose, catlike and elegant. "My headache improved this afternoon. I suppose I'll see you at dinner?" It wasn't a question; it was a command.

Katherine nodded before scurrying upstairs, relieved to evade Madelaine's brooding presence for a few more hours.

In their chamber, Gunther drew the stack of Sorchia's diaries from his satchel, arranging them on the duvet. "Do you want to read Sorchia's diaries now?"

Katherine nodded. "The sooner the better." She slid off her boots, plopping on the bed and stretching her legs before lifting the first diary from the stack and thumbing through the crinkling pages.

Sorchia's most recent diary; Katherine estimated the last entry was written shortly before Sorchia's death. Katherine flicked through the pages; the diary mostly consisted of notations about appointments, purchases, and expenses for the house and property— until she reached the last few pages.

"Gunther. Look, I've found something interesting," Katherine said, eyes sparkling.

Gunther lifted his head from the earlier diary he'd been scanning. "What did you find?"

"Read this." Katherine underlined the words with her slender finger as Gunther leaned close. "... I'll visit Natalie today. She owes me an explanation. I must find where she hid Avella, and I'm determined to meet my other granddaughter. Natalie informed me Madelaine has no powers, but she lies. I've been watching closely and seen proof with my own eyes. She might hide her secrets from Natalie, but she can't hide them from me."

Gunther raised thick eyebrow.

"... Look here...." Katherine continued. "Madelaine shows even more promise than Avella. She's might hide her gift successfully from her mother, but I know the signs. Madelaine is bold and brave; not like weak-willed Avella. The things Madelaine could learn under my tutelage are endless. The Iasian kingdom would be ours."

Katherine bit her lip. "Sorchia wanted to use Madelaine's gift..."

"To take the Iasian throne." Gunther finished Katherine's sentence.

"I wonder what happened between Sorchia and Madelaine to cause the argument?" Katherine asked aloud. "Althea said there was an altercation that left Madelaine disfigured. The accident must have been devastating; Madelaine had high aspirations at Iasian court. Natalie set her heart on her daughters marrying up—preferably the prince."

"The prince—Penelope's father? Did Natalie know..." Gunther narrowed his eyes.

Katherine nodded, subdued by the thought that Natalie was willing to sell her daughters to such a corrupt character. The Iasian king—then prince—was infamous throughout the neighboring kingdoms for cruelty and unsavoury deeds. No wonder Penelope turned out the way she did.

"Did Sorchia write any entries after that date?" Gunther asked.

Brows furrowed, Katherine flicked through the rest of the diary. "They're blank."

"So whatever happened, your great-grandmother, Sorchia never wrote another entry? Did Althea tell you know what Sorchia's gift was?"

"Althea said Sorchia's gift was growth, especially plants; that's how Sorchia trapped mother in the forest tower. She locked and barred the tower door; when Sorchia wanted access, she used her gift to grow mother's hair and use it to climb the tower walls. No wonder mother wanted to escape.... wanted to keep us away from them." Katherine's eyes were hard.

A thoughtful expression crossed Gunther's face. "Sorchia's power scarred Madelaine."

Katherine nodded, setting the diary aside. "My mother fought Sorchia and won, but Madelaine...."

"Didn't. Or not enough to get away unscathed."

"Not back then." Katherine shivered. "Her powers might have grown now."

"We just have to leave the estate without raising Madelaine's suspicions. If she follows us, she'll find your mother and sisters."

Katherine jerked her head up, eyes sharp. "Do you think Madelaine knows I'm her niece?"

Gunther shook his head. "It's hard to guess, but Madelaine's extremely smart. And determined—very determined to exact revenge on Avella." Gunther clenched his fist. "We'll leave tomorrow. We'll have to circle round; Madelaine would be suspicious if we leave the direction that we came from."

Katherine nodded, looking forward to the moment she could leave the estate and its grim secrets.

A soft knock at the door interrupted them, Katherine stuffed the diaries under a pillow. "Come in." she said, pasting a pleasant smile on her face.

"Dinner will be served in thirty minutes." The steward said, pressing his mouth in a thin line at Katherine and Gunther's dishevelled state.

Katherine tilted her head, and the steward back away with a curt nod.

"More bisque?" Madelaine asked in a stiff voice.

"No thank you, this was delicious." Katherine answered, setting her spoon down. Candlelight flickered, reflecting off the silver serving dishes. Katherine soup was whisked away and replaced with another plate. Katherine gulped, wondering how many courses she would have to sit through. Tonight's dinner felt interminable.

"Did you enjoy your walk?" Madelaine asked in a dry tone.

"Er, yes, the estate is so lovely." Katherine answered, cutting a tiny section of asparagus, she threw a glance at Gunther who seemed to have no trouble eating, he buttered a roll, taking a massive bite. He met her glance with a tiny wink.

"Thank you dear, I worry it's getting too much for me though." Madelaine sighed, "If only I had close relatives to pass the estate to."

Katherine winced as the eyes behind the veil glittered.

"I'm sure someone will be found." Katherine answered, choking out the words.

Madelaine toyed with her fork. "I suppose." To Katherine's immense relief, she waved for the maid to bring the sweet, a rich chocolate torte.

Finally, though Katherine when dinner was finally over and she could escape to her chamber, lying in the bed and closing her eyes. She couldn't wait to get out of this place.

A BOARD CREAKED AS Katherine crept through the shifting shadows down the wide staircase. She wanted another look at Madelaine's strange library. Her slippered feet whispered noiselessly over the carpet as she tiptoed down the corridor. A light shining under the bottom of the door stopped her. It must be Madelaine. Katherine wondered what her aunt was doing awake so late.

A murmur of voices drew Katherine closer; she slithered over, pressing her ear against the doorframe, shivering in awareness— if the door opened, Katherine had nowhere to hide.

"... found the healer... "Katherine strained to hear a low, rumbling voice.

Do they mean Althea? Katherine wondered, hardly daring to breathe. The voice sounded familiar. She peeked through the keyhole, but her view was limited, her vision blocked by a side table blocking her eyeline.

"... we followed her messenger and know where she lives," the voice said.

"You followed the messenger? Nothing more?" Madelaine's voice hardened with repressed anger and frustration.

"We thought you wanted to speak to your sister." The voice sounded apologetic. "You know how we feel about killing humans."

"How you feel about killing doesn't matter." Madelaine's tone dripped with disdain. "Unless you're prepared to face the consequences, I asked you to do something, and I expected you to follow orders. What about the other Rapunzel girls? I believe there were three altogether?"

"We tracked one girl to the healer's cottage but lost the trail at the cottage."

Madelaine hummed in dissatisfaction. "You've failed me there as well I see."

A low growl met Madelaine's complaint. That's why the voice was familiar, Katherine realised, her blood freezing in her veins—the wolves. She bit back a cry, driving back the urge to flee. She had to learn what they were planning next; her life, and Gunther's depended on it.

"Well, what you were to weak and lazy to accomplish, I was," Madelaine continued. "I found this— part of the girl, my guest's, cloak. It's been warded so she can use the cloak to disguise her scent. A good ward too; she nearly had me fooled. I'll take care of her, eventually, but I'm going to need her to track the other Rapunzel sisters.

"Follow the girl, she'll go directly to Avella's and Avella will have Sorchia's book; I need it. That should be a straightforward task. Avella was always weak and silly." Madelaine's voice held a note of bitter triumph. "If you can't kill them, I will... but don't think there won't be consequences."

Madelaine's response was met with another low growl, followed by a whimper. A brief silence accompanied by swishing feet followed. With a tiny gasp, Katherine realized Madelaine and Alerion were walking directly toward the door. Katherine whirled, fleeing silently up the stairs in her haste to get away unseen and unheard.

Katherine closed the stateroom door with a snick, turning the key before she leaned against it, panting.

She rushed into the adjoining dressing room where Gunther slept, sprawled on a pile of blankets. He was fast asleep, a lock of dark hair curling across his forehead.

Katherine hesitated, unused to seeing Gunther off guard. He looked relaxed, younger, without that constant air of watchfulness. She reached out a hand, resting it on his broad shoulder and shaking gently.

"Gunther, Gunther," Katherine whispered.

Gunther bolted upright, instantly alert.

"What's wrong?" he asked, alert to the frightened expression on Katherine's face.

"The wolves are here at Madelaine's estate. I heard Alerion." Katherine began stuffing clothes into the nearest saddlebag.

Gunther pulled on a tunic and grabbed his breeches. "Did you see the wolves?"

Katherine shook her head. "No, only heard them, in the library with Madelaine; I wanted to check Madelaine's books again before leaving. Their leader, Alerion, was speaking to Madelaine. Gunther—the wolves know where Avella lives. They followed Althea's messenger. They tracked the messages all the way to mother's village."

"Is Avella all right?"

"Mother's safe... for now. I don't think the wolves want to hurt morher, but Madelaine's forcing them. She told the wolves if they don't kill her, she will, and they'll face the consequences. She's threatening them; I think they're scared enough to hurt mother even if they don't want to. And that's not all... Madelaine knows Avella is my mother. She discovered a piece of my red cloak that ripped on the banister of Sorchia's manor. She knew it was warded; Madelaine knows I'm a Rapunzel." Katherine shoved the diaries into the saddlebag.

Gunther stood, sliding a sharp dagger into his right boot and strapped on his sword. "We'll leave immediately. If we get a head start, we might outrun the wolves."

CHAPTER SEVEN

"Come on." Gunther said, laying a calloused hand on Katherine's shoulder. "I won't let anything happen to you, or your family."

Gunther inched the bedroom chamber door open, wincing when it creaked. Thick silence blanketed Madelaine's manor house. "The wolves must be gone, sleeping or lurking. We'll use the servant's staircase and sneak through the kitchen," Gunther whispered. Together they crept down the corridor towards the servant's staircase. Fumbling through the murky darkness, not daring to use a candle, Katherine nearly tripped on the uneven stone steps; she caught herself, heart pounding, and continued on. They arrived in the kitchen; the glowing embers in the fireplace highlighted the courtyard door. Then they were in the courtyard, the chilly night air a welcome rush against Katherine's hot skin.

The full moon lit their way to the stable; the extensive building was warm and homey, scented with the comforting smell of hay and oiled leather. Katherine helped Gunther lead out their horses and saddle them. They spoke in whispers, not wanting to wake the groom sleeping upstairs. Heart in mouth, Katherine's stiff fingers fumbled with the tack as she fastened the saddlebags. Finally, they were ready; the horses blew and stomped, waiting for direction.

Hooves clattered against the stable yard cobblestones; Katherine hardly dared breathe, sure the commotion would wake the stable master, but the yard remained quiet. Gunther opened the gate when suddenly a gigantic shadow sprang out of the darkness.

The bear. Rearing up on its hind legs, it growled, the sound vibrating the air, making the hair on Katherine's arms stand on end. Her eyes darted to Gunther as she reached for her dagger.

"Katherine, go, now!" Gunther shouted, urging his tall black horse into a gallop.

Katherine kicked Bardot, who pawed the ground, wild eyes rolling before lunging after Gunther. Bardot and Katherine shot out of the gate like a bolt of lightning, scattering stones as he sped down the estate lane. The bear rushed after them, powerful legs pushing the ungainly body with surprising speed. Katherine leaned low over Bardot's neck, careening toward the main road as the bear gained ground. They were approaching the main road. With a thundering roar, the bear leapt, nicking Bardot's hindquarters with knifelike claws.

Bardot squealed, increasing his pace, and they sped down the road. The bear stopped, the only sound the thunder of hooves and the horses' heaving breath. Katherine swung her head—the bear stood on hind legs, weaving its head and sniffing the air. The creature grunted, then dropped to four paws and lumbered away, a pale gleaming shape in the silver moonlight.

"Are you hurt?" Gunther slowed to a canter.

"I'm fine, but I think the bear got Bardot," Katherine answered. Trembling, she glanced behind her, noticing a streak of blood smearing Bardot's hindquarters. Gunther reached out to touch Bardot, and the horse snorted in annoyance.

"It looks superficial. I have healing salve; we can treat the injury when we rest. Do you think you can keep riding? I'm worried Madelaine's wolves will track us; we need some distance between us and Madelaine's estate."

Katherine took a deep breath and nodded; Madelaine's wolves were her primary concern. Being nocturnal creatures, the darkness wouldn't affect their eyesight. If they attacked, Katherine and Gunther wouldn't notice until it was too late.

Katherine and Gunther travelled all night, maintaining a brisk pace and only stopping when necessary to rest the horses and treat Bardot's injury.

"We'll sleep in the inn for a few hours before continuing to Iasia," Gunther told Katherine. "If we stay in a town or village, we'll be safe; the wolves won't dare touch us unless we're concealed in the forest."

Katherine pushed through her exhaustion to remount her tired horse and continue the journey. She couldn't—wouldn't— stop until everyone was safe.

As dawn brightened to daylight, they arrived in Havre, a trading village across the Iasian border. It was market day. Noisy venders were busy setting up their merchandise, shouting happy greetings across Market Square. Although small, Havre was a thriving village; its strategic location in the middle of the Lovanian and Iasian trading routes afforded it a constant stream of trading caravans. The lively marketplace attracted merchants and venders from both sides of the Lovanian border.

Gunther and Katherine paused in Market Square for a hasty breakfast of fried dough and hot milk sweetened with honey and cinnamon before going on to Havre's main inn. Katherine gazed longingly at a few of the fabric stalls, greeting several of the fabric venders she knew from guild business as she hurried by the colourful stalls toward the inn.

Katherine leaned across the desk to the innkeeper of Mary Lou's Brew. "I want a room of my own and a bath," she insisted, narrowing her eyes as the innkeeper gave her a suspicious look. No wonder; Katherine gave her stained and dingy cloak a rueful look.

"Fine, but private baths costs extra because Jean has to heat and lug water buckets to the tub upstairs in the room," the innkeeper huffed, tossing her frizzy brown hair in annoyance.

"That's fine." Katherine would have paid anything to feel clean. In spite of Madelaine's luxurious accommodations, she couldn't bathe in a shared chamber with Gunther and was eager for a luxurious hot soak.

Tired and aching, Katherine sank into the dented metal tub with a sigh of satisfaction. She dipped her head under the water, rubbing the soap into her hair. It wasn't the fine floral scented soap she was used to, but it was pure heaven after being stuck in the grubby red cloak. Katherine rinsed and stood, rivulets of water splashing into the tub. Shivering, she rubbed herself dry. There wasn't time to wash her clothes. She gave them a sad look as she squeezed water from her damp hair.

After dressing, Katherine collapsed on the narrow cot and fell into a heavy sleep, not waking until noontime sun glared through faded checkered curtains.

Refreshed, Katherine made her way down the wooden staircase; Gunther was waiting.

"There you are. Feeling better?" Gunther's dark eyes met hers.

"Much." Katherine plopped onto a hard wooden chair.

"I bought you this. I don't know if you'll like the color but I figured with the travelling, you'd need something clean." An uncomfortable expression crossed Gunther's face as he shoved a squashy package into Katherine's hands.

Katherine took the package, untying the brown wrappings with curious fingers to reveal a beautiful fabric.

"You bought this for me?" Katherine let the fabric slide through her fingers. The deep, rich blue wool was soft and warm. She held it against the light, admiring the fine stitchwork and the velvet ribbon that held the hood in place. A cloak— an expensive one, Katherine's practiced eye noted.

"There's a dress too, but I'm not sure about the fit. I know you ladies use tailors and dressmakers for that," Gunther's voice was gruff, a tinge of pink staining his ears.

Katherine unfolded the dress, the same rich blue but a lighter material.

"I love it." She stroked the dress with her fingers. "You shouldn't have," Katherine scolded Gunther gently.

"It was nothing," Gunther said, swallowing. "If we want to keep ahead of Madelaine's wolves, we should to leave immediately. I've paid the innkeeper already."

Katherine changed into the blue dress, sighing as the soft, clean material brushed against her skin. She folded her old clothes and stuffed them in her saddlebag. As Katherine tied the new cloak over her shoulder's, she paused. It wouldn't do to have the wolves trace her scent. Regretfully, she placed the fine new cloak in the satchel next to the old dress and threw the red cloak over her shoulders. It would do until they could get her mother to safety.

Katherine met Gunther downstairs, noticing a flicker of disappointment flashed through his eyes when he saw her descend the staircase. "Didn't the clothes fit?"

Katherine flicked back the edge of the red cloak to reveal the blue dress underneath. "It did, but Althea warded the red cloak. I don't want the wolves to track us. Hopefully Althea's ward will hold until we rescue Avella."

"Wise." Gunther nodded, taking Katherine's arm and leading her to the stable. "Now let's ride before they catch up to us."

Besides the blue dress and cloak, Gunther stocked up on supplies, leaving them well prepared for whatever the trail might bring. Katherine wondered how Gunther accomplished so much on so little sleep. He must be exhausted.

The road was pleasant, the weather taking a turn for a better. If it weren't for the threat of sharp teeth and claws looming over her, Katherine would have enjoyed herself. Gunther stuck to well-travelled roads, explaining to Katherine that wolves were unlikely to attack in plain sight. Katherine had reservations, but she felt safer with other travellers. They headed for a part of the country she'd never been to before. The Western border was mountainous; its rocky terrain was home to Lovanians mining communities.

Katherine and Gunther threaded through the mining villages toward the Arborvue town Avella called home. It was surprisingly busy, since it was the first port from the Eowin kingdom. From there, caravans brought the goods through Lovan to Iaisia. Katherine couldn't wait to explore this harbour town; the most beautiful fabrics came from over the sea, richly patterned silks and velvets that left Katherine drooling with envy over their lush textures and brilliant colours.

After two days on the road, the pleasant weather broke; thunderclouds rolled in— dark, thick, menacing.

"We're in for some a severe storm." Gunther turned in his saddle, face creased in concern. "Do you want to wait it out?"

"We should keep going." Katherine clutched the red cloak around her, protecting herself from the whipping wind. "If the wolves attack now, we wouldn't hear them coming." Although they were making steady progress, the wolves were fast and smart, and Katherine knew they would take advantage of any opportunity Katherine and Gunther afforded. She shivered as a bolt of lightning crackled across the darkening sky; the thunder crashed right on its heels. A few fat drops of rain landed on Bardot's saddle, followed by more, until the heavens opened, unleashing torrents of rain so heavy it was hard to see more than a few feet ahead of Bardot's flattened ears.

They pressed on, the jittery horses cautious on the slippery road. Lightning shot down from the sky; Bardot squealed, rearing as a tree crashed on the road directly behind them.

"Are you all right?" Gunther shouted above the din of the storm. Flashes of lightning lit up the rivulets of water running down his face. Katherine nodded, knowing if she spoke, Gunther would hear the fear in her voice.

"There's a farm up the road; we'll stop and ask to shelter until the storm passes. It's too dangerous out here." Gunther pointed toward a glowing orange point of light gleaming through the lashing rain.

Katherine bit her lip, shivering under her soaked clothes. Rivulets of freezing cold water dripped down her hair and into her eyes.

They rode into the farmyard, and Gunther dismounted, knocking on the door of a small thatched cottage.

"Hello?" the door opened and a young woman peered out, pulling a patched dressing gown tight around her slight figure.

"We were wondering if we could shelter until the storm passes." Gunther stood back, allowing the woman to see Katherine, who was dripping and shivering in the rain.

"Katherine? Is that you?" the young woman peered out, squinting through the sheets of driving rain.

"Hello Sylvia," Katherine stepped forward.

"Why are you travelling in this weather? Is this about the silkworms?"

"No, this is personal business; we're travelling and got caught by the stormy weather," Katherine said, blinking the water from her eyes.

"Oh, come in." Sylvia suddenly realized Katherine and Gunther were standing in pouring rain. "There's room in the barn to rest the horses."

Gunther led the horses to the barn as Sylvia ushered Katherine inside the cozy cottage. A large loom took up one corner of the room; Sylvia was one of Katherine's best weavers. Katherine itched to go see what new patterns Sylvia was weaving, but refrained, sitting politely by the crackling fire. There'd be time enough to talk about weaving techniques and patterns later.

"Let me take your cloak, its soaking." Sylvia spread the red cloak next to the fire to dry, taking a moment to admire the colour, still cherry bright after the long journey.

"Tea?" Sylvia scooted the kettle over the hottest part of the fire.

"That would be nice." Even by the blazing fire, Katherine still shivered from the cold. She briefly wondered if the wolves' thick coats protected them from the wild storms in this part of the kingdom before forcing her thoughts to more cheerful topics.

"I have to ask... is that Lord Gunther you're travelling with?" Sylvia lowered her voice, even though Gunther was in the barn, stabling the horses.

Katherine sighed, hoping Sylvia wasn't the type to start rumours.

"Yes," she admitted. "We bumped into each other on the road, so he offered to accompany me."

"So chivalrous of him." Katherine could tell by the glint in Sylvia's eyes she was entertaining romantic ideas.

"Gunther and I are just friends; there's nothing more than that going on," Katherine said, ignoring a twist in her gut the words gave her.

Sylvia raised an eyebrow.

"Believe me, it's true," Katherine's voice was dry. Gunther had been wonderful, a gallant companion, but she knew his real loyalty was with Prince Frederich—his motivation had nothing to do with her. Gunther had a previous attachment, and Katherine couldn't forget that fact, no matter how gallant and thoughtful he was.

Sylvia threw her a suspicious look but said nothing as she poured steaming tea into three clay mugs. She handed a fragrant mug to Katherine, who cupped it in both hands, enjoying the warmth as much as the hot drink.

"The storm's getting worse out there." Gunther burst through the door, rivulets of water pouring off him and forming a puddle on the wooden floor. He took off his dripping cloak and took the other chair at the fire.

"Where are you travelling next?" Sylvia asked Gunther, handing him his tea.

Gunther and Katherine exchanged a glance. Not that Katherine didn't trust Sylvia, but other than the weaving, she didn't know the girl. The last thing Katherine and Gunther needed was for Sylvia to inadvertently lead the wolves to their trail.

"We're traveling to my country estate," Gunther broke in before Katherine could answer. "I'm redecorating and I needed Katherine's opinions on fabrics... for curtains. She kindly agreed to accompany me there before the next leg of her journey." he shot Katherine a glance, letting her know she should play along.

Katherine nodded enthusiastically, relieved Gunther had provided a plausible explanation, and Sylvia seemed satisfied.

As the conversation continued, Katherine yawned. The tea had made her sleepy and the hectic days were catching up with her.

"You're tired." Sylvia busied herself gathering the empty mugs. "I only have one extra room..." her voice trailed off.

"That's fine. I'll sleep on my bedroll by the fire. It will be a palace compared to the storm out there," Gunther insisted.

Sylvia led Katherine to her spare room, where hot bricks left the bed toasty warm. Lulled by the sound of rain beating on the thatch, she pulled the soft worn quilt over her head, fell asleep, and didn't wake until morning.

After a breakfast of hot porridge topped with honey and nuts, Gunther went to prepare the horses for the day's journey.

"Are you sure there's nothing going on between you two?" Sylvia gathered the breakfast dishes, placing them into the metal dishpan.

"Oh, I'm sure," Katherine answered.

"I don't mean to interfere," Sylvia backtracked. "It's just the way he looks at you..."

In spite of her unsettled feelings toward Gunther, Katherine's heart skipped a beat. But before she could answer Sylvia, Gunther was back, stomping the sticky mud off his boots before stepping into the cottage. The storm had passed during the night, leaving puffy white clouds drifting through the clear blue sky; droplets sparkled on every surface of the garden, a shimmering whirl of green and pink.

"Are you ready?" Gunther placed a calloused hand on Katherine's shoulder.

"Yes." Katherine stood hastily, avoiding Sylvia, who stared pointedly at the Gunther's hand.

Soon, they were off, the horses picking their way down the muddy road.

"We should reach your mother's by nightfall," Gunther told Katherine when they stopped to let their horses drink from a rippling brook. "Did Althea tell you which house was Avella's?"

Katherine shook her head. "She lives outside the city, near the bay. Althea said to ask for Ella at the apothecary."

The road gradually got busier; occasional farmers and merchants giving way to a steady stream of traders—all headed for the harbor. The smell of salt and seaweed filtered through the air as the thick forest thinned, broken by sandy marshes and salt flats.

"Look, the sea." Gunther pointed left through a gap in the landscape. A brilliant line of blue dotted with foamy whitecaps as the tossing sea glittered in the sunlight. Around the next bend, it stretched before them in all its glory, wide open and expansive.

"It's beautiful. Wild," Katherine gazed at wide blue water sparkling before her.

Gunther nodded. "And dangerous." Come, we have a few miles until we reach the port.

The bustling port teemed with activity. Fishing boats unloading their catch for the day, cargo ships anchored in the deep harbour, bobbing against their thick ropes. Sailors and fishermen alike bustled about the docks.

Katherine watched as they spread fish on racks to dry. Later, the fish would be packaged and sold. The smell of fish hung thick and heavy over the entire village. Merchants and traders supervised as dockworkers loaded wagons with cargo, spices, fabrics, and all manner of exotic goods from across the sea.

"We can leave our horses at the tavern and then find the apothecary," Gunther told Katherine, raising his voice to be heard over the clamour.

"Wait a minute, is that the apothecary?" Katherine asked, pointing to a dilapidated sign hanging over a weathered door. Boards nailed over the door signalled the owners didn't intend to return. "Excuse me, is this the only apothecary in town?" Katherine asked, flagging down a weathered fisherman dragging a pile of nets to his boat.

The fisherman scratched his chin. "Yep, we have to go to Pinker when we need treatments now. They up and left a week ago, left us all in the lurch." He yanked the nets over a rough stone.

Katherine turned her horrified gaze to Gunther.

"I have an idea." Gunther steered Katherine toward the Fish Head, a tavern located directly across from the harbour. The Fish Head was small, but thriving, its prime location making it a haven for fishermen and sailors alike. Gunther handed their horses to a groom and strode inside, taking a place at the bar; Katherine slid onto the scarred wooden stool beside him.

"Gunther. Haven't seen you in ages." The tavern keeper slapped Gunther on the back. "How are you keeping... I see you're not alone? Is this your lady?" his eyes roved over Katherine.

"No, nothing like that... we're just... on business," Katherine jumped in before Gunther could answer. Out of the corner of her eye, she could see his ears turning pink. She firmed her lips; he had no business thinking he had a claim on her.

"Well, you're very welcome here." The tavern keeper grinned, displaying a row of shiny white teeth.

"Two bowls of fish stew; I've told Katherine yours is the best, and two pints of your best mead," Gunther told the tavern keeper.

"Coming right up," the tavern keeper answered with a wink.

"I thought you had an idea?" Katherine crossed her arms in front of her chest.

"Of course, but I'm starving, and The Fish Head makes the best fish stew you've ever tasted. Besides, this tavern is the best place for information," Gunther promised with a grin.

Katherine rolled her eyes, eying the earthenware bowl suspiciously. It smelled good. She took a cautious bite.

"You're right, this is delicious." She hummed in approval, sticking her spoon back in the bowl. Katherine's lunch had been a few strips of dried meat and dry bread, and the fish stew was delicious—warm, creamy, and filled with salty delicate flavour. Katherine scraped her bowl clean and washed the stew down with the last dregs of mead.

"Another two bowls, please." Gunther raised his hand to catch the tavern keeper's attention. He set a two silver coins on the table in front of them.

"You're overpaying me." Pascal glanced at the coins.

"The other one is for the information," Gunther told the man. "We're looking a woman named Ella... friendly with the apothecary?"

"Ella." Pascal drew his eyebrows down and pursed his lips. "The only Ella is a woman who repairs fishnets. She's quiet, keeps to herself. Her cottage is about a mile down the road that way, you can't miss it; you'll see the fishnets hanging in the cottage garden. She's not about much anymore—I can't remember the last time I saw Ella. Is your business with her?" His eyes slid toward Katherine's fine clothes, no doubt wondering what she would have to do with a woman who repaired the village fishnets.

"One more thing..." Gunther continued, ignoring Pascal's nosiness. "We're looking for a group of four, suspicious-looking characters, probably wearing long grey cloaks."

Pascal scratched his cheek. "I can't say that I've seen anyone like that about. But I can keep an eye on newcomers."

"We'd be grateful," Gunther lowered his voice, leaning forward, "It's crown business, you know."

Pascal puffed up. "What do you want me to do if I run into them? Are they dangerous?" his voice sounded hopeful.

"Very," Gunther advised. "They're shapeshifters so I wouldn't engage. But if they try to find us—or Ella—send them in the opposite direction. We can take it from there."

Pascal winked, "You can count on me." He slid Gunther's coin back across the wooden bar. "You can hang on to your coin; this service is for the crown." He walked off, shaking his head, muttering choice words about magical creatures under his breath.

Gunther slid the coin into his bag before tossing back the last drops of mead and grinning at Katherine. "And that's how to gather information. Tavern keepers and innkeepers—they always know everything."

Katherine and Gunther emerged, blinking into the bright sunlight. Leaving the horses stabled, they strolled toward the end of the bay. It was quiet at this end of the town. The elderly cottages were small, but surrounded by flourishing garden plots, with goats and sheep grazing on the hardy grasses.

"Do you think that's Avella's cottage?" Excitement throbbed in Katherine's chest as she pointed toward a small, thatched building perched on the edge of the pebbly beach. Fishnets were piled in untidy heaps in front of the door and strung along the garden fence.

"Looks like it," Gunther said, giving Katherine an encouraging smile. "Are you ready?"

Equal parts fear and panic gripped Katherine. What was she going to say? Her steps faltered.

"Are you all right?" Gunther paused. "You're very pale."

"I'm fine... it's just..." Katherine didn't enjoy explaining her feelings at the best of times.

"Come on. You'll be fine." Gunther took Katherine's hand and led her up the garden path. He knocked on the weathered door. They waited and waited with only the crashing waves on the beach and crying seagulls breaking the silence.

"Maybe Avella's not home." Defeated, Katherine wondered what she was going to do next.

"We'll check the back garden." They continued around the side of the cottage, toward the back garden. There, among the neat rows of vegetables, was a woman weeding the carrots. An enormous straw hat obscured her face. But Katherine knew this was Avella, the mother she'd been searching for and longing for.

"Avella?" Gunther asked.

The woman lifted her head. Other than some faint lines and streaks of grey threading the golden hair, she could have been Katherine's sister.

"Mother?" Katherine's voice trembled. "Is it really you?"

The woman froze, dropping the clump of weeds clenched in her fist.

Katherine ran toward her, her arms outstretched. "Mother, I can't believe it's you." Her cheeks were wet with tears as she embraced the other woman.

Avella sat still for a moment, then slowly her arms went around Katherine. She was slight, thin, and wiry from years of labour. "I thought I'd never see you again." Her face was full of wonder.

"Is it.. Katherine? I can tell by that golden hair. Your sisters have your father's dark hair, but yours is exactly like mine." Avella held Katherine by the shoulders, searching her face with teary eyes. "Come inside, we'll talk." Avella picked up her vegetable basket, carrying it to the back door of the cottage.

Katherine looked around Avella's cottage with curious eyes, eager to see the place her mother made home for the past twenty years. The cottage was neat, clean. Pots of herbs sat on sunny windowsills, and a cheerful rug covered the floor in front of the fireplace.

Avella moved the large tabby lounging in the chair by the fireplace. "Here, sit down; I'll boil the tea."

Katherine and Gunther sat while Avella bustled around the tiny kitchen, putting leaves in the pot and setting out a tray of bread, jam, and cheese.

"You received the message?" Avella poured tea into three colourful mugs.

Katherine nodded, "Lucie and Marion have children, so we decided I would be the one to come find you."

"Lucie? Children, I still can't believe it. She was a tiny baby last time I saw her. I've missed so much. Althea sent messages as much as possible, but it wasn't the same. And what of Pierre—your father?" Avella brought the tea tray, setting it on the wooden table.

Katherine took a mug of tea. "Father is good. Busy with the guilds, but he loves it."

Avella pulled up a chair from the kitchen table, taking a slice of bread in her tanned hands. "It was all worth it to see you now. Alive and safe," she smiled tenderly at her daughter.

Katherine swirled the tea in her mug. "Mother... it's not safe in this village.. not anymore."

Avella nodded. "I was afraid Madelaine would catch up with me one day."

"Did you know about Madelaine's gift with the animals?" Katherine filled Avella in on what they discovered at the manor house. Avella listened, her face thoughtful.

"Madelaine had a gift with animals; although, few knew. It only makes sense her gift would become as twisted as she is. Madelaine never liked me—she was jealous—always wanting to be one step ahead of me." Avella sighed. "I just wanted a sister. Someone I could talk to; someone I could trust. I suppose it was my mother's fault, because Natalie always pitted Madelaine against me. With Natalie's interference, we never had a chance. I hoped if I were out of the picture,

Madelaine would leave you girls alone. I wanted you to have chances I never received— to be a real family."

Katherine put her hand in her mother's. "I'm grateful we had that chance, but now it's your time. Come home mother. Madelaine knows where you are and she's coming. She's sent wolves—shifters. And they were tracking us; Madelaine sent them ahead of you."

"How far behind you?" Avella froze, instantly alert.

"The wolves are fast, and they left Madelaine's estate when we did," Gunther broke in. "If we're going to keep ahead, we'll have to leave today."

Avella stood, brushing dirt from her rough linen tunic. "I've been preparing for this moment. We can leave immediately." She disappeared into the bedroom, returning a moment later with a large rucksack.

"Do you have a horse?" Gunther asked.

Avella shook her head. "I had little need for one, and mending nets doesn't bring in enough income to justify its keep. Although I have money to buy one if needed from some of my inheritance."

Something told Katherine her mother's pride wouldn't allow her to let her pay for her so she merely nodded. Without a backward glance, Avella locked the cottage door and the three set off along the road toward the harbour.

CHAPTER EIGHT

Katherine, Gunther, and Avella wove through the crowd in the Fish Head; Pascal was still at the wooden bar, wiping it with a greasy cloth. Pascal spotted the trio, raising a finger for Gunther to wait. Katherine's stomach lurched at the expression on Pascal's face.

"Have the strangers appeared?" Gunther leaned forward, seeing the concern flaring in Pascal's eyes.

"The ones you looked for arrived five minutes after you left. Grey cloaks and all. I did what you said, told them I hadn't seen you, and sent them the opposite direction. But unfortunately, I wasn't the only person they spoke to." Pascal's voice was low and urgent.

A muscle in Gunther's cheek twitched. "Which direction were they headed?"

Pascal jerked his head away from the harbour. "East, but I fear they might circle around; they had a woman with them—a rich Iasian, very well dressed."

"A woman?" Katherine asked, her heart flopping in her chest. "What did the woman look like?"

"I didn't get a close look at her, she didn't take her veil off. She was probably about your height. Had a fancy Iasian accent, and fine jewelry; not someone you'd usually see in The Fish Head."

"Madelaine." Katherine felt the blood drain from her face. "She travelled with the wolves." She turned to Gunther. "If we travel by road, they'll catch us for sure."

"We'll take a different route." Gunther turned back to Pascal. "Are any ships leaving soon?"

Pascal scratched his chin thoughtfully. "Which way are you headed?"

"We'll board the earliest ship available, ideally one sailing toward the capital. We can disembark in the nearest harbour, then the castle's only an hour's ride away."

"Leave it with me." Pascal disappeared, leaving them standing at the bar. A few minutes later he returned, a tall sunburnt man in tow.

"Captain Kain of Lucie Marie at your service." The man smiled, whipping the cap off his head. "I hear you're interested in a passage east? We're headed to Florin."

"Are you willing to make a stop near Corvan?" Avella asked.

"For the right price; it'll cost you extra." The captain perused Gunther and Katherine's fine clothes as his sharp eyes glinted with the possibility of earning gold.

"How much?" Avella countered, her face set.

"Twenty gold pieces."

Avella didn't flinch at the price. "I'll give you half now and the other half when we arrive."

The captain nodded, clasping Avella's tanned hand in his weathered, calloused one. "Fair enough."

"When do you sail?" Avella asked.

"With the tide." The captain answered, "We should be able to set sail in a few hours."

Avella nodded. "We'll need to stay on board until we leave harbour, somewhere out of sight."

The captain raised an eyebrow. "Right then, follow me."

They threaded through the harbour toward Lucie Marie, a large wooden vessel with square sails. The ship was being loaded with cargo; a flurry of last-minute preparations were being carried out for departure. They skirted a flock of seagulls squabbling over a pile of fish entrails as they picked their way across the docks. One of the birds turned to look at Katherine, its beady eyes staring with a strange sort of intelligence.

"Did you see that?" Katherine whispered to Gunther, wondering if it was her imagination.

"What?"

"That bird, I think it's watching us..." She pointed to the gull which was still staring at her, head cocked to the side.

Gunther paused, "It looks like a regular seagull to me, probably doesn't want to share."

Katherine turned again, but the strange bird was gone. *You're letting your imagination run away with you,* she scolded herself as she followed Gunther up the gangplank. But she couldn't shake off the disquieting feeling that something wasn't right.

Captain Kain led the trio to a wood panelled stateroom. "I've only got one extra stateroom." He explained, indicating the narrow bunk. "One of you can use the pallet, and no interfering with my crew while sailing." He gave Avella and Katherine a hard look. "I'm not as suspicious as most sailors, but I need my crew sharp—especially if we're making an extra stop. I pride myself on reaching port on time with my cargo."

"We won't get in the way. I promise..." Katherine began, but the captain had already left. The door swung shut, leaving the three in gloomy darkness. There was nothing to do but wait.

Katherine sat gingerly on the edge of the bunk. She had little experience with ships, and the gentle rocking made her unsteady on her feet. *Are ships supposed to creak so much,* Katherine wondered, eyeing the sparking water bobbing out the porthole.

"We'll lie low until we leave port, and Madelaine and her pack will be none the wiser. It'll be hard for the wolves to track us by water. Too many fishy smells." Avella comforted her daughter as she sat beside her.

"Is that why you came to live by the sea?" Katherine turned to her mother, hoping the conversation would distract her from that sickening feeling in her gut.

Avella laughed. "Goodness no. I had no idea the wolves existed, much less that Madelaine would think to use them to hunt us. Although, Madelaine always was clever about twisting people—and animals—to accomplish her goals."

Gunther paced the room, hand on his sword. Waiting was not a pastime Gunther enjoyed. "What time did Captain Kain say we were sailing?" he peered out the porthole.

"A few hours," Katherine answered, joining Gunther at the porthole. "What are all those seagulls doing?" A gigantic flock of seagulls was hovering over the Lucie Marie, fighting for space on every surface and line of rigging. Their squawking and squabbling filled the air with raucous cries.

"Seagulls?" Avella's head jerked up. "Didn't you say one of the seagulls was acting strange earlier?"

Katherine nodded. "He was staring at me, like he knew who I was."

"Madelaine," breathed Avella. "Come away from the porthole." Avella grabbed Katherine, dragging her back from the porthole.

"Madelaine's using the gulls to find you," Avella explained, draping a blanket over the porthole. The three travellers were cast in gloomy darkness, only broken by the increasingly deafening cawing of gulls. Avella inched back the makeshift curtain and peered through the crack.

Gunther dashed to the door, sliding the bolt across. "How did Madelaine tell the gulls to follow us?"

Avella shrugged. "Promised them fish probably, gulls aren't exactly loyal."

Something thumped against the porthole, all scrabbling claws and beating wings. "They found us." Avella clenched her fists in her lap.

Outside the thin wooden walls, they heard shouting. Gunther pressed his ear against the door. "The crew is panicking out there. You know how superstitious sailors are. The captain's telling them to weigh anchor, anyway; fortunately, the tide is on our side."

"It could still be hours before we're properly at sea," Avella answered, barely able to hear her own voice over the thrumming of wings and the screeching of gulls.

A rapping at the door interrupted them, and Gunther cracked it open. "Captain Kain?"

Gunther widened the door to reveal Captain Kain with an uneasy expression lurked in the captain's eyes. Fear, Katherine realized. He's terrified.

"I don't know if you've done anything to bring infernal birds. But if you have — it doesn't happen again. They scared Lucie Marie's crew witless."

"Are they attacking?"

Captain Kain shook his head. "No, just staring. Like they're waiting. Planning something. There's something infernal unnatural about those birds."

Katherine shivered, wondering what Madelaine had planned. They hadn't left harbour yet; if the captain removed them from his ship, they would be at Madelaine's mercy.

Gunther motioned for the captain to approach. "This is crown business—you understand? If Lucie Marie get us safely out of this harbor and to Corvan, there'll be a rich reward for you—you have my word. Just beware, if an Iasian woman or anyone wearing a strange grey cloak arrives, don't let them board ship. They're extremely dangerous."

The captain paled. "Crown business?" He knew he couldn't argue with crown business; if he refused now, he'd never be allowed to dock in Lovan again.

"I'll tell my crew." The captain slid the door open.

Katherine peeked through the blanket covered window. "The gulls are moving." Thundering wings rattled the glass in the porthole. A commotion flared on deck— shouting followed by a thud— then silence. The three exchanged looks, eyes wide. The sickening feeling in Katherine's stomach intensified as her blood drummed in her ears.

"Madelaine's here; stay in the cabin," Gunther told Katherine and Avella. "I'll go help." He slid his sword out of the scabbard as he opened the door and slipped away.

Katherine fumbled with her satchel, opening the clasp with shaking fingers.

"What are you doing?" Katherine heard panic in Avella's voice. She forced herself to focus; she couldn't worry about that now. Not with everyone in danger. The fight on Lucie Marie's deck increased, growing louder, more intense.

"I'm going to help Gunther." Avella snatched the thin dagger Gunther had given her. She slid it out, the metal cold against her palm. "Take this. Whatever happens, don't let Madelaine get her hands on it." Katherine shoved the book into Avella's hands. Avella opened her eyes wide with questions at the sight of this stark reminder of her past. However, before Avella could argue, Katherine dashed away, rushing up the dark stairs.

It was worse than Katherine expected.

The wolves had shed their human forms. A terrifying blur of teeth and claws. Gunther was an excellent swordsman—one of the best. Even so, he was hard pressed, fighting against the formidable wolves. Madelaine's black veiled figure stood watch nearby, stark against the bright sunlight.

The crew was nowhere to be seen—hiding below deck. Katherine glimpsed a figure crouching behind a pile of boxes. Unnoticed, Katherine edged around the mast until she was behind Madelaine. She gripped the dagger tightly—she would only have once chance to strike; it had to count. She was close—so close to Madelaine she could almost feel the heat of her skin and smell her expensive perfume. Her breath caught in her throat. Katherine had never hurt anyone intentionally before.

"I wondered when you would show up," Madelaine's voice dripped with icy disdain. "Just in time to see my pets destroy him."

Katherine leapt at Madelaine, brandishing the dagger, but Madelaine batted it away, sending it clattering harmlessly to the deck.

"That's sweet to be so protective of him." Madelaine flicked her finger at the wolves. "But you're not the only one with a weapon." One of the wolves broke away from Gunther.

"Don't kill her—yet—she has something of mine," Madelaine said to the wolf, who snarled in response, pointed white teeth gleaming.

The wolf rose on hind legs, shoving Katherine down. She tumbled to the rough wooden deck, smacking her head on the boards. The metallic taste of blood filled her mouth. Black spots swirled in her vision. Golden eyes and sharp teeth flashed. Familiar eyes. Katherine blinked away the searing pain, focusing on the golden irises.

"Eleonor?" Katherine gasped.

The wolf paused, frozen in shock. That second of hesitation was all Katherine needed to act. She kicked hard. Snap. Katherine's foot met flesh and solid bone. The wolf whimpered, golden eyes closing. Using all her strength, Katherine shoved the heavy body away from her, scrambling toward the fallen dagger. Her fingers brushed against smooth metal. She strained to grab it, but the ship lurched, and the dagger slid away.

"Eleonor—you know the cost of disobedience," Madelaine's commanding voice rang through the air.

Tail between her legs, the wolf slunk toward Katherine, who still lay flattened against the salty boards. Reluctance etched the wolf's every movement. Katherine squeezed her eyes shut, her heart thudding above the crash of the waves. Everything stilled; the sounds of the fight dimming as Katherine focused on Eleonor's face.

"I'm sorry." The rumbling whisper was so faint, Katherine almost thought she imagined it. The gulls whirled overhead, their shadows flickering in Eleonor's eyes.

"Eleonor. Now!" Madelaine screeched.

Eleonor crouched, preparing to pounce.

"Stop." Eleonor froze.

Avella stood at edge of the deck, holding Katherine's book high above her head.

"Hello, sister." Avella stared at Madelaine, a tumult of emotions racing across her face. "I believe you're searching for this?" She waved the book over the water.

Madelaine narrowed her eyes, Eleonor forgotten.

"Call off your dogs and this is yours. Don't and I'll drop it." Avella held the book over the churning water.

"You wouldn't dare," Madelaine challenged. "It's your only leverage."

Avella raised an eyebrow. "Wouldn't I? I've done a lot of growing up since you've known me.... learned some things. I'm not that sad little girl you knew anymore, Madelaine."

Madelaine raised a finger. The wolves slunk to her side; the gulls stopped mid-flight—lining every inch of rigging in utter silence. "Fine. I'm listening. What do you want?"

"Leave this ship and take your birds and your dogs with you."

"And if I don't?"

Avella let the book slide an inch toward the salty foam. "I don't have any leverage—but if you hurt one hair on my daughter's head, this is going straight into the ocean. Your choice, sister."

Madelaine jerked her head, sending the wolves skulking to the wooden dingy bobbing in the water. The birds sped away, whirling into the sky like autumn leaves.

"Board the dingy and pass up the oars; I'll throw the book down to you."

Madelaine hesitated before lowering herself into the dingy with the wolves. She untied the rope, and the dingy began to drift away from the ship.

"Now, the book; or next time your daughter won't be spared," Madelaine said.

"Catch." Avella tossed the book into the dingy, and Madelaine scrambled after it, cradling it like a precious jewel.

"This isn't finished." Madelaine glared at Avella as a salty wave crashed over the bow of the dingy.

Avella ignored her sister as she picked up the fallen dagger and handed it back to Katherine. "Now, where are Captain Kain's crew hiding? The tide's just right and the wind's perfect; we should be sailing." There was a nervous edge to Avella's voice as she gave the disappearing dingy an uneasy glance.

Captain Kane emerged from his hiding place below deck. "Are the creatures gone?" the captain's face was pale and shaken.

"Mother, I can't believe you gave Madelaine the book." Katherine hurried to Avella's side.

Avella smiled grimly. "If Madelaine had bothered to examine the book before leaving, she would have noticed it was actually Captain Kain's repair log. I switched the outer covers."

"But what if Madelaine comes back?" Katherine was equal parts impressed by her mother's ingenuity and aghast at the risk she took.

Avella shook her head. "She can't. The ship's been moving; they'll be lucky to get back to land as it is."

"We'll go to the capital and send men after her." Gunther joined them. He had a long streak of blood smeared across his tunic—Katherine didn't know who's— and was limping. "If we make good time, we should arrive in Corevan before her."

"What about Althea? The wolves know the location of her cottage." Althea's cottage was so isolated, it would be easy for Madelaine to attack her there.

"Althea's cottage is too far; we'd never reach her before, Madelaine. We'll just have to hope she wants the book more. Althea knows she's welcome at my estate if there's any trouble. My men will protect her. And something tells me Althea's not as weak as she seems."

Katherine worried her lip, considering Gunther's words. A whirring of wings, steadily louder, distracted her from the conversation.

"Take cover," Captain Kain shouted.

The gulls. The noise of thousands of beating wings filled the air as the gulls hovered above the ship. Katherine, Gunther, and Avella rushed to the stateroom.

"What are they going to do?" Katherine shouted to be heard above the din. Everything in the cabin rattled and vibrated.

"I don't know," shouted Gunther. He took her hand in his. The gulls hovered, their cries so loud Katherine felt her ears were going to explode. Then, as quickly as they appeared, the birds were gone in a dark sweeping cloud that disappeared over the horizon.

Katherine ran to the porthole. The only sight was the expanse of deep blue water, broken only by a thin strip of land fading into the distance.

"They've gone." She turned to the others.

"A warning," said Gunther. "Madelaine's opened the book."

CHAPTER NINE

Katherine sat in Lucie Marie's cabin, chewing on a hard dry roll. Jumpy and suspicious after the run in with the seagulls and Madelaine's wolves, the Lucie Marie's crew members made it clear the travellers weren't welcome on board the ship. Understandable, considering the gulls returned daily—a dark cloud shadowing the Lucie Marie. Madelaine was making no secret about keeping a close eye on the traveller's whereabouts. If this concerned Avella, she kept it to herself, but Katherine thought she saw worry lurking in her mother's eyes.

"Escaping from deck unpleasantness?" Gunther plopped in the leather chair at the small desk.

"I don't think Captain Kain likes me much." Katherine bit into the bread roll. It was hard, chewy, and tasteless. She forced it down with a grimace and a gulp of tepid ration water.

"Captain Kain doesn't like any of us much." Gunther lounged, propping his elbow on the edge of the wooden desk. "The captain only has to tolerate our presence a few more days. Everything's fine; we'll arrive in Corvan before you know it."

"What's fine?" Avella opened the door and perched on the bunk beside Katherine.

"Katherine's worried about the crew's nerves and ill manners," Gunther explained.

Avella nodded. "They are out of sorts about the seagull business. I can't say I'm comfortable with it myself—nasty flying rats. But the gulls don't seem to be able to hurt us, so maybe Madelaine can't control the birds as much as she believes."

"Is that why Madelaine wants the book, to strengthen her magic?" Katherine said aloud, imagining the damage Madelaine could wreak with even more control over her beasts.

"Definitely, although I don't know how Madelaine discovered the existence of Sorchia's book if they had no contact."

"The diaries," Katherine gasped, bolting to her feet so suddenly she bumped her head on the top bunk. How could she have forgotten about them so easily, she chided herself, rubbing her bruising scalp. "I found Sorchia's diaries in the old estate house—and I brought them with me." Katherine slid her hand under the bunk, pulling out her satchel. "I meant to finish reading them sooner, but we fled so quickly, I forgot."

Katherine reached into the satchel, pulling out the stack of diaries. "Sorchia must have written her secrets somewhere in these."

"I'll help read." Avella took the diary on the top, fingering the mouldering leather. "Are these all the diaries Sorchia wrote?"

"We had so little time to search—one of Madelaine's creatures attacked us. We were lucky to find these." Katherine shivered, remembering the crazed look in the bear's eyes as it reared over her.

Avella opened the diary, examining Sorchia's spidery handwriting. "This diary is from when Natalie still lived in the estate with her. See?" Avella drew her finger across the page, underlining the text. "... much as I have tried, Natalie shows no sign of gifting. So disappointing, I'd hoped to find her a sponsor and send her into court. So pretty, yet somehow so useless."

"Sorchia doesn't sound terribly motherly." Katherine frowned.

"That explains a lot about Natalie," sadness coloured Avella's voice. "She wasn't terribly motherly herself."

"Does the diary say anything about Sorchia's book?" Avella opened another diary, skimming the pages. Gunther joined them, picking up one of the leather-bound volumes and poring over it; his large fingers thumbed through the aged pages with care.

"Nothing in this one—wait—I might have found something." Katherine pointed to a section of writing, reading aloud. "Today, I finally have it... my true inheritance. My mother wanted to steal it from me... along with the house and the lands and give them to my father's niece, a mere infant. But I discovered their plan and stopped the whole thing before it was too late. This gives me the power I need to take back what's rightfully mine. I found the key to unlocking the power of the book."

"Sorchia says she has the key to the book, but she never writes what the key actually is." Katherine huffed in frustration, slamming the diary shut.

"Maybe it's really an actual physical key." Gunther glanced up from his diary. "Did Sorchia carry anything that resembled a key?" Gunther turned to Avella who tapped her chin.

"It seems familiar, but it happened such a long time ago..." Avella closed her eyes, her brow furrowed.

"If it was an actual key, Sorchia would have kept it close to her. On her person or locked away somewhere safe."

"The necklace." Avella set her book down with a thump. "Sorchia wore a necklace with a little gold key hanging from it. She kept it tucked in her dress, but I saw it once. I thought it was strange because Sorchia didn't wear much other jewelry."

Katherine set down the diary, "Madelaine must have the key now; that's why she's so desperate to get her hands on that book. She must realise grandmother wanted to take over the kingdom...."

"... and Madelaine plans to finish what Sorchia started," Gunther continued. "Whatever happens, the book needs to stay safe. If there's even a hint Madelaine might get near it, it needs to be immediately destroyed."

"I kept the book on my person." Avella drew a small volume out of her pocket. Without its cover, it fit snug in her palm. The three stared at the tiny object, until Avella shuddered, sliding it back out of sight into her pocket. "I can't touch it for too long. It feels...slimy." She grimaced, rubbing her hand on the fabric of her dress.

A flurry of noise and activity drew their attention away from the book. "What's happening?" Gunther opened the door and peered out. The deck was in an uproar; crew members lined the port side, peering over the railings and muttering anxiously.

"What is it?" Katherine dashed to the side of the ship, clinging tight to the railing as she leaned toward the salty waves. Deep blue water topped with streaks of foam met her eyes.

"There's something down there." One crew member, a tall, gangly man with a scraggly red beard, forgot his dislike of the interlopers as he pointed at the water. "Something huge." His eyes were wide with fear and suspicion.

"Like a whale?" Katherine squinted through the water, wondering how frightened she should be.

"No, a sea dragon."

"I'm pretty sure sea monsters don't... oof." Katherine's words were cut off when Avella elbowed her in the side.

"What was the sea monster doing?" Avella cut in, meeting the sailor's pale blue eyes with an urgent expression.

"I'm not sure.... Killian spotted it." The sailor pointed at the first mate.

"Does Captain Kain know about the sighting?" Gunther broke in, addressing the first mate.

"I do." Captain Kain strode across the deck, sun glinting off his polished sword.

"Did the sea monster see the ship?" Avella asked Captain Kain. With a shock of fear, Katherine realized Avella believed the sea monster was real—and dangerous.

"Sea monsters rarely bother ships, much less attack them." Captain Kain's brave words and firm tone didn't match the barely disguised panic in his eyes.

"Rarely?" Avella shot the Captain a stern look.

"We'll post a double watch in the rigging to be safe. The wind is on our side; you'll arrive in port within two days... until then, I suggest you lie low. The crew is increasingly restless. And If I find this sea monster malarky has any connection with those blasted seagulls, I'll toss you overboard myself, crown business or not."

Avella tightened her lips. "Come on." She marched back toward the cabin. Katherine followed, turning to look over her shoulder. Captain Kain's rigid figure stared at the glinting blue water, shading his eyes with his hand.

CHAPTER TEN

"Do sea monsters actually attack ships?" Katherine questioned her mother, following her back into the cramped stateroom. Her stomach cramped as she realized how helpless they were in the vast blue water.

"Captain Kain's right, it is rare for sea monsters to attack ship, but only because they live in the rocks and rarely encounter them. I've never heard of a sea monster leaving a ship intact... strange." Avella's troubled eyes were distant, thoughtful.

"You think Madelaine influenced the sea monster to find the ship?" Katherine asked, searching Avella's face. "But why not attack the Lucie Marie outright?"

"Madelaine wants Sorchia's book, she wouldn't risk it falling to the bottom of the sea." Gunther stared out the porthole at the glimmering water. "And we still haven't learned how the book works."

Later that afternoon, Captain Kain's first mate brought them their rations, making it clear the trio were unwelcome on deck. In the meantime, they threw themselves into Sorchia's diaries, scouring every page for answers. Answers that refused to be found.

"I've read this stupid diary three times and still haven't got a clue," Katherine huffed, tossing the volume on the bunk. The ship rocked, sending the book sliding off the edge of the bunk and shooting it under the desk. Katherine crawled under the tiny desk where the book lay splayed open on the floor.

"Oh dear, I think I tore the cover." The dried leather of the diary had cracked, a split running the length of its spine. Katherine prodded the crack, pulling the two sides together.

"Katherine, let me see that diary." Gunther held out a hand, an urgent expression crossing his face.

Katherine shrugged, handing Gunther the diary.

"Look, something's hidden under the cover. May I?" Katherine nodded, and Gunther's strong fingers tugged, tearing the ancient leather from its underpinnings. Katherine and Avella leaned forward, eyes fixed on what they saw. Between the leather and the inside cover sheltered a single sheet of yellowed parchment—so old it was ready to crumble with a single breath.

"We've found it." Gunther said as he placed the parchment in Avella's waiting hand.

"Can you read the writing?" Katherine leaned over Avella's shoulder.

Avella squinted at the parchment. "This isn't Iasian script—it's older. I can only make out occasional words, not enough to translate."

Disappointed, Katherine flopped back on the bunk.

"The Lovanian castle has an extensive library," Gunther said. "Someone there will translate it. Lucie can advise us; after all, she practically lives in that library. Whatever happens, we can't let Madelaine get her hands on this parchment, or the book," Gunther said, clenching his fist.

"Can you keep them safe for us? Madelaine's not trying to kill you." Katherine raised her eyes to Gunther's.

"If you're sure you want to trust me with them." Gunther met Katherine's gaze, questions in his eyes. Katherine met his dark eyes with her own blue ones; wordlessly, she handed Gunther the parchment and Sorchia's book, still safely ensconced in the cover of Captain Kain's logbook. Gunther tucked the parchment into the logbook and placed them in a leather case hanging from his belt.

The next day dragged by slowly. The weather was sweltering, and the tiny cabin was stifling and breathlessly hot. Katherine longed for a breath of fresh air, but the thought of facing the angry crew of the Lucie Marie kept her inside. The seagulls arrived four times that day; even the usually unflappable Captain Kain seemed jittery, tossing their rations in the door before scurrying off.

Katherine sat next to the porthole, staring at the endless waves. "Is that land over there?" She pointed at what seemed to be a narrow peninsula jutting into the sea. A gleam sparked in her eyes, a lighthouse perched on the end of the peninsula, afternoon sun glinting from glass windows.

"That the Bay of Thieves." Gunther joined Katherine at the porthole. "A smuggling point during the Great War—I guess the name stuck. They never built a port because the tides are far too dangerous; they'd drag a ship right into the rocks."

Katherine shivered. "The smugglers didn't mind the danger?"

"Risk takers," Gunther answered. "The good news is, Thieves Bay isn't far from the Harbour; we should dock by tomorrow morning." He raised his voice to be heard over the gulls, their gleeful cries drowning out his voice.

Katherine cast a doubtful eye through the porthole. The gulls swooped low, their beating wings vibrating the Marie Lucie's wood framed hull. "How many creatures can Madelaine control at once?" She turned to Avella.

"I don't know." The grim expression on Avella's face made Katherine's pulse race. "But grandmother Sorchia called up a nest of thorns the size of the Marie Lucie in an instant. The Rapunzel gift is powerful." Avella's eyes were troubled. The gulls hovered over the ship before disappearing, speeding toward land, their screams echoing across the water.

Avella watched the birds as they faded from sight before something else caught her eye. Something under the water. Huge. Sleek. Fast. The creature was speeding toward the ship, leaving a thin wake trailing behind it in the foamy sea.

Katherine wasn't the only person who had spotted the massive creature. Shouts and thuds were heard on deck, the panicked cries of the crew as they raced to respond.

"Gunther, Mother, the sea monster, it's back." Katherine pointed a shaking finger at the churning water. The long lithe creature sped toward the ship, rippling through the sea like a comet. A spiny black fin ran the length of its back, and the rest of the vast, liquid body was a deep glittering green. It got closer and closer, cutting a line directly for the ship's bow. The panic above deck intensified.

A gaping red mouth spread open, displaying rows of gleaming pointed teeth. Dark wet eyes stared right at Katherine's white face; then the monster disappeared.

"It's under the boat," Avella murmured.

A jolt almost knocked them off their feet— too big to be a wave. "The sea monster," Katherine gasped, struggling for balance.

"It's slamming the Lucie Marie," Gunther said, brow furrowed.

The ship rolled again, sending Katherine crashing to the floor. She sat up, rubbing her bruised elbow. "Should we go on deck and help the crew?"

"We'd be in the way," Avella told her. "We'll have to wait it out here."

The creature relentlessly nosed the ship toward the bay, where thundering waves crashed on the rocks of the narrow inlet. At times, the ship heeled over so far, the three travellers were nearly sideways. The Marie Lucie drifted closer to the lighthouse; so close Katherine could count the windows on the top floor. But somehow, the Marie Lucie stayed afloat, barely missing barnacle encrusted rocks jutting above the surface of the boiling water.

A banging at the door pulled their attention from the porthole.

"Open up. It's Captain Kain." The Captain's strained face showed the turmoil of the last hour.

"We're lowering a lifeboat." Captain Kain's expression grew more grim. "You three are going on it."

"Is the ship running aground?" Katherine asked, every muscle rigid.

"No, but the situation is precarious. The crew is revolting if you're here any longer—we'd lose everything."

"How do you expect us to survive that?" Avella demanded, gesturing toward the swirling waters; she stumbled as the ship suffered another rough shove from the sea monster.

"You have two choices, either go willingly or be dragged out; one way or another you're leaving this ship, crown business or not."

CHAPTER ELEVEN

Stinging saltwater crashed against Marie Lucie's bow as the crew struggled to heave the frail lifeboat over the side of the ship. The lifeboat was merely the size of the sea monster's head. The creature was at the bow of the boat, shoving the creaking wood hull steadily forward with its nose. Miraculously, the Marie Lucie had missed the rocks as it forced her through a narrow inlet.

When the lifeboat settled, rocking and precarious, into the waves, the monster turned, liquid eyes glinting with recognition. Katherine's heart clenched. They had been noticed. The creature left the Marie Lucie, rearing its head out of the water. It was so close Katherine could see every scale, every rivulet of water running down its muscled neck, pouring into the sea in foaming waterfalls.

"Here, use the book." Gunther shoved the artifact into Katherine's hand."

Katherine held up the book, trying desperately to remember how it had worked when the other animals had attacked. Nothing happened.

"What's going on?" Avella said.

"I'm doing what I did before." Katherine said, hands trembling.

"Now she knows you can use it, Madelaine's probably set a ward against it." Avella said, watching with horrified eyes as the sea monster drew even closer, the tiny boat rocked wildly as the waves crashed against it.

Just when Katherine thought the creature was going to crash down on the tiny group, it slowed, gently pressing its nose against the lifeboat.

"It's pushing us," Katherine said, flinching from the bottomless black eyes. The lifeboat powered through the water, leaving the Marie Lucie to flounder through the waves. The tiny craft slid on, gliding through the inlet and into the bay where the water calmed, gently rocking the little lifeboat.

"So, this is Thieves Bay." Gunther's attentive eyes took in the sight, searching the treelined shore. The bay was quiet after the roar and crash of waves on the rocks. The sea monster pushed the boat past soaring cliffs toward a sandy beach at the southern end of the bay. Four familiar figures stood gathered on the sandy shore; long grey cloaks whipped in the wind as they waited for the lifeboat to reach shore.

"The wolves," Katherine said, gripping the edge of the boat. "Madelaine must be nearby too."

One last shove pushed their craft through the surf, directly toward the waiting wolves. With a flick of his tail, the sea creature slid away, scaly green body disappearing under the waves.

"Use the oars," Gunther shouted, "Maybe we can get away. He grabbed two pairs of oars from the bottom of the boat. Katherine and Avella each took an oar and began to row.

Faces grim, the three strained, pulling the oars against the current, but it was no use. The tide was sweeping in, pulling them relentlessly toward the sandy shore. The wolves stood unmoving, silhouettes against the sky. Waiting.

With a bump, the boat hit the sandy shore. The wolves sprang, flashing into wolf form before Katherine could blink.

"Where. Is. The. Book?" the largest wolf growled at Katherine.

Katherine whipped her dagger toward the wolf's face. Snarling, the wolf batted it out of her hand and shoved Katherine to the bottom of the boat.

"I know what Madelaine did to you," Katherine's voice shook as she stared into unblinking yellow eyes. "She's your enemy too, isn't she?"

He grunted, sharp claws digging into Katherine's shoulder; razor-sharp teeth snapped inches from her face.

"She'll never let them go," Katherine continued. "Never."

Katherine whimpered as teeth grazed the side of her neck.

"Katherine, no..." Gunther started.

"Madelaine will keep using and using..." Katherine said, interrupting Gunther. "And when she's done, you'll end up exactly like them. Who are they? Brothers? Children?"

The wolf paused, closing his yellow eyes. "My sister."

"My Mother." Another of the wolves stepped forward. Eleonor, Katherine recognized the timbre in her voice.

"You'll never get them back. Unless you fight against Madelaine. Join us.... It's the only chance.... their only chance."

The pressure on Katherine's chest eased as the wolf inched back. The largest wolf snapped, and the pressure increased again.

"Madelaine has them locked and chained, and her guards are the only key holders. Her eyes and ears are everywhere."

"We have influence. If you help us, we'll help you," Katherine answered.

"Yes." Eleonor stepped forward, after another long pause. "I'll join you and fight against Madelaine."

"Eleonor. Hush—you don't know what you're doing," the enormous wolf said, reprimanding her in a gruff voice. "We decide together, as a pack."

Eleonor growled low in her throat, the hair on the back of her neck raised. "I've made my decision. I refuse to be Madelaine's pawn any longer."

"You defy me?" The wolf leaped off Katherine, rushing Eleonor. He must be Alerion, Katherine realized. He surged toward Eleonor and they were down in a howling blur of sand, fur, teeth, and blood.

Without pausing, Zelia and Jules jumped in the fray. To Katherine's shock, they were on Eleonor's side, and Alerion, unable to withstand the three of them, was pinned to the ground.

"Submit," Jules growled, nipping Alerion's neck.

Alerion narrowed his yellow eyes, his chest heaving. "I submit." He said, his voice a reluctant growl. The wolves released him, and he stood, shaking his fur and licking his torn skin.

"Fine, we'll help you, but on one condition. You use your royal connection to free our families."

Katherine blinked. The wolves were once again in human form, blood streaking Jule's tunic, and Alerion cradling a wounded arm.

"What is Madelaine's plan?" Gunther asked, reaching to help Katherine step over the edge of the boat.

"Madelaine wants the book. And she wants you and your daughters dead." Jules turned to Avella. "We were to meet you here, get the book, and take you prisoner until Madelaine met us."

Gunther pressed his lips together, concern flitting across his face. "When was Madelaine to meet you?"

"Tomorrow," Jules answered. "But, Madelaine has messengers everywhere." He threw an uneasy glance toward the forest.

"We'll move fast. Where's the nearest village, somewhere we could obtain horses?"

"Chauville is two miles east; nothing more than a farming village."

"Where there are farms, there are horses— for the right price." Gunther grabbed his satchel and joined by the wolves, set off across the beach, long strides eating up the ground.

Katherine scampered after them, her satchel banging against her hip. "Do you think we'll make it to the castle before Madelaine?"

"I hope so," Gunther replied. "Madelaine will have help from her animals, but we made good time on board the Marie Lucie."

The town of Chauville was tiny, a single narrow street with a row of cottages. They headed for the single tavern next to Market Square.

"Franc's got horses." The tavern keeper chewed the end of his pipe. "He'd be willing to part with them... for a price, obviously. His farm's at the south edge of the village. You can't miss it; he has a yellow door on his cottage."

"Of course," Gunther replied smoothly. They walked down the dirt packed street, where, as promised, stood a thatched cottage with the yellow door. Stacks of wood covered the bare front yard and a promising well-kept barn squatted behind the cottage.

Avella followed as Gunther and Katherine strode up the garden path, startling a clucking flock of chickens. They knocked at the yellow door. The wolves paused at the gate; solemn golden eyes watched before slipping down the road and melting into the forest.

"Horses, you say?" Franc eyed the salt crusted ragtag group suspiciously.

"Yes. Have you any to spare?" Katherine stepped forward. She was used to dealing with farmers in the guild, and Franc looked like someone who loved to barter.

"Aye, I have horses in the barn yonder," Franc said, strolling toward barn; he jerked a calloused thumb, beckoning them to follow. Inside the spacious barn, two tidy rows of stalls greeted them. Velvety noses poked over doors; liquid eyes followed the strangers entering their domain. Franc's rugged face softened at the view as he patted a tall bay on his velvety nose.

"They seem good stock," Gunther said, admiring the bay. "We're in a bit of a hurry, but we'll pay with gold."

"Gold?" Franc's eyes lit up as he turned from the bay.

"Gold," Gunther repeated. "But we need the horses now, the fastest and sturdiest you've got."

Franc scratched his chin. "Well, there's Marigold there; she's a right goer." He pointed at a bright chestnut mare. "And, Violet and Thorn." Franc led out the horses. "This is going to cost you. Are you sure?" he peered suspiciously at Gunther.

Gunther nodded.

Franc raised an eyebrow and led out the three horses. Gunther chose Thorn, a tall blue black; Avella rode Violet, a mild-mannered grey mare, and Katherine took Marigold.

Gold exchanged hands, and they rode away, meeting the wolves at a stone bridge past the southern end of the village.

"We'll keep to the woods; if we're seen on the path, it will cause a spectacle," Jules informed them. The four wolves evaporated into the thick woods, silent shadows that flickered along beside them as they rode.

The road was easy, and the horses were fast; Katherine was lulled into a sense of security until a shadow flitted across the path, startling her horse; an eagle wheeling overhead. "Did you see that?" Katherine asked Gunther, a sense of disquiet stirring in her gut. He glanced up, uninterested.

"That eagle's been following us for a while." Avella shaded her eyes, peering into the sky. "I wonder if it's Madelaine's."

The thought sobered them, each wondering what other creatures Madelaine had at her disposal. They rode hard, only stopping when the horses needed rest.

"We'll reach Corvan tomorrow," Gunther said. As sunset approached, they stopped to make camp in a clearing. Katherine and Avella gathered sticks for the fire as Gunther watered and fed the horses.

"Do you think we're still ahead of Madelaine?" Katherine chewed on the dried meat they'd bought in Chauville. There was no further sign of Madelaine's eagle, but the group was watchful, alert. Every rustle in the underbrush could be a potential enemy— every flurry of wings, spying eyes for an evil mistress.

"We should be," Gunther replied. "But, we'll need to keep watch tonight. We can't take any chances of being caught by surprise."

The wolves spotted the fire and approached. Tired from their travels, Gunther, Avella, and Katherine ate in silence and fell asleep. The wolves curled in their wolf forms by the fire. Katherine and Avella were wrapped in their cloaks on the ground, while Gunther opted to take the first watch.

The night passed uneventfully. Katherine stretched her arms overhead, easing her muscles, stiff from lying on the hard ground.

"No sign of Madelaine or her minions?" Katherine asked, turning to Gunther.

"Not that I could see." Gunther handed Katherine a chunk of bread.

Katherine nibbled the hard bread. In a few hours, she would arrive in Corvan; her silkworms would hatch any day, if they hadn't already. Katherine was surprised the thought hadn't crossed her mind earlier. The silkworms had been her obsession for so long; she sighed.

"What's on your mind?" Gunther asked, swigging water from his canteen.

"It's going to be so different returning home. I can see why Lucie changed after she met Frederich at the Chateau and with Penelope."

"We're not out of danger yet," Gunther answered, "We still have to contain Madelaine."

Sobered by the thought, they began tacking the horses. Time was tight, and they needed to warn King Erich.

A few hours later, the castle gates loomed before them. They rode the back lanes through Corvan, but even so, the wolves drew stares and muttering, loping beside the three of them in wolf form. An unfortunate necessity; it would take too long to reach the castle in human form.

"Gunther? Katherine?" King Erich's guards rushed to open the gates.

"We must speak to King Erich and Queen Isabelle at once," Gunther ordered. The horses clattered to a stop in the castle courtyard.

They swung down, handing the reins to the grooms and followed by the wolves, headed directly for the castle entrance.

"King Erich is in the audience hall receiving citizens," the castle steward protested as they strode past.

"It's an emergency," Gunther said, giving the steward a hard look. "We received news that Princess Lucie and her family are in grave danger."

Convinced, the steward stood aside. After rescuing Prince Frederich from captivity, Lucie could do no wrong in the eyes of Lovanian castle staff.

"Gunther, what's this about?" King Erich's tall figure strode across the room. They had been escorted to a small side room leading off King Erich's audience hall. King Erich gave Avella and the wolves, in human form again, a sideways glance and nodded a greeting to Katherine.

"We've discovered a plot against Lucie," Gunther said, eyes tight. "She and her family are in immediate danger."

A grim expression flashed through King Erich's eyes. "Who is it?"

"Lucie has an aunt— an Iasian noble woman who has the gift of communicating with animals. She has been pursuing us relentlessly with her band of creatures from Iasia. Even now, Madelaine approaches the Lovanian castle; we ourselves were attacked by a sea monster under Madelaine influence. These wolves are her former servants; they can tell you more."

Jules bowed, eyes grave. "Your Majesty, Lord Gunther speaks the truth that Madelaine is a formidable enemy, determined to shed the blood of Lady Avella and her three daughters. Indeed, she can communicate with animals and use her gift to influence them to do her bidding. We ourselves were at her mercy when she kidnapped our relatives, keeping them captive until we obeyed her."

"Tomas, call a council meeting this afternoon. Whoever is in the city should attend," King Erich said, turning to his steward. "We must act immediately to protect Lucie and her family."

"Forgive me, Your Majesty, but I fear even now there isn't time to discuss the matter in detail with the council. Madelaine is due to reach Corvan today," Gunther said.

King Erich nodded, turning back to the steward. "Inform the general we must deploy all available fighting men to defend the castle and the city. And dismiss the citizens. Tell them to go home and be safe; no one should travel the streets of Corvan today."

Tomas nodded, rushing off to do King Erich's bidding.

"Come—tell me everything."

Soon, the castle was in an uproar. King Erich's men, bristling with weapons, were teeming everywhere. Lines of archers were stationed on the castle walls, and within the hour, the gates were locked and barred, with strict instructions to only allow council members or known guests entrance. A contingent of soldiers was sent to collect Marion and her children and transport them to the safety of the castle. King Erich holed up with the four wolves and Lord Gunther to discuss strategy, leaving Katherine and Avella on their own.

"Miss Katherine, will Lady Avella be residing at the castle?" Tomas asked politely.

Katherine flashed her mother a questioning glance. "We'll both stay in the castle," Katherine decided. "For safety," she explained, turning to her mother.

"Can I..?" an uncertain look flickered in Avella's eyes. "Can I see Lucie? And the children?"

"Of course. Why didn't I think of it? Follow me."

Katherine led Avella to Lucie and Frederich's apartment. Katherine turned to her mother, placing a finger over her lips. "The baby might be sleeping," she warned, rapping the door softly.

Lucie peeked out, her brow smoothing when she saw Katherine. "Come in." She took her sister by the hand, pulling her into the room. She raised an eyebrow when she saw Avella hovering behind Katherine. "Is that..." Lucie's voice trailed off uncertainly.

"Lady Avella, our Mother," Katherine answered, smiling at Lucie.

Tears welled in Lucie's eyes as she flung her arms around Avella. "I can't believe you're alive."

"You're not angry?" Avella's lip trembled.

"Yes. No. I don't know. I have children of my own now... I would do anything for their safety. I'm just glad your safe," Lucie babbled, pulling Avella on the settee next to her.

Avella reached out a tentative hand, stroking Lucie's dark hair. "So like Pierre's," she murmured.

"Tell me everything," Lucie demanded. "Does it pertain to the ruckus outside, because soldiers have been marching those corridors like Hades is chasing them."

Avella's eyes dimmed. "I'm afraid your aunt Madelaine is after us; she's gifted."

A shadow crossed Lucie's face. "I'll get the sceptre." She rose immediately. "Come, the nursemaid will take the babies."

"So it's true, you wield the Lovanian sceptre?" Avella asked.

Lucie nodded, the weight of responsibility evident on her face. "I have the Rapunzel family gift."

Avella and Katherine followed Lucie down a long stone corridor; at the very end stood a wooden door leading to the library. Lucie opened the door, striding past towering shelves. Thousands of books lined the surrounding walls on every side. At the end of the library, Lucie turned abruptly, drawing a key out of her pocket. Metal scraped metal as she twisted the key.

"My office," Lucie explained to her mother, leading them inside. "I love the library so much that Erich gave me this study to use." Lucie's office was crowded with more books. Ignoring the books, Lucie pulled a painting off the wall, revealing a metal door set into the stone wall.

Lucie plucked a tiny key from a bunch of keys in her pocket and opened the metal door. "Here it is, the Lovanian sceptre." She cradled a small velvet pouch.

"Can I—see the sceptre?" Avella asked.

Lucie pulled away from the velvet, revealing the jewelled sceptre. Even in dim light of her office, the sceptre reflected prisms of light that danced and shimmered around the tiny study.

"I can feel it," Avella murmured, half to herself. "It's been years since I've felt that."

Katherine closed her eyes briefly, then opened them. "Feel what?" she gave her mother a puzzled glance.

"The magic," Lucie replied. "It moves across my skin..."

"Like fire," Avella finished her sentence for her. "I had the gift too... once. Althea sealed it to keep us safe."

"Would you ever unseal your gift again?" Katherine turned to Avella, questions in her eyes.

Avella paused. "It was the best day of my life when we sealed the magic. The relief. But as the years passed, I realised the magic wasn't the problem. It was how the gift was used. Or how it wasn't used. If I had the choice, I believe I would unseal it again." Her eyes glowed. "I would fight my sister."

A resounding crash broke the quiet hum of the castle library.

"We need to go, now." Lucie locked the study carefully before they crept through the maze of shelves. Tension hung thickly over the palace. Threatening. Ominous.

"Madelaine must be close now... if she's not in Corvan already," Avella whispered. The stillness was broken again, distant shouts trickling from above.

"It's on the roof," Lucie whispered. "Follow me, I know a shortcut." Lucie turned abruptly, steering them toward a recessed door in the side of the stone wall; behind the door rose a narrow staircase.

"This goes to the south turret," Lucie explained. The steep staircase, rarely used, was festooned with spiderwebs and layered with thick, choking dust. Katherine felt along the undressed stone with trembling fingers as she stumbled up and up.

As they rushed to the turret, the noise grew, a terrible screech and a slow rhythmic thud. Unlike anything Katherine had heard before, her gut twisted as she wondered what dangers Madelaine could possibly have brought to the castle door. A faint stench—burnt metal and singed rock— drifted down the stairwell.

Avella halted at the top of the staircase. "It's me Madelaine wants," she whispered, nudging Lucie aside and flinging open the door.

A fantastic sight met their eyes. A dragon, grey as a thundercloud, was spitting enormous bolts of fire that rained down on the castle. Clinging to the dragon's neck, her black veil billowing against the smoky sky, was Madelaine.

Avella didn't flinch as she stepped fearlessly into the landing at the top of the turret. "Looking for someone, sister?" she asked, fixing her eyes on Madelaine's veiled face.

The dragon whirled, a white-hot spit of fire narrowly missing Avella as it cracked the stone. Strangely clumsy for a dragon, and now that Katherine got closer, the dragon wasn't as big as expected. Its big yellow eyes were strangely murky, rolling in its head as Madelaine directed it.

"You!" Madelaine hissed at Avella from under the veil. "You're not slipping away this time."

Katherine's heart thudded against her ribcage. Her body was numb with fear; she watched as Avella stood firm, her cloak whipping in the hot, sulphurous winds created by the dragon's wing.

"Tell me, sister," Avella raised her voice to be heard. "What is it like?"

Madelaine paused, unclenching her fists from the dragon's neck. "What is what like?"

"To be so consumed by dark bitterness you have nothing else left. That's what this is, isn't it? What happens when you finally accomplish your goals? Will you go back to hiding in your crumbling manor alone? What happened after the accident with Sorchia? Did mother reject you like she did me? Because you didn't fit into her perfect little plan anymore?" Avella took another step forward.

"How dare you?" Madelaine's voice dripped ice. "Yes, mother loved me, but at what price? At least you had your freedom. I had to coddle Natalie, follow her whims at every moment, bend over backwards to please her. And it all came to nothing. I lost everything because of you."

"No Madelaine, you lost everything because of Sorchia. Grandmother did that to you, not me."

Madelaine laughed. A cold, bitter laugh. "Sorchia would have stayed out of our lives if you had been able to control your gift. And now you will pay. But, I'll spare your daughters for one thing."

"What's that?"

"The book. I know you have it. And don't think you can switch the covers again." The dragon lowered itself to the roof, but Madelaine remained seated on his back— a cold, proud figure rigid against the sky.

Avella wavered; Madelaine had pounced on her one weakness—her daughters. Sensing hesitation, Madelaine pressed harder. "Just think, Avella, your grandchildren can grow up with their mothers. Not like your daughters did, the poor, motherless creatures. It's a wonder they turned out as well as they did."

Madelaine had gone a step too far. A low cry burst out of Avella's mouth; pulling a dagger from her waist, she sprang at Madelaine. With a feral scream, Madelaine shouted at the dragon, who drew in a deep breath, preparing to spew liquid flame. Avella leapt out of the path of the dragon's flame. To her surprise, the dragon fire was instantly quenched by a bolt of blue flame, thin and powerful. The electric taste of magic was thick in the air. Tingling, sharp, acrid.

Lucie's hand was outstretched, holding the Lovanian sceptre. She pointed it at the dragon's flame, and the magic licked the molten flames away. Lucie walked steadily toward the dragon, who remained motionless, stunned by the sceptre's power.

Closer and closer, Lucie was now mere inches away from the dragon. She touched its nose gently with the shining sceptre.

"Be free," Lucie whispered to the dragon.

The dragon closed its huge eyes and shook its head, a shudder traveling through its large body. The milky eyes cleared to a bright, shining yellow.

"What happened? What is this strange weight on my back?" the dragon's voice was youthful. It was still a child, Katherine realized, as a dart of sympathy shot through her.

Madelaine howled in anger, muttering in a desperate attempt to regain control of the creature, but Madelaine's gift was no match for the power of the sceptre. Katherine and Avella joined Lucie at the dragon and Katherine even patted the dragon's nose gingerly, wincing at the dry, scaly heat.

"You were under a spell… or a curse… whichever you prefer to call it," Lucie answered the dragon. "What was your last memory before flying to the castle?"

The dragon narrowed great golden eyes and blew out a puff of steam. "I was with my mothers; they must be frantic."

Temporarily distracted by soothing the dragon, the three didn't notice Madelaine stealing her hand into her thick cloak, until a flash of motion caught Katherine's eye.

"Duck, Madelaine has a dagger," Katherine shouted. Instinct took over, and her arm flew up, knocking Madelaine's cruel black dagger to the ground. The dagger skidded across the rough stone, sliding halfway across the turret.

Madelaine threw herself off the dragon's back, both arms outstretched in an attempt to reach the dagger first. But Katherine was closer. And quicker. Katherine snatched Madelaine's dagger, raising it above her head in one breathless motion.

Madelaine yelled, jerking Katherine's head back by the hair, but Katherine held tight to the dagger. Slowly, slowly, she forced the dagger to Madelaine's chest, pressing it until a drop of blood welled up, splashing to the ground. Heaving, Madelaine softened her grip.

Shaking, Katherine stood, gripping the dagger tight as Avella rushed forward and wrapped her belt around Madelaine's wrists.

"I wish it didn't have to be like this, sister." Avella's eyes filled with tears as she bound her only sister's wrists together.

The next few moments were a muddle of activity. The guards shot onto the roof, accompanied by Prince Frederich, pale and shaken when he saw his wife calmly stroking the dragon's neck. They quickly wrapped a cloth around Madelaine's mouth before she was pulled away by the guards. No one wanted to take the chance of letting Madelaine using her gift to call more creatures to her aid.

Katherine stood next to the dragon with Avella and Lucie as he regarded them with bewildered eyes.

"I've never seen humans up close before." He blinked. "Are you always so busy?"

Katherine laughed. "Goodness, no, we're usually much calmer. Madelaine was using you as a weapon to attack the princess."

"Oh. I'm sorry." The dragon turned his head, fanning them with his fiery breath. *Like standing in front of an oven on baking day,* Katherine thought, leaning away from the sulfur scented heat.

"Where are your mothers?" Katherine asked the dragon.

"Iasia.... Is that far away?" the dragon asked, a boiling tear hovering at the corner of his eye.

"No, sweetheart, you're in Lovan. Would you like someone to accompany you home?" Motherly instincts aroused, Avella stroked the dragon's neck.

The dragon snorted a babyish snuffle, accompanied by a spurt of flame. "Yes. I miss my mothers."

Frederich beckoned to one of the soldiers, a gangly youngster. "Harry, will you organise for..." he turned to the dragon. "Excuse me, what is your name?"

"Bernard." Another hot tear rolled down the dragon's cheek, splashing on the stones where it steamed and bubbled.

"Will you please organise for Bernard to be returned to his mother?"

Harry saluted. "Fly down the courtyard, Bernard; I'll make sure you get home safe." With a clumsy flap, the dragon flew off, landing in the courtyard with an awkward hop.

Frederich turned to his wife, embracing her in a fierce hug. "You need to stop scaring me like that," he whispered into her hair.

Katherine turned away, wishing someone felt like that about her. She wished Gunther felt like that about her. The thought whisked through her head, taking her by surprise before she could shove them away. Since when had she entertained these thoughts about Gunther? Sure, she had a childish crush on him, but those feelings disintegrated to bitter ash the moment Katherine realized he belonged to another. *Not yours,* Katherine chastised herself sternly. Even with the scolding, Katherine couldn't tear her eyes from the dark square.... The doorway that led to the steps. But it remained empty. Quiet. Gunther wasn't coming, and Katherine was alone.

".... We'll have to make sure she's all right," Lucie was finishing her sentence.

"Who?" Katherine turned to her sister.

"Althea," Lucie continued. "We have to bring her to the castle where it's safe. Who knows how many minions Madelaine has skulking around Lavon; the wolves can't possibly be her only creatures here. Madelaine knows where Althea lives and I would never forgive myself if anything happened to her."

Avella nodded. "Just because we have Madelaine doesn't mean we're out of danger yet."

"Do you think we could ask the dragons to help?" Katherine turned to her sister. "After all, we're returning their stolen child. They're bound to be grateful."

Lucie tapped her chin thoughtfully. "If the dragons don't burn us to a crisp first. We'll have to ask Frederich to advise us about the dragons, because he knows far more about their habits than I do. If only Frederich's sister, Princess Celine was here to help; the dragons adore her after that time she rescued their egg."

The three headed toward the staircase.

Still no Gunther, Katherine thought, fighting the stabbing disappointment that lanced through her gut.

Lucie led Katherine and Avella down the main staircase. King Erich's council members were filing into the council chambers when they arrived at the bottom of the stairs. Katherine caught sight of the back of Gunther's head, chatting with the others. She turned to hide the disappointment in her eyes.

"Katherine, I know you've only recently arrived back and haven't had time to refresh yourself yet, but would you join Gunther to report your findings to the council? And the Lady Avella as well, if your willing." King Erich bowed his head as Avella curtsied. Even in her worn linen shift, Avella was elegant and poised.

"Of course, Your Majesty," Avella murmured, following the others into the council chambers.

Lucie squeezed Katherine's hand. "I'm going to check on the babies, but come up later and we'll talk."

Katherine took a seat at the polished wooden table in the council chambers. Because of the short notice, several council seats remained empty. She glanced up, catching Gunther's eye before lowering her eyes. Obviously, now his obligation of duty was fulfilled. She was out of the picture, Katherine thought. It stung, but she should never have expected anything different.

"Let the meeting begin." A grave expression settled on King Erich's face. "We have gathered today because an enemy of Princess Lucie and her family has attacked the royal castle. I'm sure you're aware of the juvenile dragon in the west courtyard?"

The council members nodded, curiosity in their eyes.

"That dragon is the work of Lady Madelaine, an Iasian. She has the power to influence animals by bending them to her will. As a result, she is extremely dangerous, even detained as she is now. Lord Gunther and the Lady Katherine have had more intimate dealings with her and will now report their findings."

King Erich turned to Lord Gunther, who proceeded to detail their experiences with Lady Madelaine. Katherine glanced around the room, seeing shocked and surprise crossing the faces of several council members.

"Our next step will be to request the Iasians investigate the Lady Madelaine's estate further. We believe there are gifted animal shifters imprisoned on her estate grounds against their will." King Erich continued. "And we will also request that because of the crimes committed on Lovanian lands, she be detained here in Lovan for trial. If found guilty, we will request Lady Madelaine's gift be sealed."

"Seal the gift?" Lord Hadyn glanced up, surprise flashing across his face. Sealing the gifted was a last resort, not something done to someone from across the Iaisian border.

King Erich frowned. "The Lady Madelaine attempted to kill the Princess Lucie. It is a reasonable punishment."

"But how can we possibly seal Madelaine's gift? Only Iasians know the secret of performing a sealing ceremony."

Avella cleared her throat. "There is someone in Lovan who can perform a sealing ceremony."

Heads turned, all fixated on the humbly dressed woman seated next to Katherine.

"Althea. She sealed my powers."

A murmur went around the table.

"Then we approach Althea immediately and issue a request." King Erich's piercing gaze roamed the table. "Do all agree?"

A chorus of agreement made its way around the circle.

"And tonight," King Erich continued, a slight smile creasing his features. "We celebrate the return of the lady Avella. Lucie's mother."

Avella smiled politely, but Katherine saw by the slight tremor in Avella's hand that the attention made her nervous. After Avella's introduction, the council broke up, the members scattering.

"A ball?" Avella turned to Katherine, panic leaping into her eyes. "I've never been to one before. Whatever will I wear?"

"Don't worry." Katherine laid a hand on her mother's arm. "This is my speciality."

King Erich insisted Katherine and Avella stay in the castle; Madelaine might be detained, but they weren't out of danger yet. After sending a messenger to the manor house to check if her silkworms were hatching, Katherine turned her attention to finding a suitable dress for her mother.

"I hate causing you extra work," Avella insisted as Katherine led her to the castle workroom.

"Trouble? Katherine lives for this." Lucie laughed.

Katherine took in a deep breath as she entered the workroom. Her workroom. She greeted the seamstresses before ushering Lucie and Avella to the bolts of fabric that lined from floor to ceiling against one wall. Katherine curated the fabrics personally; nothing entered this room, except under her approval.

Katherine scanned the fabrics, eyes skimming over the bright jewel-like colours.

"This one," she decided, pulling out a bolt of bright white— soft, flowing silk, with a faint sheen that caught the light. She let the fabric run, simmering through her fingers before holding it up to Avella. "This would look beautiful on you."

The white fabric made Avella's smooth tanned skin glow. She motioned to the head seamstress, who came hurrying over. "I want everyone you have working on this dress. If I use one of the patterns we have already, could it possibly be ready for tonight?"

"It's not really necessary..." Avella protested, but Katherine interrupted her.

"It is necessary, mother. I'm only alive because of what you did, your sacrifice. The least I can do is make you look beautiful. Besides, Father will be here tonight. Don't you want him to see you at your best? Your most beautiful?"

Avella's breath caught it the back of her throat. "Pierre?"

Lucie nodded, putting a hand on her mother's shoulder. "Yes."

Avella swallowed hard. "It's been so many years.... I'm not young, like I was when I left him. And I don't know if Pierre will forgive me." A tear hung at the end of her lashes.

Katherine held Avella by the shoulders, "You are a beautiful woman. Besides, Father never looked at another woman after he lost you. He misses you still. Every day."

Avella sighed, wiping her eyes. "All right, I'll wear the dress, but only if you and Lucie wear something equally beautiful."

Katherine smiled. "Of course, Lucie has stacks of dresses; she's never even worn a lot of them. I have my eye on a blue velvet." Katherine grinned.

After the workroom, the ladies went to their respective staterooms, where much welcomed baths were waiting. Katherine sighed, dipping her head under the floral scented water. Tendrils of steam rose to the ceiling, and Katherine tilted her head against the back of the tub, watching them drift in lazy circles; it had been too long since she'd been able to relax like this. Katherine swirled her hand in the water, leaving a trail of bubbles in its wake. A rap at the door interrupted her thoughts.

"Come in," she called. Katherine stood, letting rivulets of water run back into the tub before she wrapped a towel around herself. A lady's maid peeked in the door.

"Princess Lucie sent me to do your hair. And Lord Gunther sent this." The girl held out a small velvet box.

"He did?" Curiosity won, and Katherine took the box in both hands, tightening her towel before sitting at the vanity to investigate. She caressed the blue velvet before she cracked the box open, peeking cautiously inside. A sparkle inside met her eye. Her breath caught it her throat as she removed the lid.

"It's beautiful," the maid gasped before quickly covering her mouth with her hand, embarrassed at the outburst.

"It is." Katherine set the box aside. "But I'm afraid I can't accept it."

The maid cast a disappointed eye at the gleaming item, but remained silent, respectfully standing with her hands folded in front of her until Katherine found a robe, throwing it on and sat back at the vanity.

The maid began combing her hair; it was knotted from so many days on the road, and it took a while to loosen the stubborn snarls. Katherine winced as the maid worked on a particularly painful knot. Her eyes drifted to the blue velvet box. Longing. If only she could accept Gunther's jewels. She picked up the box, lifting out the shining necklace, pretending for a moment it was really hers— a fine gold chain, with an intricate pendant hanging from it. She placed it back in the box and pushed it away.

Katherine's eyes met the maid's in the mirror. "I won't be his second." The maid remained silent, expert fingers steady, soothing Katherine's hair.

KATHERINE EXAMINED herself in the mirror. She was with Marion and Lucie. The white dress had been pressed and delivered to her mother's room, and Katherine couldn't wait to see how it looked.

She glanced to her two sisters, so alike yet so different. Marion was in a jewel green that suited her shining dark hair, and Lucie in a pale blue. Katherine had opted for a deep rich burgundy that set off her fair hair. The material drifted around her, giving her the confidence to go out—to face her, Gunther's real partner.

Lucie glided over to her sister, squeezing her hand. "I have to say I'm a little excited. I usually eat in the nursery with the babies. It's exciting to have a chance to dress up." She cast a glance toward the nursery where the nursemaid was telling a rousing bedtime story.

"Something tells me they'll still be up when you get back." Katherine smiled at her sister, squeezing her hand.

Settling a wrap around her bare shoulders, Katherine accompanied her sisters to the hall. Tonight's festivities, organised by Queen Isabella, would begin in the banquet hall and end in the ballroom.

"We have to give Avella a proper welcome back," Isabella had insisted, before dedicating all her staff to making tonight a night to remember. As a result, the Lovanian castle had bustled and heaved with preparations all day; it was a hive of activity dedicated to the evening's festivities.

Katherine hesitated in the door to the banquet hall.

"You're seated next to Lord Gunther," the steward ushered her to her seat. Katherine flushed, wondering why Queen Isabella had seated Lord Gunther next to her, instead of Mirabel... his intended. Across the great hall, Mirabel caught her eye, glaring. Katherine gave her a tiny shrug. It wasn't like she decided on the seating. Lord Gunther was already in place. His eyes darkened when he saw Katherine.

"You look beautiful." Gunther swallowed.

"You're just used to seeing me in my dirty old travel clothes," Katherine kept her voice light, but her heart raced at the compliment. *Not yours,* she reminded herself again, accompanying the reminder with a tiny pinch on her arm. Mirabel's glare became more obvious. Her mouth pressed into a fine line, her eyes narrowed. Katherine turned her head.

Gunther's eyes lingered on Katherine's bare neck. "Did the necklace not suit you?" His voice caught.

"No." Katherine lowered her lashes. "I just didn't think it was appropriate... considering..." her eyes flashed to Mirabel, who continued to stare, ignoring her dinner partner.

Gunther lowered his brows, eyes confused. "Considering what?" his voice was low.

"Considering... her." Katherine didn't want to draw attention to Mirabel... lipreading was a court pastime. She didn't dare say the name out loud.

Gunther opened his mouth, about to ask another question, but they were interrupted by the tinkling of a bell. Queen Isabella stood, a poised smile on her elegant face.

"Thank you all so much for coming at such brief notice. I'm sure you heard all about the events of this afternoon. But that's not what tonight's festivities are about." She cleared her throat daintily. "What we are here for tonight, is to welcome Avella, our dear Lucie's mother. Separated by unfortunate circumstances, she has returned to us, and we're overjoyed to welcome her back." She wafted an elegant hand; Avella stood, glowing and beautiful in the white dress, covering her nervousness with a gracious smile as a smattering of applause greeted her.

"Thank you," her voice was quiet in the enormous hall. "I'm delighted to be among family and friends, and look forward to reuniting with all of you." Avella smiled again, smoothing her dress and taking her seat. Katherine noticed her hands shaking slightly as she fidgeted with her glass.

"She nervous," Katherine whispered to Gunther, forgetting about their earlier conversation. "I think she's worried because Pierre hasn't arrived yet."

"Where is Pierre?" Gunther scanned the room. "He should be here by now. He was due back in the city this afternoon."

Katherine shrugged. "I haven't heard from him. Do you think.... Madelaine?" her eyes met Gunther's, full of concern.

Gunther shook his head. "We have Madelaine under constant guard and made doubly sure she has no possibility of contacting any of her... minions."

Katherine nodded, relieved, but still an uneasy feeling lurked. She wouldn't feel safe until Madelaine's magic was sealed, her estate of horrors destroyed.

Dinner dragged on. In her travels, Katherine had forgotten about the niceties of royal life. The many courses, the polite chitchat. The gloss of manners and protocols. No wonder Gunther escaped whenever he could; if not to his estate, then on whatever business King Erich would send him on.

Finally, dinner was over.... They drifted to the ballroom, where faint music wove through the crowd, enticing them to dance.

"Would you care to dance?" Gunther held out a hand to Katherine.

"Are you sure?" Katherine hesitated. "I don't mind if you want to dance with someone else," her eyes darted to Mirabel.

"No. Not really," Gunther spoke bluntly.

Katherine took Gunther's offered hand. She couldn't help but feel small and petite at the way his large, calloused hand swallowed her own small one. They swept onto the floor, joining the crowd as they glided and twirled across the polished floor. They sailed past Lucie and Frederich, lost in their own world, enjoying a night off from childrearing duties.

Katherine looked across the room, "Look Gunther, it's Father."

Pierre stood in the ballroom doorway, his eyes searching the crowd. Finally, his eyes found the object of their pursuit. Avella, chatting with one of the court ladies. Avella glanced up and froze, a multitude of expressions flashing across her face. Fear, hesitation, shyness, regret.

"Why isn't she going to him?" Katherine whispered, her heart aching.

"She doesn't know how Pierre will react," Gunther said. "Sometimes, people don't want to wear their heart on their sleeve—in case it gets stomped on."

Pierre shook himself from his stupor, striding across the ballroom floor. Avella dropped her head, but Pierre didn't stop. He wrapped her small form in his, holding her close. Slowly, slowly, Avella melted into Pierre's embrace.

The crowd who had been holding their breath, watching the reunion as if their life depended on it, gave a collective sigh of relief. The music came back into focus; a new dance began.

Katherine sighed, blinking back the tears gathering in the corner of her eye. "After all this time.... They waited for each other." She sniffed.

Gunther nodded, a faraway look in his eyes. "They're the lucky ones. Some people have to wait alone. At least they waited together," voice thick, he turned away from Katherine, leaving the dance floor.

Katherine stood, watching him go.

"What bee stung him?" Marion glided to her side, giving Gunther's disappearing form a curious look.

Katherine shrugged. "I don't know, he was watching mother and father and then just.... left." Confusion flitted across her face. Was it something she said, Katherine wondered.

"Is there something happening between you two? He followed you all the way across the country. What happened between you two out there?" Marion's voice was gentle.

"Nothing. Absolutely nothing," Katherine's voice was firm.

"Are you sure?" Marion pressed. "I thought that feelings were blooming between you two once. Then, it stopped. Very suddenly I might add."

Katherine's voice dripped with bitterness. "That's because Gunther was engaged to someone else."

Marion gasped. "No, why have I never heard this?"

Katherine nodded. "Secretly engaged."

Marion lowered her voice to a whisper. "If Gunther was engaged, why didn't anyone know?"

Katherine rolled her eyes. "I just told you, silly, it was a secret."

"Yes, but how did you discover Gunther was otherwise engaged?"

Katherine pressed her lips together, her mind drifting—back to that night.

"Ages ago, Lucie had been sucked through the mirror, and Gunther and I were in the chateau together. I was terrified, and he was gentle, understanding. When we travelled together back to Corvan, with Fluer and King Erich's soldiers, we got to know each other. I missed Lucie terribly. We thought we would never see her again. I thought at the time Gunther was paying me special attention. Singling me out."

Marion nodded. "I thought Gunther singled you out also; he never looked at me the way he did you."

Katherine swallowed hard, the words coming out slowly. "Then we arrived at the castle. King Erich and Queen Isabella welcomed us. I wanted to see Gunther, to thank him. At least that's what I convinced myself. Really, I wanted to see his face, to see if there were feelings... Silly of me... We were mere country girls. There was nothing special about us."

"You know that doesn't matter to Gunther," Marion said, her eyes flashing.

Katherine sighed, "I know, but at the time there were chasms of difference existing between Gunther and me. That's when I found him," Katherine's voice caught, as she hesitated. "I found Gunther in the salon, with someone else."

Marion gasped. "What, who?"

Katherine scoffed. "Not in an entirely compromising position. But they didn't notice me at first. I had time to.... observe."

"And what did you see?"

"They were close. He was holding her, and not in a brotherly way—whispering in her ear. I couldn't hear much of what they were saying. The blood was pounding so hard in my head. I didn't realize until that moment how deep my feelings for him ran. I paused in the doorway, not sure where to turn… and I heard him… talking about their engagement."

Marion covered her hand with her mouth, eyes wide. "Then what did you do?"

Katherine shrugged. "I ran. As far as I know, Gunther never saw me. After that, I avoided him. To let him know I had feelings would be humiliating beyond measure." Katherine blinked away the haze of tears covering her eyes.

"Who was the girl?" Marion scanned the ballroom, searching for marriageable candidates.

Katherine lowered her voice. "Maribel."

Marion furrowed her blow. "Why did they never marry?"

Katherine shook her head. "How would I know? She obviously still has a claim on him. Did you see how she was shooting daggers at me at dinner tonight?"

Marion rubbed her sister's shoulder. "Have you thought to speak to him? Ask him what happened."

Katherine pulled back. "Never."

Marion gave her sister a stern look. "You're too proud, sister. You need to either ask him, or put this behind you. From what I can see, he's never given her a second look. But you, darling. He looks at you as if you hang the moon and stars in the sky."

Katherine lowered her lashes. "But wouldn't that be intentional…. If it were a secret engagement?"

Marion scoffed. "If it's an engagement, he's certainly let it drag on long enough. You need to find out what he's thinking."

Katherine drew back. "How? Ask him?"

Marion rolled her eyes. "Leave it to me. Maribel's sister and I have tea together every Tuesday. I'll find out. And next time…. Don't leave it for so long. We all love you too much to let you suffer in silence."

Katherine embraced her sister, a weight lifting from her chest.

That night, Katherine lay in her comfortable chamber, grateful for the soft bed, the smooth sheets, the warm blanket. Her eyes drifted closed. Tuesday... Tuesday... she would find out how Gunther felt. The thought drifted through her mind, soft and silken as a butterfly's wings.

CHAPTER TWELVE

Katherine glanced out the window as horses clattered into the courtyard, followed by one of King Erich's carriages. Althea. She dropped her task—sorting bolts of fabric for the guild—and raced down the nearest flight of steps, completely ignoring the fact that it was the staff staircase— steep, dusty and uneven. She burst out the back door, flying toward the shiny black carriage where a footman was already opening the door.

"She's in pretty terrible shape." One of the footmen hovered over Katherine's shoulder. "You're going to have to call the healer as soon as possible."

Katherine waved down a passing servant. "Call Aric. Immediately," she said. The servant heard the urgency in Katherine's tone and rushed to do her bidding.

Katherine's heart pounded against her ribcage as she stuck her head in the carriage, wondering how bad Avella's condition really was. The woman in front of her was barely recognizable. They had swathed Avella in makeshift bandages, and what little skin showed was black with blood and bruises.

Katherine gasped. "What happened to her?" she clambered into the carriage, taking Avella's frail knobbly hand in her smooth one.

"A wild animal—my best guess would be a bear. There are... claw marks."

A tear ran down Katherine's cheek as she gently touched the woman's forehead. "Get a stretcher and carry her into the infirmary; we'll attend to her needs there." She scrambled out the carriage, hovering as King Erich's men swung into action. Within moments they produced a stretcher, and gently, very gently, lifted the frail woman, moving her to the castle infirmary.

Thankful someone had the foresight to put the infirmary on the ground floor, Katherine stuck to Althea's side as she accompanied her to the infirmary. Aric the healer rushed in, still tying on his apron.

"What is it?" Aric assessed Althea with a practiced gaze.

"A wild animal attack her; the injuries are serious," Katherine explained, watching anxiously as Aric examined Althea.

"I'll mix up some poultices and give something to help her sleep; rest is the best healer. For now, we'll remove the bandages and make sure they've cleaned everything properly; you might want to step back for this," Aric said, shooting Katherine a warning glance.

Katherine shook her head, standing firm. "No, I'm staying. Let me help."

"It won't be easy," Aric said. "Althea's wounds are critical, but I would appreciate some help with the bandages."

Katherine bit her lip, eyeing the blood-spattered bandages and dreading what lay beneath them.

"I'll do it," Katherine said, straightening her spine.

"Fetch me a bowl of clean boiled water and put a few drops from that green bottle in it," Aric said, gesturing toward a neat row of bottles.

Katherine rushed to do Aric's bidding. When the bowl arrived, he dipped a clean cloth in the water before loosening the first bandage.

Cleaning Avella's wounds was a long, tedious, gruelling ordeal; the bandages stuck to the dried blood, so removing them was an arduous and time-consuming process. Althea didn't stir through the entire process. The only sound was the whispering of their breath hissing faintly through the infirmary.

"She's so still," Katherine breathed, placing a soiled bandage onto the growing pile.

Aric nodded, eyes dark with concern. "The sleep will do Avella good; we'll continue the treatments in the morning. I'll have someone sit with her tonight in case she wakes up."

"I'll stay," Katherine volunteered. "Send word to my mother and sisters because they'll want to know Avella's arrived." But Katherine's words were too late as Avella, Marion, and Lucie came bursting into the infirmary.

"How is she?" Avella's face fell when she saw Althea, lying still and white on the infirmary cot. Her white hair trailed around her head in ragged wisps.

"Not good," said Katherine. "Aric says she needs rest. The wounds are terrible. I don't know how she survived at all."

Avella stroked Althea's forehead, calloused hand gentle on the delicate skin.

"We'll take turns staying with her," Avella told Aric. "I owe Althea my life, and her injuries are my fault." A tear hovered at the corner of her eye.

"I have the babies, but I'll stay with Althea a few hours during the day. The nursemaid won't mind," Lucie insisted.

"I'll do the same," Marion said, her eyes soft as they travelled across Althea's face.

They decided Katherine would take the first shift, so Aric provided her with a pillow and a blanket for the small cot next to Althea's, ears tuned for any slight change in her condition.

It wasn't until the grey predawn light crept through the window that Katherine heard a sound; stirring and a faint moan came from the Althea's cot.

Katherine bolted upright, lighting a candle with shaking hands, before peering at Althea's face. Underneath the eyelids was a faint movement, and another groan wrenched from deep withing Althea's chest.

"Althea," Katherine whispered, taking her hand. "Althea, it's Katherine, you're safe at the castle with me, Avella, Lucie, and Marion. We're all here."

Althea's eyelashes fluttered and cracked open, mere slits in the swollen skin. "Katherine." She groaned. "Thirsty."

Katherine rushed to pour fresh water from the jug. She propped Althea up, helping her sip from the cup. Water puddled at the corner of her mouth, dribbling on the blanket. Katherine gently wiped Althea's face before lowering her to the cot.

"Go to sleep, Althea," Katherine whispered. "You need to rest."

"No," Althea groaned. "Can't sleep, have to warn you."

A wave of fear pricked across Katherine's skin. "Warn us about what? Madelaine's been captured."

"Warn you about Madelaine, she's gathering an army," Althea said, her eyes fluttered as she rasped the words from her bruised throat.

"Madelaine's in the dungeon; you're safe now," Katherine said, soothing Avella's clammy skin.

"Her soldiers aren't in the dungeon," Althea said, her eyes drifting closed. "Need to unseal Avella's magic."

Katherine paused, waiting for Althea to finish, but she was asleep. Katherine sat on the edge of her cot, deep in thought. Avella's tone was urgent, so urgent that Katherine wondered if she should call for help. But call who? Katherine desperately wished Gunther was there to ask for advice. He would know how to respond.

Katherine threw on a wrap, shoved her feet into slippers, and padded into the corridor. Knocking on Aric's door, she asked the bleary-eyed healer to watch over Althea before silently slipping down the hall toward Avella's room. Avella came to the door immediately.

"What's wrong?" Avella's eyes filled with concern. Katherine could see by the dark circles, Avella hadn't been sleeping.

"Althea woke up... she said... she said you have to unseal your magic. Madelaine's sending an army," Katherine said, her eyes searching her mother's face.

Avella pressed her lips together. "But how? Avella's not well enough to perform an unsealing ceremony."

"Could we go to Lucie's office? She keeps magic manuals in her study. Maybe there's something that will tell us more, something that will explain what to do."

Avella nodded, pulling her hair over her shoulder and shoving her arms into the sleeves of her dressing gown.

The library was empty. Silent. The lamp cast eerie shadows; looming shelves towered above them as Katherine and Avella crept through the grey light toward Lucie's study. The sky was lightening, but the castle remained silent.

"Lucie hides a key inside this book," Katherine explained, opening a leather bound volume of poetry. A tiny key glittered against the creamy page; Katherine fit it into the lock, which clicked immediately. They were in.

Katherine made a beeline for the tall bookshelf that took up one end of the small study and Avella headed to Lucie's desk.

"Are you sure Lucie won't mind us rifling through her things?" Avella hesitated over a stack of journals.

"No." Katherine shook her head. "Lucie's not like that." She flipped through a book, History of Magic. "Do you see anything promising?" she asked, turning to her mother.

Avella shook her head. "No. This is mostly related to the mage guild."

After an hour of searching, Katherine sat in the deep leather chair, head propped in her hands. "I don't even know what I'm looking for. Lucie's bound to be awake by now. The babies rise early. We should go ask her because she knows this library inside out." Carefully locking the door behind them, they left the study, replacing the key in its hiding place.

"Katherine," a deep voice called outside the library called. Katherine turned, her eyes meeting Gunther's.

"You're still at the castle?" Katherine blushed, pulling her wrap tightly around herself. Even after weeks of travelling together, she felt shy of her undone appearance.

"King Erich wanted an early council meeting," Gunther explained. "What are you doing awake so early?"

"It's Althea." Katherine explained what Althea had said. Gunther's face grew more and more concerned.

"We should inform King Erich right away. I'm on my way to the council chambers. Would you join me?"

"Yes, but can you give me five minutes to get ready? I can't attend a meeting in my nightdress," Katherine said, crossing her arms over her chest.

Gunther ran his eyes over her, swallowing as for the first time he realized Katherine was wearing her dressing gown.

"Five minutes, I'll meet you in King Erich's study."

Katherine nodded, rushing down the corridor.

Five minutes later, Katherine was rapping on the door to King Erich's study.

"Come in." Ensconced in a deep leather chair, King Erich was fully dressed in spite of the early hour. The early morning sun peeked in the tall window, throwing patterns on the carpeted floor and across the king's polished wooden desk.

Katherine's feet whispered across the thick carpet as she crossed the floor and sat next to Gunther, soaking in the comfort in his steady presence. Her eyes flitted to the tapestry covering one wall, absently wondering if she could replicate that shade of green in a pattern she was working on.

King Erich threaded his fingers under his chin, his eyes shadowed as he thought.

"Lord Gunther filled me on Madelaine's intentions," King Erich said, his voice rumbling across the space.

Katherine nodded. "Madelaine's been planning for years, her entire life. She's intelligent, determined, and strong. She'll have contingencies in place; probably contingencies for the contingencies."

King Erich nodded. "We suspected that."

"Has Madelaine given any trouble to the guards in the dungeons?" Gunther asked, leaning forward. His voice was still rough from the early hour, his thick hair tousled from rushing.

King Erich shook his head, his face grave. "The prison guards said Madelaine's calm, too calm. Completely unconcerned about her own welfare."

Gunther frowned. "In any case, we need to prepare the troops for whatever Madelaine sends us. And you, your sisters, and your mother need to lie low. Keep as safe as possible. We're expecting a messenger from Iasia within the week; we'll know then what Madelaine's estate held."

"Did you tell the Iasians about Madelaine's estate?"

Gunther nodded, eyes shadowed. "Every detail; they'll send a mage to free the wolves' relatives and break the wards Madelaine used on the locks."

Katherine let out a deep breath. "All we can do is wait until Althea fully wakens."

"How is Althea?" Gunther turned to Katherine.

Sadness flitted across Katherine's face. "Very frail. Althea's wounds were deep. If she does heal, it's going to take time."

A maid rapped at the door with coffee and pastries on a wheeled cart. Katherine took a cup of coffee, sweetening it with honey and adding a healthy dollop of cream. The pastry was flaky, the filling a sweet raspberry, just tart enough to complement the buttery crust. She swallowed and took another.

"Althea seemed to think she would be the one to unseal Avella. Why is that?" Katherine asked. This question had been tugging at the edge of Katherine's consciousness since Althea had woken.

King Erich paused, cup halfway to his mouth. "She did?" The king furrowed his brow, deep in thought.

"Surely the Iasian mages could unseal Avella's gift?" Katherine wondered out loud.

Gunther nodded, "They could, unless Avella's gift was sealed in such a way that only the person who sealed it could unseal it."

"How so?" Katherine turned to Gunther.

"First is if Avella and Althea were blood relatives, but there must be other ways as well."

Katherine tilted her head. Related? No, they couldn't be... her mother or Avella would have mentioned it. Katherine sipped her coffee, letting the hot liquid warm her. "Althea and Avella are from the same Iasian town...." she said, mulling the idea over in her head.

Gunther sat upright. "It would explain why Althea was devoted to your mother and you girls for so long. She followed you from Iasia, gave up a thriving healing practice, her own apothecary, to become the local herb woman in a tiny village. Buried herself in obscurity."

"I'll ask Avella." Katherine was already setting down her cup.

"I'll come with you." Gunther stood, hand at the small of Katherine's back. They quickly nodded to King Erich before hurrying to the infirmary, footsteps echoing in the corridors. A few servants were about, delivering trays to the various staterooms. Katherine dodged a young maid carrying a giant tea urn toward the breakfast room.

She held her finger to her lips as they came to the infirmary. Inching the door open, Katherine peeked inside. Avella sat in a high-backed wooden chair next to Althea's cot. Althea was still sleeping; her face slack as her slight chest rose and fell.

"Any change?" Katherine asked Avella, studying the elderly woman.

Avella shook her head. "No, but Aric said she's stable and to give it a few days."

"There's something that came up, something important we have to ask you, mother." Katherine said, hesitating.

Avella turned inquiring eyes toward her daughter.

"Avella said she was the one who would unseal your gift. We were wondering why? King Erich says there are other mages who can perform the unsealing ceremony. The king thinks there's a vital reason that only Althea can unseal the magic."

Avella gazed at Althea. "I wish I knew. You girls had more time with Avella. I spent most of my life trapped at the manor house with my mother and Madelaine. Avella ran the apothecary, and she was always kind—especially to me. Then when I moved from Iasia to Lovan, I only knew her through occasional messages we sent back and forth. I always wondered why Althea's loyalty was so unwavering. She never swerved, never wished herself back in Iasia."

"King Erich said one reason could be a blood tie. Is Althea related to us?"

"My father—your grandfather's family was nobility, so they would have no ties to Avella. But my grandmother Sorchia—my mother's mother—married a commoner, a merchant I believe. He would have been my grandfather; I know little about Sorchia's family though."

Katherine's eyes rested on Althea, swimming with regret. Althea had so many secrets, so much lay hidden under that wrinkled skin. Katherine's hand rested on the faintly moving blanket, wishing she could turn back time and do things differently.

"I hope we find out someday." Katherine choked on the words, tears clouding her vision.

"Find out what?" A scratchy, hoarse voice said.

Katherine whipped her head around. Althea's eyes slid open, the pale blue orbs watery and weak. Weak, but alive and lucid.

"How are you feeling?" Avella rested a cool hand on Avella's forehead, stroking the soft, bruised skin.

"I've been better," Althea said, blinking.

"You should rest, we'll worry about politics later," Avella said, patting the wool blanket.

"What were you talking about?" Althea said, struggling to sit up.

Katherine sighed, knowing Althea wouldn't be content until she had a satisfactory answer. "We were discussing likely reasons you have to be the one to unseal Avella's magic."

Althea's eyes fluttered shut, exhaustion creeping across her face. Exhaustion and resignation, Katherine realised.

"Are you.... Are you... family?" Katherine asked, still not believing the prospect. She peeked at her mother's face; Avella was holding her breath, skin pale under the deep tan.

Althea sighed. "Yes." The answer was simple. Powerful. Expected, yet surprising.

A silence settled across the room—thick, heavy, and tense.

"How?" Avella asked, breaking the awkwardness.

Althea cleared her voice, then spoke in a low voice. "Your grandfather had a sister, Marie; she was my mother."

"How did I never know?" Avella asked.

"Natalie, your mother, didn't want you to know. Status was everything to her, and she couldn't stand having any links to the likes of us commoners. I never had an opportunity to tell you I was your aunt because Natalie watched me like a hawk," Althea said, her voice still weak.

"But you could have told *us*," Katherine scolded.

Althea's eyes fluttered closed. "I never took the chance; you girls were so happy and content with your lives in Annecy. Until Pierre lost the business. The last thing they needed was an Iasian mage for an aunt.

I stayed close. They were my nieces; I didn't want to interfere with them."

Tears pricked the back of Katherine's eyes. "I wouldn't have minded," she insisted, taking Althea's withered hand in hers.

Althea's tired eyes fluttered open, a spark flickering behind the tiredness. "Would you?"

Katherine lowered her lashes. She searched her heart, realizing she didn't know how she would have responded if she'd discovered Althea was her aunt back in Annecy. Where being Lovanian, being like everyone else in the tiny village, was key. Would she have accepted her? She didn't know. But she knew now.

"Althea, are you the only person who can unseal Avella's magic?" Katherine asked,

Althea's eyes inched shut. "Tomorrow."

Avella and Katherine exchanged uneasy glances. Tomorrow seemed an age away, but Althea's exhaustion was obviously too much for her.

"Do we have time?" Avella whispered to Gunther, who until now had stood silent, absorbing everything.

Gunther's face was stone. "We'll have to."

All day, Althea hovered on the edge of awareness. Sometimes lucid, sometimes asleep, sometimes muttering— tales of her past life as far as Katherine could tell. Katherine left Althea's side that evening after dusk had fallen. The lamps were lit, casting pools of golden light across the stone corridors. She made her way to Lucie's apartment. Eager to see Lucie and Frederich's children, to have everything feel normal, if only for a moment.

Katherine paused in the doorway, absorbing the scene of domestic bliss. The smell of warm bath, soap, a hint of steam, and wet baby was in the air. One child, little Frederich, was in his dressing gown, damp hair curling at his neck. Little Red was finishing his bath, being fished out by the nursemaid. Lucie held a large heated towel, ready to wrap around the squirming body.

"Auntie Katherine." Little Red ran toward her, pudgy arms outstretched. He threw himself into her arms, little body damp and warm. Katherine held him tight, resting her cheek on his soft hair.

"Auntie Katherine, did you bring me anything?" Little Red tilted his head back, a gap-toothed grin on the little face.

"Frederich?" Lucie's voice was appalled.

"Not this time." Katherine laughed, tweaking a curl. "I've come from the infirmary. I don't think there's anything in there that would appeal to you."

Little Frederich frowned.

"Sorry." Lucie gave her eldest son a stern look. "What have we talked about? You can't ask people if they brought you presents. Instead, say thank you if they did."

Frederich hung his head. "Sorry, Mummy. I forgot." He tilted his head at Katherine, the long lashes still wet from his bath.

Katherine laughed. "I'll bring you something next time. I promise." She smiled at her sister. "He's grown, even in the past few weeks."

Lucie smiled proudly. "I know. Mother was shocked when she saw them. She couldn't believe it. It feels so strange to say the words... mother."

Katherine nodded. "I know. And how is Marion feeling about Mother's return?"

Lucie frowned. "She's... cold. I thought Marion would be the most excited. After all, she knew mother the best."

Katherine nodded. "Marion felt it the most when mother left. Remember, she carried the burden of raising us while Father travelled with the caravans. Marion essentially lost her childhood."

Lucie tipped her head. "I suppose. But she could have been more welcoming. Av—Mother's feelings were hurt. I saw her eyes."

Katherine pursed her lips. "What can we do? Marion won't listen to us."

"She'll come round." Lucie bundled a small round body into a cosy nightdress, pulling sleeves over chubby arms, rubbing the wet hair. "There. Now give Aunt Katherine a kiss and go with Nursie to bed."

The children enveloped Katherine in exuberant kisses and wriggling bodies before the patient nursemaid ushered the children to their room for the night. Katherine threw them one last kiss before turning to Lucie.

"Althea said tomorrow she'll unseal Avella's magic."

Lucie sucked in a breath. "What kind of magic does Avella have?"

"Fire. Like yours," Katherine answered.

"After so long…" Lucie's voice was filled with wonder.

"What's it like?" Katherine draped the damp towels by the fire. "Having the gift of fire?"

Lucie sighed. "Fire isn't my first choice. Instead, I'd prefer something useful. Something to build, not destroy— like you."

"Me?" Katherine choked out a laugh. "I don't have a gift."

"Not a magic gift." Lucie hesitated. "But you're always creating, always making beautiful things— finding beautiful things where they didn't exist before."

Katherine rolled her eyes. "You're my sister; you have to tell me they are pretty things."

Lucie froze, an armful of dirty clothes halfway to the basket. "Katherine. The guild, the weaving, the patterns, the beautiful clothes. No one in the entire kingdom creates like you do."

Katherine sighed. "But it's not magic. You have the same gift that mother does—did. That's special." She opened the door for the maid.

Lucie put the soiled clothes in a basket, then grabbed Katherine by the arm. "Come on, let's sneak down to the kitchen. Nursie can watch the babies." Lucie led Katherine toward the main kitchens. Even at the evening hour, they were busy. Evening tea and chocolate was simmering on the big range, trays of pastries and sandwiches lined one table. Lucie pulled out a wooden chair for Katherine. She busied herself stacking ham sandwiches, pastries, and two giant slices of ginger cake on the plate, plonking it in front of them.

"What is this really about?" Lucie handed Katherine a fork.

Katherine took a forkful of ginger cake, letting the flavours mingle on her tongue. Cardamom, spice, and nutmeg all blended together in a dark sugary deliciousness. She licked the fork.

"It's Maribel," Katherine finally admitted.

"Maribel?" Lucie scrunched her eyebrows.

Katherine sighed. "Marion said Maribel and Gunther aren't really engaged..."

"They're not," Lucie agreed, biting into a ham sandwich. "Maribel is engaged to Frederich's cousin. The one who lives down south." She wiped a mustard covered crumb from the edge of her mouth.

"She is? How did you know this?"

"It's supposed to be a secret?" Lucie wolfed down the other half of her sandwich. "I heard Queen Isabella talking about it. She said it was about time. Maribel chased Gunther forever, but apparently she's finally given up. Probably figured out his thing for you isn't a passing fancy." Lucie licked her fingers, then chose a pastry, a custard filled tart. She examined the sugar and nutmeg topping, then popped it into her mouth.

"But that's just it." Katherine toyed with the fork. "I don't think he is serious about me."

Lucie nearly spit out the custard tart. "How could possibly think that? Gunther dropped everything to rush after you the minute you left to find Mother. I know he pestered you until you took him with you to Madelaine's in Iasia then halfway across the country to fetch mother."

Katherine lowered her lashes, picking at the candied ginger in the icing. "I thought I ran into him accidentally."

"Pshaw," Lucie scoffed. "King Erich complained about how he took off in the middle of a council meeting. You know that's not like him."

"I suppose...." Katherine hesitated. "But why hasn't he said anything?"

Lucie shrugged, polishing off another pastry. "He's probably given you a signal, and you missed it."

"A signal? The necklace?" Katherine felt suddenly stupid.

"He gave you a necklace?" Lucie leaned forward, eyes sparkling with interest.

"Yes... it's in my room. He only just gave it to me before the ball." Katherine filled her in quickly, seeing Lucie's expression of exasperation. "I thought he was with Maribel."

"Wear the necklace," Lucie told her sister, scraping her chair back. "The poor man might be good at speaking in King Erich's council, but he has no idea how to express his emotions. Especially when you're so..."

"So what?" Katherine gave her sister a hard look.

"Well.. not very demonstrative," Lucie filled in, averting her eyes. "Look, I have to go back to the babies. Nursie can only take so much from Little Frederich. Wear the necklace tomorrow. See what he does. And stop holding everything in; you can always come to me and Marion... and mother." Lucie balanced her plate of treats, carrying a fresh cup of tea in the other hand.

Katherine sat at the table, picking at her cake until only a pile of crumbs remained.

CHAPTER THIRTEEN

The time for the unsealing ceremony arrived.

"I'm ready." Avella sat in front of Althea in Lucie's small office. They decided this would be the most discreet place to unseal Avella's magic. Althea could now walk short distances with the help of a walking stick. Lucie arranged for her to be moved from the infirmary to a stateroom near her apartment where Aric attended to her daily, changing the dressing on her wounds. Well acquainted from the days Althea lived in Corvan, the two enjoyed reconnecting. Aric peppered her with questions about herbs and tinctures.

"Do you remember how the gift felt?" Althea asked Avella.

Avella nodded. "I had trouble controlling my gift, and it was so volatile and dangerous. Until grandmother gave me a herb tea that dulled the fire."

Althea nodded. "Seneca and honey pods. I was the one who taught Sorchia about that tea. I've had Aric mix some up for you."

"Why..." Avella paused, dark memories flitting across her face. "Why couldn't I control my gift when Madelaine and Sorchia could?"

Althea sighed. "Fire magic is tricky and difficult. Lucie is lucky her fire never came to life until she found the sceptre and accessed training. My guess is your gift was too strong for you. Madelaine's gift is easier to control. Some say those with fire magic have dragon's blood running through their veins." Althea laughed, then grabbed her side. The wounds still pained her when she moved too suddenly.

"Now, take my hands in yours and keep your eyes closed. Unsealing won't hurt as much as sealing, so don't worry." Althea's face was gentle and kind.

Avella closed her eyes, resting tanned, calloused hands on top of Althea's knobbly, wrinkled ones. Althea clasped her hands, closing her eyes with every muscle frozen in place. A look of concentration settled on her face; her eyes flickered behind pale blue veined lids. A cool breeze darted around the room, rustling stacks of paper on the desk, tugging at tapestries, whispering in the air.

Moments passed. Althea's hands tightened, her mouth moving. Avella squeezed her eyes shut, and Katherine and her sisters held their breath, eyes glued to the two women. Then it was over. Avella inched her eyes open.

"How do you feel?" Katherine studied her mother's face.

"I feel.... free?" Avella's expression lightened as she smiled. "I feel good."

Althea smiled, although her face looked weak and tired. Katherine could see the unsealing had taken more effort than she wanted to admit. "Now, we wait."

They didn't have to wait long. That afternoon, the messenger appeared from Iasia, interrupting their family luncheon. King Erich took the message and read it, trying, but failing, to hide the worry growing in his eyes.

"What is it?" Frederick asked.

"King Ruben sent men to investigate Madelaine's estate. Things are worse than we feared."

CHAPTER FOURTEEN

"Did the soldiers find Madelaine's barn and rescue the animals?" Katherine asked, hovering on the edge of her chair as she hardly dared breath.

King Erich nodded, his face grim as sadness mingled with concern in his eyes. "That wasn't Madelaine's only barn at the estate."

"Where else? Madelaine had no other estate buildings," Katherine said, eyes widening.

"The forest?" Gunther lowered his brows, his face tightening.

King Erich nodded. "I believe so."

"What was in Madelaine's other barns?" Katherine asked.

"Mostly magical creatures, Lindwurm, a baby dragon, shifters—I assume Madelaine has their relations out working, locked in cages. Also, the soldiers found countless animals of the more common variety, wild and tame." King Erich rubbed his hand on his face. "The Iasian army freed what animals they could, but the main problem is, we don't understand yet what hold Madelaine has over these poor creatures. The Iasians transported some of the more helpless creatures to be cared for and recover elsewhere. Liliana and Landry offered to maintain them in their mountain estate until they heal or further decisions are made. They'll be far enough from Florin that Madelaine can't capture or destroy them. The Iasians agreed to deploy their army for protection until we get Madelaine sorted."

"How did Madelaine manage to escape Iasia's notice so long?" Gunther said, raising his incredulous voice.

"Madelaine kept a quiet profile at court. The Iasian court barely remembered her; her estate is far enough from Florin that no courtier's visited the estate. And Madelaine wore her veil when she travelled to town. The court merely assumed Madelaine was eccentric— more tragic than dangerous. Of course, some people knew about Madelaine's barns. Builders, trappers, merchants, but Madelaine chose people who could be easily bribed to keep their mouths shut."

The horror of the situation washed over Katherine as she wondered how someone could grow so evil, so twisted, they could spend their whole time life bent on revenge.

"What will the Iasians do with Madelaine?" Katherine asked, doubting anyone could curb Madelaine's insatiable thirst for destruction.

"Because Madelaine's a traitor to the Iasian crown, they're leaving the decision in our hands. If we kill Madelaine, it may unleash something she's organised that we haven't predicted. Who knows what evil she's put in place with her gift. And now that Madelaine knows who you, Lucie, Marion, and Avella are... where you are... we can't risk freeing her. Not until Avella controls her gift better. With Avella's gift and Lucie's power with the Lovanian sceptre, we'd have a chance against whatever darkness Madelaine's planning. We'd use the book, but if Madelaine's warded against it, we have no assurance it will be effective against her."

"How long until Avella learns to control her gift?" Gunther asked, turning to Katherine.

Katherine shrugged. "With Lucie's gift, it was within weeks. But Lucie used the sceptre, and Althea trained her gift all day, every day. Althea's too weak to train Avella at the moment, and Avella's magic is unstable."

Gunther furrowed his brow as he mulled this over.

"Avella can call her fire, but they arrived without warning. Althea mixed Avella a special tea that dampens the fire gift, otherwise..."

"The entire castle could blaze up in flames," King Erich finished Katherine's sentence.

"Isn't there anyone else who could train Avella's gift?" Gunther turned to Katherine.

"Lucie, and a single fire mage down south; she's not powerful, but it's possible she could help train Avella. If we can wait for someone to fetch her."

"I'll bring it to the council later this morning." King Erich stood, dismissing Katherine with a nod.

THAT AFTERNOON, KATHERINE accompanied Gunther to the stables. They had returned Bardot to the castle stables by ship that morning, and Katherine was eager to be reunited with her beloved horse. Katherine carried a bowl of carrots from the kitchen to treat Bardot.

Bardot poked his velvet nose over the stable door, nickering a greeting as Katherine entered the castle stable. Katherine sighed in satisfaction; the stables exuded a warm, welcoming air, filled with the scent of clean straw, oiled leather, warm horse, and the sound of shuffling hooves and animals murmuring to each other in low, horsy voices.

"Were you a good boy?" Katherine held out a carrot, smiling as Bardot leaned down, his warm breath tickling her fingers. Then, suddenly, everything changed; Bardot drew his lips back, revealing long, yellowed teeth, and struck, sinking his teeth into Katherine's gloved hand.

"Bardot!" Katherine jerked back her hand, the glove already filling with blood that dripped down her arm, smearing across her dress.

"What happened?" Gunther flew to Katherine's side.

"Bardot bit me." Stunned by the unexpected attack, Katherine peeled back her glove, crimson blood splashing on the straw covered floor.

"Let me bandage your hand." Gunther took his kerchief out of his pocket and expertly wrapped Katherine's hand. The wound was deep, blood soaking through the makeshift bandage.

"You'll have to go to Aric immediately; that wound needs stitches. Hold it up; that will slow the bleeding." Leaving the abandoned carrots scattered across the stable floor, Gunther helped Katherine to the castle infirmary.

"I don't understand; Bardot's always been gentle and well-mannered. Do you think the ship upset him?" Katherine winced and gritted her teeth as Aric pinched her torn skin together.

Gunther shook his head. "The stable master said the horses have been restless all week. But Bardot's aggression surprised him too. Bardot's so gentle, he's never given anyone an ounce of trouble."

"Do you think Madelaine caused Bardot's temper?" Katherine said, sucking in her breath. Although Aric was being as gentle as possible, but the stitching hurt.

"Madelaine must have assumed we left our horses at the harbour," Gunther said the words slowly. "But it seems like a waste of Madelaine's time to influence Bardot to take an occasional nip. Madelaine's plans are bigger than that."

Katherine nodded. "I suppose." But she couldn't shake the uneasy feeling that something evil loomed on the horizon. Something dark.

Aric finished stitching Katherine's hand, wrapping it in a huge white bandage and warning her against overuse. Fine for Aric. *How am I supposed to hold a spoon or fork with this awkward monstrosity?* Katherine thought, holding her clumsy bandaged hand in front of her as she went back to her chambers.

Gunther had returned to the stable; he wanted to question the stable master further. Katherine had a feeling Gunther suspected

Madelaine's influence had somehow reached the castle stables. Horses were the lifeblood of Lovan's army. Without them, there'd be no cavalry. No speed. Katherine sensed Gunther's mounting concern as they parted ways in the corridor.

"What happened?" Lucie emerged from her apartments, little Frederich in tow. She eyed Katherine's bandaged hand with wide eyes.

"An accident at the castle stable; Bardot bit me," Katherine said, cradling her injured appendage.

"Bardot?" Lucie's mouth dropped. "Impossible, Bardot's gentle."

Katherine bit her lip, throwing little Frederich a cautious glance. "There's one obvious reason…"

"How would Madelaine gain access to the castle horses?" Lucie said, lowering her voice and glancing down the empty corridor. "They have not left Madelaine alone in her cell; not even for a single second. No one's noticed suspicious behaviour; she sits in the corner, hard as stone."

"I'm scared," Katherine confided in her sister. "Even Gunther looked nervous when he saw Bardot attack me."

"Gunther was with you in the stable?" Lucie shot her sister a curious glance.

Katherine shrugged. "Gunther wanted to see his horse too, so we went together."

Lucie gave Katherine another suspicious glance.

"What? He did," Katherine said, her cheeks tinging pink.

"Well, I suppose we can discuss that later. First, we have to tell King Erich about Bardot; he's in his study, waiting on word from the dragons. The flyer who returned the baby dragon is due back today. He's hoping the dragons will join us to fight Madelaine. Dragon warriors would be a tremendous advantage."

"Do you think the dragons will agree?" Katherine asked.

"I don't know; the dragons love Celine, and dragons are loyal to anyone who looks after their young. We have a good chance of swaying them. On the other hand, they're dragons and dragons are fickle. Come on, I'll walk you to King Erich now."

Moments later, for the second time that day, Katherine found herself sitting in King Erich's study, explaining the events that happened in the stable. King Erich steepled his fingers under his chin, eyes thoughtful.

"Our only recourse is to question Madelaine again. Maybe she'll leak a clue about what she's planning. I'll send Frederich and Gunther; they're experienced and the most likely to get answers from her."

"But what if Madelaine attacks them?" Lucie's eyes widened.

"We'll ensure Madelaine's cell is well secured. It won't be possible for her to attack without her minions, and the gates will stay firmly shut so the animals can't breech the castle."

Lucie nodded, still hesitant but unwilling to argue with King Erich.

Katherine and Lucie left King Erich's study, heading toward Althea's chambers. They found her ensconced in a deep, comfortable chair next to the bay window; a plaid wool blanket was draped across her knees. Avella sat across from her, pouring the tea.

"Hello, dears," Althea greeted them.

Katherine knelt by Althea's side, taking her wrinkled hand in her unbandaged one. The yellowed bruises were fading. Slowly.

"How are you feeling, Althea? Can we get anything to make you more comfortable?"

Althea shook her head. "No, thank you, I'm grand. I'll just be glad to get my old bones back to my cottage. It appears, I'm not the only one suffering an injury; what happened to you?" Althea asked, her sharp eyes taking in Katherine's bandaged hand.

"Just a run in with one of the stable horses," Katherine said, shaking off the question. "Althea—Avella we have a question." Katherine began. "I don't want to dredge up painful memories, but we were wondering if you could tell us more about Madelaine's history; it might help learn what she's planning."

Althea stared out the window, watching a flock of birds as they swooped and dove across the duck pond.

"I never understood Madelaine." Avella's voice was faded with exhaustion. "She had everything when we were children; she was my mother's obvious favourite—beautiful, accomplished, clever. Everyone loved Madelaine, yet it was never enough; Madelaine always wanted more. Even the little attention mother gave me, she was jealous of, determined to steal it away. She hasn't changed. Nothing will be enough for Madelaine."

The girls were silent for a moment, pondering Avella's words.

"Madelaine wants to fulfil Natalie's plan; she wants to rule, doesn't she?" a troubled look flickered in Lucie's eyes as she asked the question.

Avella nodded. "Power was Sorchia, then Natalie's ultimate goal. Now, it's Madelaine's."

They turned their heads as a quiet rapping sounded at the door. The wolves, Jules followed by Eleonor and Zelia, slunk into the room, grey capes wafting as they glided across the carpeted floor.

"Where's Alerion?" Katherine asked, eyes flicking from one wolf to the other. A heavy silence filled the room; a thick blanket of tension settling like a cloud. Katherine froze, stomach churning as she realized by the wolves' expressions that something was deeply wrong.

"Alerion..." Zelia hesitated. "Alerion's gone."

"What?" Katherine and Avella bolted upright. "When did Alerion leave? Where could Alerion possibly go?"

"He slipped out last night. We found out when he didn't come for breakfast—but Alerion's been surly lately. We merely thought he was sulking. But we checked his chambers a few minutes ago, and it's empty. All his things are gone."

"Maybe he moved chambers?" Even as the words left her mouth, Katherine knew the truth; Alerion had returned to Madelaine. Alerion made it clear he never wanted to leave Madelaine in the first place.

He'd been dragging around the castle with a sour face since the wolves arrived. Pouting.

Lucie shot the wolves a sharp look. "Where would Alerion go? And *why*?"

Jules rubbed his chin. "Iasia, Madelaine's estate, probably. Madelaine has a greater hold on Alerion than us... Alerion was always fascinated by Madelaine's power."

A strange thought niggled the back of Katherine's mind. Something important. She looked at Eleonor. "How did you contact Madelaine while you were in the Lovanian forest?"

"Alerion was the only one allowed to contact Madelaine, but I watched him once, he used a messenger," Eleonor answered. "Madelaine's bird. A raven."

Katherine turned to Lucie. "Is there a window in Madelaine's cell?"

"No, the guards were careful, just an airhole, and a waste pipe," Lucie answered.

"Wastepipe?" Avella narrowed her eyes. "What size is it?"

Lucie put her thumb and forefinger together, about two inches apart.

"That's how she contacted Alerion, with mice... or rats. When I was young, Madelaine used to scare me with mice and rats as one of her favourite forms of entertainment. She's sent word to Alerion through them. If it was dark, and Madelaine was quiet, she could sneak messages right under the guard's noses."

"Alcrion's the general of her new army," Althea said, shivering, as she clutched the blanket tight around her knees. Despite the sun streaming in the window, the room felt dark and grim.

Lucie's eyes flashed. "If we search immediately, we'll find him. King Erich will send messengers through all of Lovan and Iasia."

A shadow crossed the window, flickering across their pale faces. "I think it's too late."

Katherine looked out the window, horror in her eyes. "Bats."

Hundreds, thousands of bats. Thousands of beating wings and high-pitched shrieks filled the air as Madelaine's horde ascended over Corvan, focusing their attention on the castle. They circled overhead, the black mass shifting and coiling as it blotted the sun, as they circled and flew away.

"What was that?" Katherine stared after the shrieking bats—an oily cloud with ragged edges, fading into the blue sky.

"A warning," Avella said. "Madelaine wants attention; she likes to play."

"What about Sorchia's book? Couldn't we learn to use it, maybe it would it add to our power?"

"It might be our best chance." Althea turned to Katherine. "Do you have Sorchia's book with you?"

Katherine reached into the secret pocket sewn into the waistband of her dress, drawing out the book. Its faded pages were showing signs of wear from its long journey—edges shabby and still in its makeshift cover.

"Here, and there's the page from Sorchia's diary too." Katherine handed the book to Althea, who took it in her gnarled hand.

"Lucie, have someone bring me all the magic books from the library. There must be some reason Madelaine is desperate to get Sorchia's book. Katherine, didn't you say you had the rest of Sorchia's old diaries? Bring those; it's not like I have anything else to do." Althea shifted, her face revealing a twinge of pain at the sudden movement.

They quickly scattered, the wolves going to share the news of Alerion's defection with King Erich and Queen Isabella, who were meeting with the council; Lucie organized the books to be delivered to Althea's room. Avella and Katherine let themselves out.

"I was wondering..." Katherine hesitated. "If I shouldn't return to Sorchia's house to search again. I know we have the diaries, but we were interrupted. I could wear the red cloak and Alerion wouldn't be able to scent me that way."

Avella gave her daughter a sharp look. "You're not sneaking off on your own again."

Katherine stiffened her spine. "I'm a grown woman, Mother, and Lovan needs our help."

"What I mean," Avella interrupted her, "is I'll go with you; I lived in Sorchia's house. And I know where her tower is, and it's so deep in the woods that its possible Madelaine never discovered its location. If Althea wards me a cloak, I could stay unnoticed for the journey."

Katherine nodded as they continued down the corridor. "But we can't tell anyone we're going, especially not Gunther because he'd insist on joining us."

Avella nodded. "We'll keep it among us."

"What about Gunther?" Lucie asked the question that stopped Katherine in her tracks.

"What about Gunther?" Katherine repeated, her throat caught, her eyes flicking between Avella and her younger sister. "I've no claim on Gunther, so why should he care where I'm going?"

Lucie rolled her eyes. "Have it your way, but Gunther won't be happy you didn't think to tell him you're rushing into danger again."

Katherine knew deep down that her sister had a point. But what should she tell Gunther? Everything was on the brink of disaster; this was hardly the time for exploring the depths of their relationship. The kingdom was at stake. Katherine shoved her reservations away and merely turned and shrugged. "I'll leave Gunther a message."

In reality, leaving Corvan was not as quick as Katherine and Avella planned. First, they needed to gather supplies discreetly to avoid suspicion. Bedrolls, food, clothes. Althea, with the help of Aric, warded Avella's cloak against discovery. Katherine used her red cloak because in spite of the tear, Althea said the ward should hold the length of their journey.

Finally, they were ready. Early morning, the two of slipped down to the stable, taking the servant's staircase to avoid detection. Frederich was waiting in the stable.

"Did Lucie tell you?" Katherine should have known Lucie would share their plans with Frederich. Lucie never could keep secrets from Prince Frederich. Katherine glanced around with a sigh of mixed disappointment and relief; fortunately, Gunther didn't seem to be around.

"I'm sending some soldiers after you—to keep you safe. They won't cross the Iasian border, but at least it's something. Alerion's dangerous, and we don't know what help he's gathered," Frederich explained, leading out two horses.

"Take the back gate; I've left it unlocked for you. You should be able to ride through the Corvan without being recognized if you keep your heads down. There's money in the saddlebags. Stay out of the forest after dark; you'll be at your weakest and Alerion and Madelaine are at their strongest."

The enormity of their mission was dawning on Katherine. She swallowed hard, taking the reins of the horse. Oblivious to Katherine's hesitation, the horse chomped his bit, blowing hay scented breath in Katherine's face. She set her face, swinging determinedly into the saddle. This would work; this must work. There was no other choice.

Katherine and Avella led their horses through the courtyard toward the rear of the castle grounds. Everything was quiet; they halted in a grove of trees clustered around the rear castle wall before slipping out the side gate and blending into the city streets.

When they reached the center of Corvan, Katherine and Avella drew their hoods over their heads. The back streets— lined with taverns, shops, and apartments— were busy enough that they didn't draw notice, melting into the bustling crowds. Katherine's shoulders didn't relax until she reached the edge of the city where spreading farms and cottages replaced the people and horses.

It was near evening when they reached the town of Chettra. There was nothing unusual about it. A single tavern, The Swan's Nest, doubled as an inn. Market Square was quiet. All market stall venders had closed shop for the evening.

"Do you have any free rooms?" Katherine strode across the dimly lit interior of the Swan's Nest. *More like the Swan's Final Rest*, she thought to herself, eyeing the dingy interior. Cobwebs edged the corners and grit squeaked under her feet—apparently cleaning was not a priority here.

"We've got one room." The innkeeper, rotund and balding, looked Katherine up and down, assessing her ability and willingness to pay for a dingy space for the night. "Two silvers." He leaned a lazy elbow against the counter.

Katherine set two coins on the sticky wooden surface. "We'll take it."

The innkeeper swept the coins into his pocket. "Follow me." He led Katherine and Avella up a creaking wooden staircase. Katherine flinched as a low hanging spiderweb brushed the side of her cheek. The room was tiny, two narrow bunks with a tiny space between. Katherine sat gingerly on the bed, wondering when the grimy bedclothes were last washed. She frowned at a large stain staring up at her; maybe she could spread her bedroll on the floor.

"At least the inn's safer than the forest," Avella said, setting down her satchel and wrinkling her nose.

Katherine nodded, overcome by a sudden wave of exhaustion and hunger. She sat on the narrow bed and stretched her legs in front of her. "Should we risk dinner?"

Avella nodded. "We'll save our own food stores for when we're travelling."

After wiping her hands and face, Katherine and Avella headed back downstairs. A few tavern patrons had arrived. Early drinkers, judging by the row of tankards sitting on the table in front of them. Katherine and Avella drifted toward the empty side of the room and sat at a sticky wooden table. The stew was bland, but at least it was hot, and the bread was decent, served warm with with plenty of butter. Katherine broke off a chunk, dipping it into the stew and chewing slowly.

Katherine watched from the corner of her eye as the long table across the room grew increasingly boisterous. The row of empty tankards grew and noise increased as more people joined the noisy table. Mostly farmers, a few merchants, and one or two travellers like themselves. Katherine eyed them curiously.

"Most of them are local," Avella said, leaning close and speaking in a low voice. "But that one—in the leather jerkin. He's not from here and he doesn't look like a trader either."

Katherine checked the man with her eyes. Avella was right; he didn't seem local, sitting at the end of the table, aloof from the rowdy drinkers. He scanned the room, cool, ice-blue eyes meeting Katherine's. She twisted her head, letting her hair swing in front of her face.

"One of Frederich's guards?" she whispered to Avella.

Avella answered with a slight nod.

They finished their food in silence, leaving the tavern and the mysterious stranger as they went up to their room to sleep.

The next evening, Katherine and Avella reached the Iasian border. Now that they had no guards, the danger would increase. They stayed the night in Harbon and crossed the border early in the morning.

"It doesn't feel any different in Iasia." Katherine took in her surroundings. Arching trees surrounded them on every side; thick underbrush left plenty of places for a lone wolf to hide. Katherine shivered, pulling the red cloak tight around her shoulders. Behind her, she felt the eyes of Prince Frederich's guards watching; they would ensure she and Avella crossed the border safely. After that, it was up to them.

Katherine gripped the reins, urging her horse through the slanting morning light. "Let's go."

Avella followed Katherine through winding pathways, passing villages and towns— always keeping their heads down and their profiles low. They were getting closer to the Rapunzel estate; Avella grew quieter and introspective, lost in tangled memories of the past.

Finally, they arrived in Lilice.

"Will anyone recognise you?" Katherine asked Avella, studying her mother's face; Avella was pale and drawn. Her confidence disappeared by the mile, replaced by radiating tension that seeped from every pore.

"I thought it was all over, that I could move on and forget, but it's all coming back to me," Avella said, her shoulders tight around her ears.

Katherine glanced around the tiny village. So far, everyone ignored them— just two ordinary travellers passing through.

"Come on," Katherine urged Avella as the horses clattered past Market Square—the same Market Square where Katherine had recently admired the fabulous weaving.

"Not far now." Katherine broke the silence as they rode down the narrow lane, thick brambly hedges rising on either side of them. Close, suffocating like black needle sharp fingers reaching for them.

"Sorchia had plant magic; she made things grow instantly," Avella explained. "I guess the plants didn't forget."

Katherine gazed at the magnificent trees soaring overhead, casting them in shadows. The hedges pressed closer as they neared the estate.

The rusted iron gate was ajar— an invitation. Avella caught her breath at the sight of the crumbling manor. She dismounted, expression dazed, as she walked toward the front door.

"I remember the first time Sorchia brought me here. I didn't even know I had a grandmother until just before Sorchia arrived and I assumed Sorchia would be like Mary—my father's mother." A bitter laugh escaped Avella's lips. "She couldn't have been more different. Sorchia was cold, determined. And she wanted me to help her accomplish her goals."

Avella was almost in a trance as she moved up the worn steps. She gently touched the door handle, rusted metal frozen by time. The handle slid down; the door creaked open, beckoning them inside Sorchia's manor.

Ducking under a wisp of spiderwebs, Katherine followed Avella inside the entrance hall.

"Where would Sorchia have kept something important?" she whispered. The hall was dark, only lit by strands of light falling from the open doorway.

Avella shrugged. "Sorchia was full of secrets. But she loved sitting in her drawing room; we should start looking there."

Katherine followed Avella through to Sorchia's sitting room. Time had not been kind; faded wallpaper hung in ribbons from the wall, and the once grand furniture was grimy and worn. Katherine could hardly detect the brocade pattern through the layer of dirt.

Together, Katherine and Avella searched every inch of Sorchia's drawing room. But they found nothing of interest—only a series of old novels and an assortment of decrepit, old-fashioned knickknacks.

"Madelaine will have scoured this place and taken everything she could find." Avella sat back on her heels.

"Is there anywhere Madelaine wouldn't have searched?" Katherine asked her mother.

Her mother's face tightened. "The tower. Only Sorchia and I know its location. And Pierre, of course; after all, he discovered me there."

"Do you remember the way to Sorchia's tower?" Katherine was already moving toward the door, anxious to leave this sad ancient reminder of the Rapunzel family's dark secret history.

Katherine followed Avella through the woods as they wound through ravines and over trees.

"I don't remember Sorchia taking me to the tower," Avella explained. "I was asleep, but I'll never forget the way out. It's burned into my memory forever."

Soon, the trees thinned, and Katherine and Avella arrived in a small clearing where before them rose an ancient tower. Narrow and tall, the crumbling tower was made of solid stone blocks.

Katherine noticed a door at the base of the tower, fastened tight after years of disuse, but the wood was soft and rotten with age.

"Should we go in?" Katherine asked, hesitating at the broken door; she flicked worried eyes at her mother's drawn face.

Avella nodded, eyes filling with emotion.

Katherine rattled the old-fashioned door handle; the door was locked.

"What should we do?" Katherine frowned at the door in annoyance.

"We could try these keys." Avella dangled a set of worn keys in her hand.

"Where did you get those?" Katherine asked, her eyes widening.

"From Sorchia's desk." Avella took the keys, fitting each one into the door.

The fourth key turned, and a screeching sound filled the clearing as rusted metal rubbed against rusted metal. The door swung open, and they peered inside, seeing a cold dark stone interior with a twisting staircase that disappeared into darkness.

Avella's eyes shuttered when she looked inside the tower, lost in memories.

"I was young when she left me alone here." Avella murmured almost to herself; her voice was small and quiet, barely heard above the rustling wind and chattering birds of the sunlit clearing.

"Sorchia?" Katherine asked, her voice gentle.

Avella nodded, pressed her lips into a firm line, and took a step forward.

Katherine held out her hand to Avella. Together, they entered, hand in hand, up the uneven steps— twisting and turning until they reached the very top of the tower. The door at the top was locked and thick rusted nails stuck halfway out of the half rotted doorframe. Avella brushed her fingers over one of them.

"Sorchia nailed this door shut; it was one of the last things I remember before... before..." Avella cut her words off. She fumbled with the keys again, trying one after the other, until finally, one grated in the lock.

Avella went in first. One tiny window lit the tower room, casting a glow over the stone walls and floor. A small wooden table sat in the corner, topped with a large bowl; a dented bucket sat in the corner. Everything was covered with dust. A pile of what appeared to be dirty rags sat in one corner.

"That was my bed." Avella lifted one— a ragged blanket chewed by rats and covered in dust and grime.

"I don't see anything in this tower; it's empty," Katherine said, disappointment seeping into every fiber of her body. She dreaded going back to Sorchia's manor. The sad house was haunted by so many memories, so much pain and disappointment.

They searched every inch of the room. Not that there was much to search; the bed in the corner seemed the most promising and gave them nothing. Katherine fought the disappointment growing deep inside. If only there was something... a clue.

"Is there anywhere else Sorchia stored important things?" Katherine said, turning to Avella, eyes pleading.

Avella leaned on her heels; a streak of dust marked her cheek; spiderwebs caught in her hair. "No." Her eyes wandered to the window. "Unless, there's something outside we missed."

The two women peered over the stone windowsill. Trees, trees, and more trees surrounded them, hemming them in on every side, and the horses happily teared a patch of grass in the clearing.

After scouring the tower room once more, they headed down the narrow stairs, their footsteps hollow in the tall, thin space.

"Wait a minute," Katherine said, halting so abruptly Avella nearly tumbled over her.

"What?" Avella asked, her voice thin and tired.

"Our footsteps; they wouldn't sound like that, not unless...."

"Unless what?" Avella asked, sensing the excitement growing in Katherine's voice.

"Unless there was a space underneath the stairs," Katherine finished. "I didn't examine it when we came in because I was so determined to search the tower."

Katherine and Avella hurried to the bottom of the staircase. "A cupboard," Katherine shouted triumphantly, crawling under the last step. A tiny, hidden door, well enforced with strong metal, was hidden in an alcove under the bottom step. Katherine knocked. The wood was dry and solid, unexposed to elements like the outer tower door.

"We'll get a light and something to pry the door open." Katherine turned to her mother, eyes glinting.

"I have a lantern in my saddlebag; its small, but better than nothing. And we can try these keys I found."

Unfortunately, the keys didn't work. Katherine tried key after key and the lock stubbornly refused to turn. Katherine's heart lurched in her chest as her fingers closed around the last key. The iron teeth fitted into the old lock; Katherine pushed, hoping, praying it would turn. It didn't. The lock held fast, refusing to betray its owner.

"I don't suppose we have tools in your saddlebag?" Katherine asked Avella.

Avella shook her head. "But Sorchia's stable is nearby; I assume her stable should contain tools. It will only set us back an hour."

Katherine nodded, disappointment easing. In the stable, Avella efficiently gathered a collection of tools including a mallet, a shovel, a chisel, and an axe. The axe handle was worn, but still firm and steady. Strong from years of labor, Avella carried the tools with effortless grace. This time, they brought Avella's lantern to light the alcove. On close examination, Katherine noted strange inscriptions etched into the metal bands.

"Does this writing seem familiar?" Katherine asked Avella, pointing to the wavering lines.

Avella nodded. "The writing matches Sorchia's book."

The two exchanged glances, an eerie shiver passing through Katherine, knowing she was about the discover the roots of Sorchia's secret.

It was hard work, but after half an hour, they saw progress, chipping away the dry wood with the axe.

"Not long now." Avella puffed, wiping her sleeve across her forehead. A bead of sweat trickled down her temple. The small landing was stuffy, filled with the smell of age, dust, and disuse. Avella picked up the axe and swung. With a great crack, the ancient wood split open to disintegrate into crumbling pieces.

Avella reached into the dark hole, feeling around with hesitant fingers. "I can unlatch the door from inside," she explained, grabbing the metal clasp.

The door swung open and musty air poured out— cold, swirling with a strange muddy tinge. Katherine felt a tingle creep down her spine. With shaking hands, she lifted the lantern, holding it in front of her and peering inside.

"What do you see?" Avella asked, hovering over Katherine's shoulder.

"Stairs."

A narrow set of stairs— carved from solid rock—wound down, disappearing into blackness.

"Be careful, Sorchia may have set traps," Avella warned.

Katherine took a deep breath; her heart pounded in her ears, that strange tingling feeling buzzed like swarming bees, vibrating under her skin.

Down, one careful step after the next, Katherine and Avella edged down the steep, uneven staircase. Finally, they reached the bottom. Katherine held up the lantern, curious to see what mysteries Sorchia was hiding. They reached a generous room the size of Katherine's bed chamber, lined with books, strange bottles, some filled with liquids and crumbling herbal concoctions, moldering, forgotten in the darkness for decades.

Katherine drifted to the books, running a finger along their spines. "Did you suspect this room was here?"

Avella shook her head. "No. Sorchia is a mystery to me. I don't think she used this room while she kept me here."

Katherine slipped Sorchia's little book out of her pocket. "I suppose we should see if anything matches the script in here." She searched for the books. "I found more diaries." She drew out a narrow volume; aged, brittle, the edges of ragged parchment crackled as she opened it.

"These diaries have recipes in them." Katherine wrinkled her brow.

Avella peered over Katherine's shoulder. "Recipes?"

"Extremely strange recipes." Katherine suddenly felt the weight of the darkness pressing in all around her, heavy and cloying.

Thick.

Evil.

"Sorchia was.... Researching, experimenting."

The words faded away, sucked into the darkness, crouching around them.

Katherine flicked through the rest of the book, shaking by the time she reached the end.

"Sorchia wanted everything. The kingdom. The Crown, maybe more...." Katherine's eyes, luminous in the dim lamplight, searched Avella's.

Avella paled. "Sorchia and Madelaine.... how did they both turn out so twisted?"

Katherine and Avella examined the other small volumes in the pile, all filled with plans and concoctions written in Sorchia's strange spidery handwriting. But still no clues how to counter Madelaine's animal forces. After Sorchia's recipe books were exhausted, they moved their attention to the rest of the underground room; it contained hundreds of books, collected through the ages.

"This must have been the original tower. Where the Rapunzel family began their traditions," Avella murmured, almost to herself. Some books were so old, they nearly crumbled under their fingertips. The ink was faded into the aged parchment.

Katherine and Avella had been hidden underground for hours but still found nothing useful. Katherine swiped her sleeve over her forehead. She was exhausted, grimy from the rank, dusty air.

"What do you suppose these are?" Avella wandered to a shelf of glass bottles. Most appeared empty, but one or two bottles still contained a watery substance. They were separate from the ingredients; the shelf protected by a set of barred doors.

"Those bottles look important." Katherine joined her mother to investigate; she rattled the door handle, turning experimentally. To her surprise, it opened easily, swinging smoothly to reveal the bottles covered by thick dust partially obscuring the contents. She lifted a bottle, rubbing the dusty surface with the edge of her tunic. A shimmering liquid floated inside the coloured glass, swirling, iridescent, almost glowing. Katherine nearly dropped the bottle in surprise.

"What is it?" Avella leaned over Katherine's shoulder.

"I think I know what that is," Katherine gasped. "Celine saw something similar in Lord Ruben's estate."

"What is it?" Avella reached a cautious hand to touch the bottle.

"When Celine and Alex explored Lord Remy's estate, Celine described something very similar to this."

"What was the substance?" Avella picked up on the serious tone in Katherine's voice.

"Souls... or powers of souls. Lord Remy had a collection of powers; he would siphon from people he killed then store them in glass jars exactly like these."

Katherine replaced the bottle on the dusty shelf as a gloom settled over the cavelike room. Dark. Menacing.

"Did you see any of these bottles when you lived with Sorchia?" Katherine asked her mother. She rubbed her hands together. She was chilly; cold sweat pooled in the small of her back.

Avella shook her head. "Honestly, if Sorchia could do that when I lived in her estate, she would have stolen my gift."

"Do you think she tried to siphon Madelaine's gift?" Katherine asked, a hollow feeling growing in the pit of her stomach.

"I wouldn't put it past her." Avella lifted another bottle. "Sorchia must have used a system to tell them apart, nothing's labeled."

"There, on the bottom." Katherine pointed to the underside of the bottle where a scrap of paper, edges brown and curling, was stuck.

"Natalie- Fire," Avella breathed, peering closely at the scrawled writing on the label. A silent tear trickled down her cheek. "My mother, your grandmother. She was cold and cruel, but she doesn't deserve this from her own mother. No one does. Madelaine was devoted to Mother; I wonder if she knew."

"Was fire Natalie's gift?" Katherine asked, searching Avella's eyes.

Avella shook her head. "Natalie never mentioned or displayed her own gift. There was so little I knew about Mother; she loved Madelaine, maybe she shared her gift with her." Heartbreak was clear on Avella's face and crackled in her voice.

"What's on this shelf?" Katherine asked, looking under the glass bottles.

Under the shelf of bottles was a tidy stack of books, more of Sorchia's diaries recording all her horrible details.

"Instructions. Plans." Avella blew the dust from the top diary and paged through.

"This diary explains the secret of Sorchia's little book," Katherine breathed, holding up the final book. "Sorchia's book would multiply Madelaine's power tenfold; that's why she is so desperate to have it. And Madelaine wants this." Katherine waved her hand, encompassing the dungeon-like room and its contents.

"We'll have destroy these before Madelaine can gain access, " Avella continued, setting down the diary. "If Sorchia's books end up in the wrong hands, they'll jeopardize Iasia and Lovan as well."

"How?" Katherine asked, glancing at the contents of Sorchia's secret room.

"Fire." Avella set her mouth in a determined line. "But first, we're taking the bottles, those poor souls don't deserve that ending."

Carefully, so carefully, Katherine and Avella removed the fragile bottles from the room, setting them at the edge of the clearing and cradling them in a blanket.

Avella and Katherine headed back to Sorchia's hidden room; they wouldn't need tinder, the notebooks would do. She followed Avella as they cautiously descended into the darkness one last time. Cold, dank air pressed in around them, close and thick on every side. It was hard to breathe. To think.

With shaking hands, they placed the journals, books, and wooden furniture in the center of the floor.

That was it; Avella swallowed. "Stand back," she told Katherine, closing her eyes in concentration. Nothing happened.

"It won't work," Avella muttered to Katherine, "Sorchia must have warded this room."

"Try again," urged Katherine.

Avella closed her eyes again, but it was futile. "We'll have to get the flint from my saddlebag."

"Wait." Avella hushed her. "I hear a noise."

Katherine froze, her face intent as she concentrated. Silence... then a creak. Subtle, quiet. Then a shuffling of footsteps creeping downstairs.

"Someone's coming," Avella whispered. "We've been discovered."

Avella and Katherine glanced around, noticing with dismay there was nowhere to hide.

"Stand behind the door," Avella instructed. "I'll try the fire again."

They had mere seconds left.

Fear clouding the edge of her vision, Avella made another futile attempt at lighting the fire, but her efforts fell flat.

The door burst open and Katherine, armed with a thick book, slammed it on the intruder's head. It glanced off the muscled chest, barely slowing him down as he slithered into the room, feral eyes glowing yellow under the lamplight.

Alerion.

Alerion growled, leaping on Katherine.

Katherine shrieked, flinging up her arm— a poor defence against teeth, claws, and rangy muscle. She was instantly overpowered. Katherine's head rang as it struck the stone floor. Stars danced before her eyes. The last thing Katherine remembered was gleaming white teeth slavering over her. The pressure against her chest. Everything went numb.

CHAPTER FIFTEEN

Katherine was floating, rising through darkness into murky gloom with a sharp, hard pressure against her back. A pressure that was warm against the biting cold.

Her head ached; her body ached; her bones ached.

Katherine groaned, her eyes fluttering open.

"You're awake," Avella's voice was gentle, her face filled with concern as she leaned over her daughter.

Katherine's stiff muscles protested; there was a sharp pain. Teeth... no ropes. Wrapped tight around her wrists and ankles.

"What happened?" Katherine blinked as the vague, blurry shapes surrounding her came into focus.

"The wolf Alerion attacked; he had you down instantly and turned on me next, we never had a chance against him." Avella's voice was low. "Then he left as suddenly as he arrived."

"Left? When, Why?" Katherine jerked her head up, then winced as searing pain lanced through her right shoulder. She knew, even as she spoke the reason Alerion defected. He was grabbing a chance to gain Madelaine's power.

"I don't know why he left, but the attack took place over an hour ago," Avella said, shifting and letting out a weak gasp.

"Are you hurt, mother?" Katherine twisted, blinking through the shadowy darkness; looking down, she noticed she lay in a puddle of liquid smeared across the stone floor; dark and sticky, like thick honey.

"Are you hurt?" Katherine asked Avella.

"A little," Avella answered through gritted teeth. "I had my dagger, but Alerion knocked it out of my hands, and I've been trying to reach it to cut the ropes, but I'm not close enough."

Katherine tested the ropes coiled around her wrists, but Alerion had pulled them tight with not an inch of wiggle room. "Where is the dagger? Maybe I'm closer."

"I heard the dagger fall near the stairs." Avella pointed through the darkness to the stairs rising to the top of the room.

Katherine narrowed her eyes and focused on the staircase, spying a faint gleam of metal under the bottom step. "I see it; if I stretch out, maybe I can kick it to you." She strained, straining her toes, hearing a scrape of metal on stone, as inch by inch she edged the dagger toward Avella. Finally, the dagger was close enough for Avella to touch with her bound hands. She grabbed it and pulled it toward herself, cringing as the sharp metal bit into her skin.

"I'll hold the dagger steady, so you can saw through your ropes." Avella clenched the knife between bound hands so Katherine could shred her ropes. It was a slow and arduous process. Katherine's shoulders ached at the torturous work, and the agony in her head caused black spots to swim before her eyes. Something sticky trickled down the side of her cheek. Blood.

Katherine kept sawing until the ropes loosened.

"Almost there, just a few strands more," Avella grunted.

Katherine freed her hands and shook her wrists as fierce pins and needles shot through every nerve and fibre of her hands and fingers. Then she made quick work of Avella's bonds and freed her ankles.

Katherine hunted through the darkness. "I can't find my flint; it was in my pocket," she muttered.

"The flint probably won't work either," Avella informed her. "I was thinking about how Sorchia warded this place to keep it safe, but to avoid detection she probably didn't ward past the staircase."

"Can your gift work from that distance?" Katherine asked Avella, hope kindling.

Avella nodded. "And then we leave; who knows what horrible things Alerion discovered here for Madelaine to play with."

With the grim realization that Alerion was lurking outside and possibly returning any moment, Katherine and Avella examined the pile one last time.

"You go outside the tower," Avella instructed her daughter. "My gift is still pretty rusty, and I don't want to injure you."

Katherine climbed the stairs, checking the clearing carefully. The horses were gone, their ropes sliced through, and so were their precious bottles. Katherine eyed a discarded pile of blankets, a pained expression on her face. Alerion must have taken those as well. She turned to the tower, resolute.

A few minutes passed, and Avella still hadn't emerged. Katherine paced back and forth, biting her lip anxiously. Several times, she started toward the crumbling structure, but then thought better. She would wait a little longer.

Finally. Finally. Katherine heard a dull thud like far off thunder. The leaves shivered, the ground vibrated underfoot as Avella stumbled out of the broken down tower.

"It's done," Avella groaned, sinking onto the grass. Her face was pale, and beads of sweat dampened her hairline.

"We should wait to make sure it's really destroyed." Avella leaned weakly against a tree trunk.

So, they waited. Black smoke boiled into the air. Foul. Thick. Smelling of evil and bad decisions.

When the tower was in flames, Avella nodded. "Let's go." She stood up weakly, cradling her left arm close to her side. Blood darkened her tunic.

"We need to get help," Katherine told her, scanning the thick woods, reluctant to return to Sorchia's manor because Alerion would surely find them there. But Sorchia's manor was the only place within reachable distance. At least Avella could get cleaned and bandaged before they continued to the village. Her stomach tightened with tension.

"Let's go." Katherine heaved herself to her feet and offered Avella her arm.

Supporting each other, they finally stumbled into the manor courtyard, where a dented bucket next to the well served as a washbasin. Katherine cleaned Avella's wound gently before wrapping it tightly in a clean cloth. Avella's bleeding had slowed, but blood still dotted the makeshift bandage as it seeped through the flimsy material.

"Wait here," Katherine instructed Avella before darting into the main house. She remembered seeing a jewellery box on Sorchia's dresser. Maybe she'd find something of value in the manor. They'd lost the coin stored in the saddlebags when Alerion chased the horses deep into the forest.

Katherine rushed up the stairs toward Sorchia's bedroom, rifling through the scant jewel box, she grabbed a few necklaces and a ring with a green stone. She quickly pocketed them, then jerked the drawers open. Jewellery would cause questions, coins would be so much more useful. Only a few dusty ointment bottles and a tin of hairpins. The jewellery would have to do.

Katherine spun, ready to dash back down the stairs, then gasped; a large presence blocked her way.

"Gunther?" Katherine said, surprise flooding her face.

Gunther strode toward Katherine, a fierce expression darkening his eyes.

Katherine stepped back, the edge of the vanity digging into her hip.

"How did you travel to Iasia so fast?" Katherine asked Gunther in a tiny voice.

"I came as soon as I heard your plan." Gunther eyed Katherine's wounded head with a grim expression. "I hope he looks worse than you do."

Katherine nodded, a weak laugh escaping from her lips. "I hope so too."

Gunther held out his hand. "Come on, let's get you to safety and then we'll talk."

Katherine nodded mutely, avoiding the broken bannister as she followed Gunther down the stairway.

Gunther put Avella on his horse and walked beside Katherine as they went to the village.

"I have rooms at the inn," he explained.

"How did you know I was coming to the estate?" Katherine asked, tipping her head back to look at him. "Was it Lucie?"

Gunther shook his head. "I asked Lucie when I couldn't find you; she refused to give me a straight answer. I supposed you told her to keep in a secret?"

Katherine nodded guiltily. "You've already done so much..."

Gunther pinched his lips together. "I've told you already that I want you safe. Why can't you just trust me?"

Katherine shrugged, avoiding Gunther's penetrating gaze as he asked the question.

"Anyway..." Gunther continued. "When Lucie wouldn't tell me where you went; I came straight here."

"Thank you," Katherine's voice was small. "And I do trust you... It's just, I'm used to doing things for myself." She held out a hand. "I'll try. I really will."

"That's all I ask." Gunther took her hand.

CHAPTER SIXTEEN

The trio limped into the village inn, avoiding any curious glances they drew. Katherine kept her head down as she rushed to help Avella upstairs.

"I'll go to the apothecary to find salve," Katherine told Gunther in a low voice after she settled Avella on the narrow bed, covering her with a soft blanket and wedging a pillow under her head.

After splashing the worst grit and grime from her face, hands, and arms, Katherine headed to the village apothecary. The apothecary was located adjacent the busiest section of Market Square; Katherine wove through the stalls and venders to reach it. Avoiding the cloth vender she'd met on her previous visit, Katherine headed toward the two story wooden building. The last thing Katherine needed was to be recognized by interfering townspeople who might alert Alerion or Madelaine's allies.

The apothecary bell chimed as Katherine entered, and a cheerful woman emerged from the back, wiping her hands on her crisp white apron. Katherine's eyes widened in surprise. It was like looking at a younger version of Althea. *Althea's family must still own the village apothecary,* Katherine thought, curious eyes taking in the neat rows of drawers and spotless bottles holding ingredients for the cures and tinctures. So this was where Althea came from. She stepped up to the wide counter, pasting a hesitant smile on her face.

"Can I help you, miss?" Dark eyes scanned Katherine's rumpled appearance with inquisitive eyes.

Katherine nodded. "Yes, there's been a severe injury; I'll need a poultice to keep the cut from infection. Perhaps tincture for pain and fever as well."

The woman nodded briskly, reaching for a large jar behind the counter.

"We keep this prepared mixture ready," she explained to Katherine, measuring the doses into a paper packet. "Injuries are more common that you think in the farming villages. Will the patient need stitches?"

Katherine hesitated; Avella's wound was deep. "I—I don't know," she faltered.

"We can attend... discreetly." The woman glanced around the empty apothecary and leaned across the counter, lowering her tone. "Strange things happen often in this village; your patient wouldn't be the first to sustain an unusual injury."

Katherine bit her lip, hoping she was making the right decision. "I suppose it wouldn't hurt to look at the injury. When can you come?"

"Now, I'll just be a moment." The woman grabbed a canvas satchel behind the counter. "Gabby, I'm leaving for a few minutes. Can you mind the shop?"

A smiling woman appeared, dusting flour from her hands. "Certainly, Nolene." She beamed warmly at Katherine, unfazed by her unkempt appearance.

"Is your party staying at the inn?" Nolene asked Katherine as she led her to the back door.

Katherine nodded, surprised.

"We don't get many strangers visiting the village," Nolene explained. "Follow me, we'll walk this way, villagers are too nosy for us to traipse through Market Square." Nolene wrinkled her nose as Katherine followed her down a narrow walkway that wound through a back street straight to the inn, avoiding Market Square completely.

Avella lay on the bed, face pale and exhausted. The effort of traveling after the fire and Alerion's attack had taken a fierce toll on her.

"Let me see the injury." Nolene gently examined the ragged edges of Avella's wound. "We can stitch this cut up and with the poultice, it should avoid infection, but she shouldn't travel for at least a week."

Katherine nodded. "As long as she's safe and healed."

Nolene's efficient hands attended to Avella's wound, wrapping a clean white bandage around it.

"I'll be back tomorrow to check on it and change the dressing; what about your own injury?" Nolene turned to Katherine.

Katherine raised a tentative hand to her head. She had nearly forgotten about the cut on her head, but the fierce ache returned at Nolene's reminder.

Nolene sat Avella on the bed, parting her hair. "The cut won't need stitches, but if you return to the apothecary with me, I'll get you some ointment."

"Has your family always owned the apothecary?" Katherine asked Nolene as they walked back down the creaky wooden staircase. She still couldn't get over the resemblance between Nolene and Althea.

"Oh yes, our family has always been healers. It's a—gift; I suppose you could say. My aunt was the best healer." Nolene stopped, clamping her lips together.

"Your aunt?" Katherine prodded gently.

"Yes, she moved to Lovan ages ago and we seldom hear from her anymore."

Katherine's heart thumped in excitement. Nolene's aunt must be Althea.

"Why did your aunt move to Lovan?" Katherine asked, prodding in a gentle voice.

"We have relatives in Lovan, and she wanted to keep an eye on them," Nolene said, her eyes darting away from Katherine's.

"If it's not too intrusive... is your aunt's name Althea?" Katherine asked.

It was Nolene's turn to be surprised. Her eyes widened, mouth rounding. "How did you know?"

"I know Althea well, since I was a tiny girl," Katherine explained as they reached the apothecary door.

Nolene gestured for Katherine to follow her inside. "I'll get Gabby; we need to talk."

Katherine followed Nolene up a wooden flight of stairs to the apartment above the apothecary, inviting her into a warm, cozy kitchen. Loaves of bread cooled on a colourful metal tray, and checked curtains fluttered at the window.

Gabby smiled as they came in, moving an enamel kettle to the hottest part of the range. "A guest, how lovely; this calls for a cup of tea."

Soon, Gabby was serving steaming cups of fragrant herbal tea. Katherine breathed in the scent of peppermint as Gabby sliced loaves of hot bread, spreading them with butter and strawberry jam.

"Althea was mother's sister," Gabby explained. "She was a gifted healer and ran the apothecary until she left. We had family—relatives—who needed Althea's help."

"Who were the relatives? I lived in the same village as Althea my entire life, and she never spoke of family," Katherine filed through the various town's people from the tiny village of Annecy.

"The family connection was strange, and something we'd rather most people forget," admitted Gabby, stirring honey into her tea. "You know the large estate nearby?"

Katherine nodded, wondering what Madelaine had to do with Althea's Lovanian relations.

"There's another estate, a lesser known one called the Rapunzel estate."

"Do you mean Sorchia's manor?"

CHAPTER SEVENTEEN

"We didn't know either." Gabby said, placing a warm gentle hand on Katherine's. "When Sorchia inherited the manor, Uncle Elfred deserted our family and refused to have anything to do with us. We weren't told about you girls until the estate burned. People started talking then, and they couldn't keep the secret from us anymore."

"But that doesn't explain why Althea wouldn't explain she was our aunt," Katherine said, a wrinkle appearing between her eyes.

Gabby shook her head. "Althea loved your mother; she knew about Avella's gift, and she hated the way Natalie treated Avella. It drove Althea mad, but the unfortunate truth was there wasn't anything Althea could do to make Natalie stop the mistreatment. Althea felt responsible for sealing Avella's magic so she could continue safely to Lovan. But Althea never realized someday Sorchia or Madelaine would follow Avella to Lovan— helpless. She didn't want to burden you; Althea is too independent."

Katherine nodded. The idea of family—cousins felt strange to her. Pierre had distant relatives in south Lovan, but he was an only child and Katherine had never met them. As long as Katherine could remember, it was her and her sisters standing together. They sat in silence, sipping their tea while the thoughts swirled in the air.

"We'd better get you to the inn; it's getting late," Nolene said, yawning.

Katherine glanced out the window at the darkening sky in surprise; she hadn't realised how quickly time had passed. Avella would worry—not to mention Gunther. A pang of guilt pierced Katherine.

Nolene escorted Katherine back to the inn to find Gunther pacing the floor in front of the staircase.

"There you are," Gunther said, shooting forward, an expression of intense relief chasing across his face.

"Sorry," Katherine apologized. "I lost track of time. Is everything all right?"

Gunther nodded, eyes tight. "Alerion's on the move; there are reports of animal attacks."

"How did you hear?" Katherine asked, her heart clenching in her chest.

"People gossiping in the tavern," Gunther answered, his voice short. "I need to return to Lovan immediately and warn King Erich and Prince Frederich."

"Then I'm coming too," Katherine said, setting her jaw.

"What about your mother?" Gunther said, his eyes searching Katherine's.

"Avella has family here; I'll send them a message and they'll care for her until she recovers."

Gunther shot Katherine a curious look, but didn't argue. "Fine, we leave in ten minutes; meet me at the stable."

Katherine nodded, then dashed up the stairs to her room.

Ten minutes later, Katherine had spoken to Avella, explaining the situation and scrawled a brief message, addressing it to Gabby at the apothecary before rushing to the stable where Gunther waited impatiently, holding the reins of two horses.

"You can ride this mare; she's not fast, but she's sturdy and even-tempered," Gunther explained, handing the reins of the brown mare to Katherine.

They mounted quickly and rode out of the village, heading for the Lovanian border.

It was dark, and the sliver of moon hid behind a bank of dark clouds, peeking out occasionally to cast dappled silver shadows across the path. Katherine's surefooted mare and Gunther's horse pressed on.

Although the path was even, Katherine's mind was not eased; she was too worried about what else lurked in the shadowy darkness—things with eyesight better than her own. Every branch that crackled, every rustle of the forest, alerted her to danger until Katherine's nerves tingled with awareness.

"We'll be all right," said Gunther, sensing Katherine's anxiety. "I'm well armed, and you have weapons too."

Katherine let out a breath. "I'm just worried Alerion will surprise us."

They travelled on until dawn broke— cold, grey, and gloomy over the eastern horizon. Rain threatened ahead and in the distance, crackled flashes of lightning. Katherine pulled her cloak tight around her. Although they had stopped several times to rest, the horses were tiring.

"We'll make camp here," Gunther said, leaving the path and breaking into the thick trees. They camped in a stand of birch trees. Too tired to light a fire, they settled for cold bread and cheese before Katherine curled up in her bedroll to catch some much needed sleep.

"KATHERINE, KATHERINE." Someone was shaking her shoulders.

Katherine mumbled, rolling over, wincing as sharp stones dug into her back.

"Katherine, we need to go," Gunther said, nudging Katherine again.

Numb and stiff, Katherine sat up. She was tired, so tired. Gunther was tired too; Katherine noticed the dark circles under his eyes, his rumpled hair, and dishevelled clothing. But they had to keep going.

Madelaine's forces were gathering, and who knew where they would strike next.

Katherine and Gunther travelled steadily, stopping only to rest a few hours at the inn in Havre. The next day, they arrived in Annecy.

Annecy was bustling. Market day was in full swing, with venders displaying their wares at the stalls— all seemingly oblivious to the impeding danger of Madelaine's army. Katherine drew several curious glances; she was well remembered in Annecy and still visited the village often. Mary, her weaving mistress, ran the Annecy weaving guild, and several of Katherine's best weavers had set up a stall in Market Square. Katherine gave their stall a wistful glance as they passed, longing to return to a time when the guild business occupied her waking moments with the fabrics, the textures, the colours.

"We can stop at the Orc's Head for lunch; after all, we have to eat," Gunther suggested, noticing Katherine's interest in Annecy Market Square.

Katherine's ears perked up; the Orc's Head was the only tavern Annecy had. Run by Henri and Izzie, it was the center for town gossip; if there was news of Madelaine's movements, it would emerge here.

The familiar smell of savoury stew and yeasty mead greeted Katherine as they entered the Orc's Head. Long wooden tables were half filled with customers. However, the tavern was strangely quiet and subdued. Katherine glanced around, looking for Henri's familiar presence at the bar. Henri liked to stay visible because he thought it kept the Orc's Head's rowdier customers in check.

Blanchette emerged from the kitchen. Usually impeccably and expensively dressed, with her blonde hair styled into sleek curls, her red-rimmed eyes and wrinkled dress told the story of a sleepless night.

"Blanchette. What's the matter?" A concerned expression crossed Katherine's face.

"Didn't you hear?" Blanchette said, her lip trembling.

"Hear what?" Katherine asked; she'd never once seen Blanchette cry. Not even when she broke her toe by getting stepped on by a horse.

"Father," Blanchette said, gulping back tears. "Father..." Blanchette cut her words off and ran back to the kitchen, wiping her eyes.

Katherine exchanged worried glances with Gunther. "Something's happened to Henri." Katherine noticed Izzie was nowhere to be seen.

Katherine glanced around the tavern, spotting someone she knew; Davino, the brother of one of her weavers.

"Davino, where's Henri? Is he all right?" Katherine asked in a hushed voice.

"Henri's dead," Davino whispered, his eyes flicking toward the kitchen door where Blanchette had fled.

"Dead?" Katherine's eyes widened. Henri wasn't old, and last time Katherine had seen him, Henri was in perfect health. "What happened to him, was he ill?"

"A wild animal attacked Henri," Davino whispered.

"Here in Annecy?" The Orc's Head was located in the middle of the village, and wild animals rarely ventured far from their forest habitats.

Davino nodded. "In the garden out back, Blanchette found him."

Katherine sucked in a breath. Blanchette was Henri's precious daughter. She was devoted to her father; she must be devastated.

"When did the attack happen?" she asked.

"Three days ago. The worst thing is, no one knows what animal it was, and where it is now. Annecy is in a panic; everyone's locking their doors at dusk," Davino answered in a whisper.

"Have there been other animal attacks?" Katherine glanced around, noticing she was drawing attention from curious townspeople.

Davino nodded. "Mostly farm animals, Gavin's bull, some horses, sheep—big animals. They're saying to keep the animals locked in the barns at night. But even that's not working."

Katherine pressed her lips together. This smacked of Madelaine, but the last thing Katherine needed was to send Annecy deeper into panic.

Gunther, who had been listening in on the conversation, nudged Katherine, warning her with his eyes. Katherine answered with a tiny nod; turning away, she ate her stew. Blanchette never reappeared from the kitchen. Instead, they were served by one of Henri's barmaid's— a petite brunette who smiled shyly when Katherine offered her an extra coin for her service.

"Henri. I can't believe it," Katherine said to Gunther as they remounted their horses. "Henri barely ever left the inn."

Gunther nodded, eyes grim. "It's Madelaine."

"I wonder what she's planning. What is there to gain by attacking a village like Annecy?" Katherine said. They rode down the forest path, with Annecy behind them.

"A warning, I suppose. Madelaine can't reach you or your sisters in the castle. She's focusing on the closest thing to you," Gunther answered, gripping his reins with white-knuckled hands.

Katherine shivered at Madelaine's callousness and disregard for human life. "We should reach Corvan tonight if we keep a good pace; we'll question Madelaine again then," Gunther said, his face grim.

Dusk fell as they neared Corvan, throwing long purple shadows across the road. Their travels had been strangely quiet. Usually, the road to Corvan teamed with travellers at all times of day or night.

When Gunther and Katherine entered the city, every building was locked tight. The taverns, usually buzzing, lay still and silent; only the occasional orange glow at the windows told Katherine and Gunther they were occupied. A chill shivered across Katherine's skin as she scanned the empty quiet streets; even the horses snorted uneasily, their hoofbeats echoing on the cobblestones.

"What's happening?" Katherine whispered, fear rising in her throat.

Gunther shook his head, "Whatever it is, isn't good."

When they reached the castle gates, Gunther knocked. "Lord Gunther and Duchess Katherine," he said in a loud voice.

The iron peephole cracked open; a brown eye pressed against the metal grate peered out to verify their identity before the door creaked open, leaving just enough space for Katherine and Gunther to squeeze through.

The guard slammed the gate shut again. Although the guard's hands were steady, the faint twitch in his left eye told Katherine about the strain the castle was under.

The courtyard was silent, dry leaves skating across the flagstones was the only sound breaking the silence. Ghostly shadows draped them in darkness, sending an uneasy feeling creeping up Katherine's spine.

Since there was no groom, Katherine and Gunther headed directly for the stables. The horses were restless, snorting and rolling wild eyes. Katherine glimpsed Bardot, lips raised as he leaned his head over the stall door, snapping long, horsy teeth at anyone who approached.

"What's happening?" Katherine asked the groom who came to take her reins. His face was pale, hands vibrating with tension.

"I'm not sure," the groom responded. "The horses were restless all day. Even the companion goats weren't themselves today. Snappy, one of the grooms, got kicked. Then one of the castle stewards came and ordered us to lock the doors and stay inside until further notice."

"King Erich must have sent an announcement to the city too," Gunther looked at Katherine. "We need to get inside and talk."

Katherine followed Gunther across the silent courtyard. The door across the courtyard was locked, but one of the kitchen maids opened it for them, throwing them a suspicious glance as she quickly locked it behind them.

"We need to see King Erich and Prince Frederich right away, preferably together."

The maid bobbed a curtsy, leading them toward the royal apartments.

Gunther rapped on King Erich's study door.

"Come in," tension radiated from King Erich's voice. "Thank goodness you're back." His face filled with relief at the sight of Gunther and Katherine. "How's Avella?"

"Injured," Gunther answered. "We left Avella in the care of her Iasian family members."

King Erich nodded. "I'm sure you've noticed there's been a... change in circumstances." He pressed his lips together in a thin line.

Gunther inclined his head, waiting for King Erich's news.

"Madelaine escaped."

Katherine sank into the nearest chair. "How? She was guarded constantly."

"Rats, as far as we can tell. Madelaine had the rats steal the key and bring it to her through the drain. The guards were either administered a sleeping potion or bitten by poisonous insects, possibly night beetles."

"Do you know which direction Madelaine's headed?" Gunther asked.

King Erich shook his head. "She disappeared like a wraith and we believe if she's using the rats, she's gotten access to the tunnels."

Gunther's eyes darkened; the castle contained a labyrinth of secret passages leading to nearly every room, especially the important ones. If Madelaine was using the tunnels, she could easily access to the royal apartments; the council chambers, nothing would be off limits.

"Has anyone spotted Madelaine outside the castle?"

"No, but we've warned the city, just in case. The animals are restless; the horses and dogs in the castle, but also sheep, chickens, cows, are all acting strange and vicious."

"We ran into Madelaine's wolf, Alerion, in Iasia." Gunther quickly filled King Erich about Katherine's encounter with Alerion. His face tightened when he explained about the room found under the stone tower.

"So Madelaine has the bottles with the soul power?" King Erich tightened his face.

Katherine nodded. "Alerion must've recognized them, and taken them with him for Madelaine."

"We have to stop Madelaine before she uses them. It's not fair; besides, who knows what powers she'll have at her fingertips with those."

"Agreed, we should move immediately," Gunther said, his eyes hard.

"I've sent messengers to every outpost, and we're gathering the army as we speak. The council met today and agreed. This is war."

Katherine gasped. "And how will Iasia respond?"

"We've invited the Iasians to join forces, and I suspect they will. After all, if Madelaine takes over Lovan, Iasia is the next logical step."

"And the dragons, will they support the war?" Gunther asked, leaning forward to hear King Erich's answer.

King Erich shook his head. "The dragons were grateful for the return of their juvenile. But dragons are solitary and peaceable beings. They need to organize a council before they commit to war. And by then..."

"By then, it will be too late; Madelaine is moving now," Gunther said.

In all the years Katherine had known King Erich, she had never seen him as strained as he was today. Katherine shivered, as she imagined Madelaine skulking silently through the castle tunnels, her strange army at her beck and call. The seagulls alone had been terrifying. What would a full-fledged attack be like? Katherine fingered the tattered book, still safely tucked in her pocket after all this time.

"What if..." Katherine said, hesitating.

King Erich and Gunther swung their heads in Katherine's direction.

"What if we had something Madelaine desperately wants, something to use as collateral?" Katherine continued, squirming under their scrutiny.

"No, you're not using yourself as bait," Gunther said, rising from his seat.

"Not me—this," Katherine answered, drawing out the book.

King Erich stood, moving to a tapestry covering one wall. He moved the tapestry, "Is everything clear, Ulrich?" After hearing an affirmative, he returned to his seat, leaning his elbows on his knees. "How would we do that?" he asked Katherine in a low voice.

Katherine explained how desperate Madelaine was to acquire the book, watching as King Erich's eyes glowed with interest at her plan.

"It's risky, but a risk worth taking. This might actually work," King Erich said in a murmur, holding out a hand. "Would you mind if I look?"

Katherine handed the little book over, gaze intent as King Erich carefully turned the crumbling pages, shaking his head.

"All this over one tiny volume," he muttered. "No wonder the royal family banned magic for so long." King Erich returned the book and Katherine slid it back into her pocket.

"I'm meeting with the council first thing in the morning, and I'll discuss the plan. You two must be exhausted. Get a few hours of rest while you're able."

Katherine and Gunther found themselves back in the corridor. Because of the late hour, the corridor was silent and deserted, with only a few lamps casting pools of yellow light to mark their way.

Exhaustion was setting in and Katherine's entire body ached, crying for sleep. They walked silently down the corridor; Katherine to her stateroom and Gunther to the guestroom kept for his frequent stays at the castle. They paused at the juncture in the corridor before going their separate ways.

"I guess... I'll see you tomorrow?" Katherine hesitated.

Gunther reached out a calloused hand, moving a strand of hair over Katherine's shoulder. "Rest." His voice was gentle and his eyes were warm.

Katherine continued alone, glancing over her shoulder to see Gunther standing in the hallway, watching until she reached her stateroom. Katherine thought she would sleep. She was, after all, exhausted. But her restless thoughts were a turmoil in her head.

After tossing and turning for hours, Katherine got up, splashed herself with water and changed into a fresh nightgown. She paced the floor, deliberating. Too late for Lucie; she and the babies would be sleeping; Katherine didn't like bothering the castle staff for tea this late at night, so she would wait until morning. She paused to glance at the window. The curtains were drawn, blocking her view of the castle grounds.

Katherine inched the curtain aside and peeked out. The moon was high, flooding the castle gardens with silvery light, casting long shadows that seemed to curve and move. Katherine peered closer, her eyelashes brushing the cool glass. The shadows were moving like living things, swarming across the ground. Katherine stepped back with a gasp, letting the curtain fall shut.

Those weren't shadows. They were alive.

The castle was surrounded.

Katherine put her fist to her mouth, biting back a cry of dismay.

Shaking, she hastily dressed in a clean tunic and breeches and shoved her feet into simple leather boots. Slipping the book into her pocket, she rushed down the corridor and ran to Gunther's room, banging on his door.

Gunther opened the door in his dressing gown, hair rumpled. The chamber was dark; Gunther's fire had burned to a few glowing coals.

"What's wrong?" Gunther reached out for Katherine.

"Gunther, something alive is out there," Katherine said, her voice a hoarse whisper.

"What?" Gunther asked.

Katherine grabbed Gunther by the hand, leading him to his window. "Look." She cracked the curtains, standing aside so Gunther could look out.

Gunther stood silent, staring in shock at the sight before him.

"When did you first notice?" Gunther reached for the pile of clothes set over the back of the chair.

"Just now," Katherine's voice trembled. "I couldn't sleep. Something felt—wrong."

Gunther nodded, pushing his arms through his tunic. "We'll speak to the captain of the guard to see what the creatures are doing, then alert King Erich."

"Gunther, does this mean..." Katherine hesitated.

"It's started." Gunther searched Katherine's eyes.

Katherine followed Gunther to the door. He paused to grab a sword, strapping it to his side as they strode down the corridor.

Outside the castle, the ground moved, shifting as if the earth itself was alive.

They rushed to the captain's quarters, where they found him in consultation with his key men. King Erich and Prince Frederich were there, faces drawn with worry.

"Any signs of Madelaine's whereabouts?" Gunther asked.

Captain Hollich shook his head. "None. We think her general, the wolf Alerion, is leading."

"Alerion," Katherine whispered. "We need to speak to Jules, Eleonor, and Zelia. They might be able to influence him or tell us his weakness."

Captain Hollich nodded, eyes tight. He flicked his hand at a sentry who hurried off to waken the wolves.

"What exactly are we dealing with?" Gunther asked.

"Creatures. Everything Madelaine could get her hands on," Captain Hollich answered. "Mostly from the forest, but domesticated animals too. Not many dogs or cats; I suppose most are loyal to their masters and can't be persuaded. Geese and swans, I know they're poultry, but they can do significant harm and damage. Goats, bulls, and cattle, some horses. It's the little creatures we worry about— the rats, the mice. They get in everywhere and hear everything."

Katherine shivered, eyes darting to the dark corners of the room where lamplight didn't quite reach. So many places to hide, slither, and creep.

"Does Madelaine have any known strategy yet?"

The captain shook his head. "It looks like a siege. But we have to wait for Madelaine to show her hand."

"And what of the sceptre, is it safe with Lucie?"

"Lucie's been alerted. She has the sceptre at hand, ready to confront Madelaine when she appears."

Katherine clenched her hands together, wondering if Madelaine had acquired the substance in Sorchia's strange bottles yet. The thought of adding more powers to Madelaine's already considerable strength made her nauseous.

Gunther strode to the window, "Dim the lights." He peered out, cursing softly under his breath. "They're closing in. Either that or there's more coming."

Captain Hollich nodded tersely. "I think this is just the beginning."

All they could do was wait.

By morning, the castle was surrounded. The creatures surrounding them stood in eerie silence. Waiting. Watching.

Finally, Katherine fell asleep in the hard wooden chair, head slumped over. She woke with a horrible crick in her neck— her mouth cotton dry and her eyes gritty with exhaustion.

Still, they waited.

That morning, the castle was silent; the maids crept up and down the hall, delivering breakfast to fearful residents.

So far, the only casualties of Madelaine's army were two guards caught unaware. One guard cut in the head by a bear, the other kicked by a cow.

Still, the creatures gathered, pouring in from every corner of the kingdom.

Finally, when bright sunlight streamed through the cracked blinds, there was motion.

A shout outside.

Alerion.

"I wish to speak to the king," Alerion said, his voice ringing like a gong.

King Erich stood, his face pale.

Lord Gunther and Frederich leaped up. "Your Majesty, is it wise…" Gunther started.

King Erich cut him off with a sharp gesture.

"The Lovanian Kingdom is in its hour of need. If anything happens, take immediate action."

Prince Frederich flashed King Erich a pleading look, but King Erich stood firm. He settled his crown on his head, resting one hand on his sword. "Stand by."

Flanked by Prince Frederich and Gunther, King Erich strode down the corridor.

King Erich climbed the stairs leading into the ballroom, walking to the balcony overlooking the castle grounds. Straightening his shoulders, he opened the door.

A hush fell over the castle. Outside, the gathering forces froze, gazing at the balcony as if a single entity.

King Erich strode to the edge of the balcony, resting his hands on the balustrade.

Behind Katherine, Queen Isabella stifled a sob, putting her fist to her mouth. Prince Frederich laid a comforting arm around his mother's shoulder.

Before them, the sea of beasts parted. Alerion, in human form, glided through the ranks, halting below the balcony.

King Erich spoke first. "You've requested an audience; now, tell us, what are your concerns?"

Katherine turned to Gunther, confusion in her eyes. "Doesn't King Erich know?"

"Yes, but they have to say it out loud," Gunther whispered back.

"My Lady Madelaine has been deeply wronged. She demands these wrongs be righted." Alerion shaded his eyes with his hand, piercing eyes bright and green in the glaring sunlight.

"The one who wronged Lady Madelaine is no longer with us," King Erich said.

"Then the Lady Madelaine requires the next of blood as a payment for her wrongs."

Someone behind Katherine gasped. She turned, her eyes settling on Lucie, clutching the sceptre to her chest with a white-knuckled grip.

"What's wrong?" Katherine ran to her sister, helping her to the nearest seat.

"Next of blood," Lucie said in a faint whisper. "That's an ancient mage tradition."

Katherine narrowed her eyes, waiting for Lucie to continue.

"If a mage is wronged, they demand their penalty and the debt is to next of kin, like a money debt."

"That's despicable, surely that law's been erased?" An icy hand grabbed Katherine's heart as she took in Lucie's wide eyes and trembling lip. "It hasn't?" Katherine felt an impeding sense of doom crawl across her skin.

"We meant to… but changing the law takes so long, and the guild was new; we never got around to it."

"And Madelaine knows?" Katherine said, something deep inside wilting.

Lucie nodded. "She must."

"Isn't there something King Erich can do? Surely, he has the power."

"If King Erich refuses, we'll have to fight Madelaine. The guards are here and some soldiers, but the bulk of the Lovanian army was deployed to the outposts last year and won't return for days." Lucie said, sliding a panicked glace to the balcony.

"Impossible," King Erich's voice, loud and clear, carried across the castle gardens.

The crowd of creatures stirred, a rustle of wings and limbs as shivers of tension skimmed across the entire castle.

Alerion's face turned grim as a gust of wind whipped his strange grey cape behind him like a plume of smoke.

"You know what this means?" he said to King Erich.

"I do," King Erich said, returning Alerion's fierce gaze. "But I cannot allow innocent Lovanian citizens to suffer the crimes they did not commit."

Alerion inclined his head. Turning abruptly, he paced toward the castle gates.

King Erich was ushered back into the castle by his guard.

"Now what?" Katherine's heart hammered in her chest.

"War." Gunther trained his eyes toward the spectacle outside.

There was a moment of silence as the entire city held its breath.

"Charge," a voice shouted.

Chaos erupted.

Feathered wings beat the windowpanes as the castle was assaulted from the sky. Dark shapes climbed, slithered, and crawled toward the castle— scaling the walls, entering every nook a cranny.

"Hold them off," shouted Captain Hollich. The archers on the roof were rendered helpless with the attack from the sky; although, they managed to fire a few shots from the slits in the wall. But in moments, the slits had to be boarded against the slithering, crawling, and flying creatures under Madelaine's control. The castle wasn't designed to withstand this insidious enemy.

Katherine gasped in horror as a viper slithered over the balustrade, weaving along the French doors for an entrance. A crane beat against the window, which began to bend and crack under the force of his wings.

Katherine heard shrieks and screams from every direction.

They breached the lower levels first. Pandemonium soon spread over the entire castle.

Lucie jumped into the fight, pointing the sceptre at a wave of hairy black spiders swarming the castle wall. They instantly shrivelled under the sceptre's fire, leaving a putrid smell clinging in the air.

Katherine turned to Gunther, panic in her eyes.

"We have to find Madelaine now," Katherine said, raising her voice above the cacophony.

Gunther's eyes met Katherine. "Madelaine can't control them from a distance, she has to be in the castle somewhere," Katherine shouted over a loud rhythmic thud— the bull throwing himself against the castle doors. Wood splintered and shattered.

"It could take hours to search the castle. King Erich's had men combing every nook and cranny since Madelaine disappeared."

Katherine bit her lip, as an idea occurred to her.

"What if Madelaine's hiding in plain sight?"

Gunther paused, a spark of interest shooting through his eyes.

"Posing as a maid, or groom, or a member of castle staff. They come and go as needed and no one notices. Remember no one knows what Madelaine looks like without the veil."

Gunther was already heading down the corridor. It was slightly quieter here, the noise dulled by an extra layer of walls.

"We'll ask Daphne," Gunther said, already heading toward the lower levels. Katherine jogged to catch up to him.

It was louder downstairs, the battle gaining in intensity. Gunther pulled his sword, stabbing a hissing snake that writhed across the flagstones.

They found Daphne in the kitchen, bravely defending her territory with a long-handled mop. An army of rats had descended on the kitchen, as interested in the food as attacking, but distressing none the less.

Gunther pulled Daphne into the broom closet, pushing a family of mice out of his way with a foot; he slammed the door shut behind him.

"Daphne, are there any new castle staff in the past three days?" Gunther asked.

Daphne shot Gunther a wild-eyed look. "You came to ask about staff?" she pushed tangled hair from her pale face.

"It's important." Gunther pinned her with his gaze.

Daphne straightened, "We had three join last week. I hired two of them myself and Queen Isabella sent me the other herself."

Gunther and Katherine exchanged glances. "Tell us about that one, the one Queen Isabella sent," Katherine suggested, wincing as a loud clatter sounded from the kitchen.

Daphne took a deep breath. "A lady's maid, very experienced, previously worked for one of Queen Isabella's closest friends, a strange scar on her face."

"Where's her room?" Gunther said, raising his voice over the slamming of pots and pans. Something big had broken into the kitchen.

"I'll take you." Daphne cracked the door, then slammed it shut, her lips white.

"What is it?" Katherine had never seen the unflappable Daphne visibly frightened before.

"Some kind of cat, but huge and yellow with black spots."

"Leopard," Gunther muttered. "I wonder where Madelaine found him." He drew his sword. "Stay close, they're fast. And deadly."

Katherine and Daphne hovered behind Gunther as he edged the door open. The leopard had its back to them, stalking delicately across the flour strewn worktop.

Gunther motioned them forward, indicating the door leading to the main corridor. They waited until the leopard was distracted by the big range, sniffing at the flames and jerking its head back when singed.

"Now," Gunther said, leaping forward.

As a unit, they dashed across the kitchen floor, throwing themselves into the corridor. The leopard spun, yowling as it leapt toward them, claws bared. Gunther slammed the door, leaning against it. They heard the screech of claws sliding down the wood and splintering under the leopard's strength.

"Lead the way," Gunther told Daphne.

They ran down the hallway, stepping over scurrying rats. Gunther flicked away a red snake slithering toward them, flinging it against the wall.

"Down here," panted Daphne, leading them toward the servant's wing. It was darker here, lit by small windows set high in the stone walls. No paintings or rugs decorated the bare stone. Daphne skidded to a halt in front of a nondescript door.

"Here," she said, pointing to the door.

"I'll do this," Katherine pushed Gunther aside and raised a shaking hand, twisting the door handle. She took a deep breath, straightening her spine, then flung the door open.

CHAPTER EIGHTEEN

Katherine peered through the dim light to see Madelaine sitting cross-legged on the bed, eyes closed as she muttered in intense concentration. She opened them slowly, focusing on the faces at the door.

"Ahh.. there you are," Madelaine said, a bitter smile flitting across her face.

Katherine hesitated in the doorway, stomach churning. This would be Katherine's first time seeing Madelaine without the thick veil covering her features.

Madelaine turned and Katherine saw the scar— a moon coloured constellation puckered across one pale cheek. Between the webbing shone strange silvery marks. Remains of a fine white paste clung to the crevices in her skin, a paste that would have covered the scars enough for Madelaine to pose as a servant.

"You see my scar?" Madelaine said, her voice a husky croak.

"Sorchia did that to you?" Katherine asked, her eyes flitting to Madelaine's.

"Don't speak that horrible name in my presence. If your coward mother had the courage, the decency to confront that witch in the beginning, we wouldn't be forced into this situation," Madelaine said in a hiss.

Katherine remained silent, letting Madelaine continue her tirade. "Avella knew, knew what evil Sorchia was capable of and saved herself, leaving us to this fate. My mother had the life sucked out of her before my eyes." Madelaine's eyes flicked away, and it was then Katherine spotted them. The silvery fluid substance swirling inside an old-fashioned glass bottle, nested on the bed beside Madelaine.

Katherine recoiled at the madness peering out of Madelaine's eyes. Her skin crawled, her heart gripped by icy claws of fear. She gripped her hands together and stepped forward.

"Madelaine, Avella was young, a mere child. She was no match for Sorchia and she did what she could."

"That doesn't help mother, does it?" Madelaine said, spitting the words out with venom.

Another step forward. Katherine reached out a hand, imploring. "Madelaine, this has to stop. You're destroying everything, including yourself."

Madelaine smiled, the silvery marks on her cheek beginning to glow. "Good, because I've spent half my life waiting for this moment and I plan to enjoy every second."

"Katherine, look out." Katherine heard the words floating from a distance. Before she could react, a heavy, solid weight knocked her to the side. She crashed to the floor, her head smacking against the hard stone. From under the bed shot a white figure, snarling. A fierce white blur, all teeth and claws, flew over Katherine in a fury. Gunther raised his sword, plunging it into the beast. The giant cat fell, a spreading pool of blood gathering under his twitching form.

Katherine pushed herself off the floor, disoriented and shaky. The marks on Madelaine's face shifted, blazing white hot. Katherine's stomach plunged as she realised what the marks were.

"Madelaine's face," Katherine said with a gasp. "The silver lines match the symbols in the book." As if in answer, the book in her pocket throbbed, pulsing with recognition.

Madelaine narrowed her glittering eyes, a greedy look sliding across her face. "Ahh... the book. That was a nasty trick you played, hiding another in its place and switching the covers. When I get the book, my power will be complete. I'll make you suffer just like Sorchia suffered," Madelaine said, her crackling voice sending shivers down Katherine's spine.

You *killed* Sorchia?" Katherine gasped.

Madelaine smirked, raising an eyebrow. "Sadly, Sorchia was torn apart by a pack of wild animals. No one knows quite why they turned on her. Unfortunate that she couldn't give me what I needed to complete my powers."

Katherine recoiled, skimming her eyes across Madelaine's cheek, she spotted a blank space next to one last symbol by her left ear. *That's* why Madelaine needed the book, to complete the ward carved into her skin. Katherine shuddered. What evil plans had Madelaine concocted and carried out to reach this level of desperation?

"No," Katherine said, raising her head, eyes flinty.

"No?" Madelaine asked, pausing as a confused expression flitted across her face. "I killed Sorchia, slid a knife right into her chest. I can kill you too."

"You're not touching that book," Katherine said as she stood on shaking legs, avoiding the stiffening heap of blood-soaked fur lying on the cold stone floor. She slid her hand into her pocket, fumbling past the book for the dagger she had slipped into it earlier. She grasped the handle, the cold hard metal reassuring and solid against her skin. Katherine took another step forward, wondering if she could really do this. The handle of the dagger was slippery in her grasp, slick with sweat.

The marks on Madelaine's face glowed brighter, and she muttered under her breath. An almost imperceptible movement alerted Katherine, a snake slithered under the door. Tiny, but its bright yellow pattern announcing its deadliness.

The snake darted toward Daphne, who stood frozen in fear behind Katherine. The creature's mouth was outstretched, bared fangs dripping with poison.

Katherine struck a clumsy blow, nicking Madelaine in the arm, but it was enough to distract Madelaine. Madelaine screeched, more from anger than pain; the snake froze, weaving its yellow head back, black beady eyes flat and unblinking.

Katherine poised the dagger in midair, a single drop of blood sliding from its tip. Breathing slowly through her nose, she wondered if she could find the courage to attack Madelaine again.

Madelaine opened her mouth, uttering incomprehensible, terrible words in a fierce voice. The snake flicked its tail then flung its writhing body across the small room.

Katherine saw the snake fly toward her, mouth open to snap. She flung her arm in front of herself, the dagger pointed outward. The dagger knocked the snake away; it bounced against the wall with an audible thud, then lay twisting on the floor.

Madelaine narrowed her sharp eyes. Katherine raised her arm again, gritting her teeth. "This ends now," she said, her eyes locked with Madelaine's.

Madelaine screamed as a sword flashed through the air and she collapsed on the bed, blood trickling from the wound in her chest.

"She's gone," Gunther said, putting a hand in front of Madelaine's mouth to check for breath. "Strange, someone who depended so much on magic died by ordinary means."

Katherine choked out a strangled sob as Gunther gathered her into his arms.

"You—you—" she said with a hiccup.

"I had to; you would never have forgiven yourself. In spite of everything, Madelaine was your flesh and blood."

Katherine nodded against Gunther's chest.

"I feel like a coward," she answered, sniffing loudly.

Gunther barked out a laugh. "Coward, that's the last thing you are, Katherine."

Katherine relaxed against the circle of Gunther's strong arms.

"Should we go see what's happening outside?" Gunther said after a pause.

Katherine nodded. "We should," she said, unwilling to leave her comfortable position.

With Daphne in tow, Katherine and Gunther wound down a myriad of corridors, heading into the bowels of the castle. Everywhere, pandemonium had given way to confusion. The animals, no longer attacking, were dispersing into chaos. Mice escaping into every nook and cranny; cows wandering in search of juicy grasses; wild animals slinking and slithering into the fields and forests.

The castle was left in a state of total disarray; Queen Isabella's precious gardens were ruined by trampling hooves. The pond was stirred and muddied. The castle was overrun with rodents, something Katherine privately thought would soon be remedied, considering the ranks of stray cats still prowling the castle grounds.

King Erich's guard and the castle staff joined to begin the massive clean-up job.

"How did you know it was safe to fight Madelaine?" Katherine turned to Gunther.

"The script," Gunther answered. "When I saw the script marks on Madelaine's face, I realised that's what she needed the book for, to complete the sequence. She wanted to bring Natalie back. Madelaine didn't care so much about taking over, only about revenge and getting back the one person she loved."

Katherine remembered the glass bottle, now safe in the castle vault, and shivered in spite of the hot sun beating down. "Natalie wouldn't be the same person if she was brought back by such unspeakable evil."

Gunther shook his head. "You're right, but Madelaine didn't care about the cost."

"The only problem is Alerion," Katherine said, wrestling a stubborn mule into a halter. She wiped her sleeve across her forehead. This was hot, sticky work. Fortunately, a steady stream of farmers poured into the castle; all grateful for the return of their livestock. An occasional squabble broke the air, most easily settled by the king's steward.

"We've asked Jules and the other wolves, but they have no idea of Alerion's whereabouts. King Erich's sent his best men to search for him, and my guess is, he'll head back to the forest to lick his wounds or return to his family in Iasia. They should be easy to find with Jule's help."

Katherine nodded, knowing King Erich's men wouldn't rest easy until the traitor was behind bars.

With everyone working together, the animals were ushered back to the forest or corralled by nightfall. The damage and cleaning would take longer to remedy.

"WE'LL HAVE A CELEBRATORY ball at the end of the week." King Erich leaned back in his chair.

They had gathered in the royal apartments to discuss the day's events. Lucie, Marion and their children, joining King Erich and Queen Isabella. Pierre had ridden to Iasia to help Avella, where Madelaine's estate would need to be managed.

Lucie clapped her hands. "Delightful, will you organise a dress for me?" She turned to Katherine, a hopeful gleam in her eyes.

Katherine sighed through the smile, tipping the corners of her mouth. "Of course."

The next morning, Katherine left the castle early, heading to her house in the city.

"I'm back." Katherine peeked into the greenhouse, admiring the tidy baskets of cocoons, silky white and creamy yellow, that lay waiting for her loving attention. Katherine skimmed a hand over the pile, lifting a small fluffy ball between her thumb and forefinger. The cocoon was so light, it was almost transparent in its airiness. They were ready. Next, the cocoons would be sent for spinning into fine smooth thread before the dying and weaving would begin. Katherine hummed in satisfaction, locking the door behind her. *Spending the morning at home was a good idea,* Katherine thought, looking forward to the finished silk and already planning which dyes to use.

"There you are," a smooth voice greeted her.

The keys fell with a clang as a large bulky form shoved Katherine against the greenhouse, the glass cold and hard against her back.

"I wondered when you would show up... so predictable." Alerion's strange grey cloak drifted around him. His hand shot out, gripping her upper arm, and Katherine gasped, her feet dragging on the ground as he yanked her toward the house.

"What do you want from me?" she asked, as Alerion opened the kitchen door, pushing her inside.

Katherine's frantic eyes scanned the room. The kitchen was empty; the house needed little staff during her long absence. She eyed the rack of knives next to the oven. If she could just distract him....

"I don't think so." Alerion jerked Katherine into the dining room. The table was set, polished silver and gleaming candlesticks proud in their places. "You ruined everything with your infernal nosiness. Madelaine promised me her power would be hers. We were going to be equals, she and I. A pack all our own." Alerion's voice was hard; his eyes glittered yellow and bright. He threw Katherine into a dining room chair, reaching for the curtain ties with his free hand.

This split second of distraction was Katherine's opportunity. She leapt forward, snatching the candlestick and whipping it back, hitting Alerion in the head with a dull thud. He stumbled back, and she struck again. Alerion crashed into the window, spraying glass across the room. He snarled, deadly yellow eyes growing feral.

Katherine had to move fast. She would be no match for Alerion in his wolf form. She spotted a large slice of broken glass, snatched it, and plunged it into his neck. Alerion collapsed to the floor and lay still, blood pooling under his form.

Katherine clutched her hand; the glass had sliced her palm, cutting deep.

"What happened? I was upstairs and heard a noise." Sarita, the chamber maid peeked in the door, horrified eyes widening at the sight—shattered glass spread everywhere, Katherine's dress spattered with blood, the body on the floor, and the injured hand.

"Can you get me a bandage?" Katherine collapsed onto dining chair, face pale and beaded with sweat.

Sarita nodded mutely, rushing to do her mistress's bidding.

Moment's later, Lukard appeared. He flinched, pursing his lips on seeing the body sprawled on the floor. But he didn't pause, first bandaging Katherine's hand, tutting over the length of the wound, then organising a messenger to the castle to inform the king what had transpired.

Soon, Katherine was nestled next to the fire, hot drink in hand. She glanced up as a hesitant knock sounded at the door.

"Katherine?"

"Lucie?"

Lucie ran to embrace her older sister. "Why didn't you tell me you were coming to the house? I would have sent guards with you."

Katherine shook her head, tears prickling the back of her eyes. "It was silly of me. I assumed Alerion escaped to Iasia, and I wanted to check the silk. And... I guess I just wanted everything to feel normal again."

Lucie rested her chin on her sister's head, stroking her hair. "Silly."

Katherine smiled. "I know that now."

"Come to the castle, you can't possibly stay here alone after that experience," Lucie said, shuddering.

"Lukard took care of everything. I'm fine," Katherin answered with a shrug.

Lucie peered at her sister, a wrinkle between her eyes. "You don't look fine," she answered.

Katherine sighed, cupping her mug between her hands. "Well, I do actually have something on my mind...."

Lucie sat beside her sister. "I know that expression; out with it. What's wrong?"

Katherine heaved another sigh. A deeper one. "I'm worried about the ball."

"The ball?" Lucie quirked an eyebrow. "Why are you—oh, because of Gunther?"

Katherine swirled her drink in her hand, concentrating on the amber liquid. "Yes," she answered in a small voice.

Lucie scoffed. "You don't have to worry about Gunther. He'll be there, waiting for you."

Katherine nodded. "I'm just afraid he won't want to wait any longer... I've misunderstood him for so long."

"Don't be ridiculous." Lucie barked out a laugh. "Gunther would wait forever. But I don't think you should make him," she added, sliding a Katherine a significant look.

The tension banding tightly around Katherine's chest eased. "You really think so?"

"I do," Lucie answered confidently. "Now come on. You're not staying in this house by yourself. Even if it is safe now."

CHAPTER NINETEEN

The night of the ball arrived.

Candles were everywhere, and the ballroom shone with a warm golden glow.

"I'll regret this in the morning," Lucie laughed. Lucie had allowed the children to stay up extra late to enjoy the festivities. Prince Frederich was currently chasing little Frederich, trying and failing to stop him from using the ballroom floor as a slide.

Katherine laughed with her sister, although an edge of sadness and regret clung to her. She still hadn't seen Gunther, because he had remained at his estate for the entire week.

In her darkest thoughts, Katherine wondered if Gunther had tired of her. She ran nervous hands down her green silk dress, anxious gaze pinned to the ballroom door. The necklace Gunther gave her was nestled at her throat, the tug of warm metal a reminder of his devotion. *His former devotion*, Katherine reminded herself. There was no guarantee Gunther would even be at the ball tonight. Still, her restless eyes wandered back to the ballroom door, longing for Gunther's tall figure to stride in.

Gunther didn't arrive.

Katherine smiled and laughed with her sisters, hiding her heartbreak with a toss of her hair.

It was too late now, nearly midnight. The children were long in bed, reluctantly dragging their feet as their nurse escorted them from the ballroom. Only the promise of a picnic next week pacified them into acceptance of the fate of an early bedtime.

"He didn't come," Katherine murmured to herself.

"What did you say, dear?" Marion asked, her sharp ears catching the end of Katherine's sentence.

"Oh nothing, just looking at Queen Isobel's beautiful flowers," Katherine answered. Disconcerted at being caught, Katherine hid her dismay under an airy laugh.

Marion slid her sister a suspicious look; she knew Katherine far too well to be fooled by her flimsy mask of cheerfulness.

Katherine's heart sank as the evening dragged on later and later. Everything was perfect, the food delicious, the drinks refreshing, the musicians played all the favourite songs. But to Katherine it was as dull as burnt toast.

She wandered to the refreshment table under the guise of wanting another pastry. Really, it was to avoid the sympathetic looks of her sisters. Katherine picked listlessly at an iced cake, wondering if it would be rude to slip away early.

"There you are," a deep voice sounded behind her— one as familiar as her own.

"Gunther?" Katherine said, her heart freezing in her chest as she turned.

Gunther grinned, teeth flashing white in his tanned face.

"You came?" Katherine fumbled with her cake, ignoring a shower of crumbs tumbling over the green silk dress.

"Of course I came," Gunther smiled again, pointedly eying the necklace lying against Katherine's creamy skin. "I see you wore the necklace," he said, clearing his throat and shifting his gaze away.

Suddenly shy, Katherine lowered her lashes. "It's a lovely necklace. I should have said thank you."

"Wearing it is thanks enough," Gunther answered, his voice caught, and he swallowed hard.

"Would you—would you like to dance?" Gunther asked Katherine, holding out his hand. The music had started, a slow haunting tune that matched the beat of Katherine's heart.

Katherine nodded, taking Gunther's hand. Even after spending so much time together, she felt nervous, almost frozen. Her feet moved numbly to the music as she followed the familiar steps.

"I thought you weren't coming back," Katherine said, her voice low.

"Of course, I was coming back," Gunther said with a chuckle, his warm hand secure on Katherine's waist. "I got behind on estate business and lost track of time." He spun Katherine under his arm before she swirled back in a cloud of green silk.

Katherine glanced up at him. "I'm glad you did."

"Katherine," Gunther paused and held her close, sheltering her under his arm. "I need to ask you something."

"Yes?" Katherine said, raising her eyes to search his.

"I know I'm rough around the edges. Marion explained about the... confusion, and I'm sorry. Sometimes I don't say the right things. Sometimes I don't manage to *do* the right things.... But all the same.... I hope that you'll give me a chance..." Gunther said, ending the sentence in a question.

Katherine stepped closer, feeling his breath warm in her hair.

"Yes," she answered.

"Yes?" Gunther asked, a light flaring in his eyes.

Katherine nodded, a grin crossing her face. "I will," she answered in a firm voice.

Gunther lowered his face to hers; Katherine realized with a start, Gunther was about to kiss her in the middle of the ballroom floor. Her pulse pounded underneath her skin; her eyes gazing into his.

His lips were soft as they moved across hers. Katherine opened her eyes, blushing. Across the room, she spotted her sisters grinning in delight. Katherine rolled her eyes.

"Don't worry." Gunther squeezed her shoulders. "We have our entire life ahead of us."

EPILOGUE

Gunther and Katherine's wedding was magnificent. Queen Isabella and Lucie threw themselves into preparations with fever pitch the moment Katherine and Gunther announced their engagement. But Katherine enjoyed the preparation— especially the dresses. The dresses were fabulous. The guild members gifted Katherine with glorious fabric, enough for five weddings.

Pierre and Avella were at the wedding, sitting next to Althea in the front row. Katherine smiled at them through happy tears as she peeked over her bouquet of lilies. But through it all, what Katherine looked forward to was everything returning to normal. The next day, they headed to Gunther's estate, eager to spend a few weeks away from the hustle and bustle.

"I can't wait to see the manor house," Katherine said as the carriage rolled to a stop outside the door. Gunther's manor was huge, set back from the road on a wooded lane. The staff came out the greet them, surprising Katherine by calling her mistress. That would take getting used to.

Katherine peeked inside at the entrance hall, admiring the black and white marble floor. She knew she would be happy here.

"I have a surprise for you," Gunther held Katherine by the hand, leading her through the manor to an enclosed courtyard.

"Outside?" Katherine turned questioning eyes on Gunther.

Gunther nodded, eyes dancing with mischief.

Katherine followed Gunther across the courtyard toward a large glass greenhouse.

"You planted some trees?" she asked, glancing at him with puzzled eyes.

Gunther smiled proudly. "Mulberry trees, for your silkworms to eat."

Katherine gasped. "Where did you get fully grown mulberry trees?"

Gunther smiled. "I've been growing them since I met you."

Katherine turned her shining eyes to his. "Really?"

Gunther touched her cheek tenderly. "Really, I knew they would make you happy."

Katherine squeezed Gunther's hand, squealing. "Now I can continue my guild work from the manor."

Together, they walked back into the sunlit courtyard and headed toward their home, ready to start a new life together.

OTHER BOOKS IN SERIES

Free – A Fairy Tale Retelling of Rapunzel mybook.to/free[1]

Brave – A Fairy Tale Retelling of Beauty and the Beast mybook.to/bravekjj[2]

Strong – A Fairy Tale Retelling of the Princess and the Pea mybook.to/strongkjj[3]

True – A Fairy Tale Retelling of Puss in Boots mybook.to/True[4]

Loyal – A Fairy Tale Retelling of Red Riding Hood

Pretty - A Fairy Tale Retelling of the Princess Frog - *coming in November 2021*

Valor - A Fairy Tale Retelling of Jack and the Beanstalk – *Coming in December 2021*

Thank you so much for reading this book. If you want to hear more about upcoming books join my newsletter at KristinaJJordan.com

I also love interacting with other fantasy readers and authors on Facebook, Instagram, and Tiktok at @kristinajjordanauthor.

Like all other authors, I appreciate honest reviews and love hearing feedback about my books. Please feel free to leave a review.

---

1.   http://mybook.to/free

2.   http://mybook.to/bravekjj

3.   http://mybook.to/strongkjj

4.   http://mybook.to/True

Don't miss out!

Visit the website below and you can sign up to receive emails whenever Kristina J Jordan publishes a new book. There's no charge and no obligation.

https://books2read.com/r/B-A-KPEO-WZXRB

BOOKS 2 READ

Connecting independent readers to independent writers.

Also by Kristina J Jordan

The Crown and the Sceptre
Free A Fairy Tale Retelling of Rapunzel
Strong - A Fairy Tale Retelling of the Princess and the Pea
True A Fairy Tale Retelling of Puss in Boots
Pretty - A fairy Tale Retelling of the Frog Prince
Loyal - A Fairy Tale Retelling of Red Riding Hood

9 798201 535377